THE LIGHT BETWEEN WORLDS

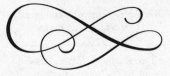

LAURA E. WEYMOUTH

HARPER TEEN

An Imprint of HarperCollinsPublishers

HarperTeen is an imprint of HarperCollins Publishers.

The Light Between Worlds
Copyright © 2018 by Laura E. Weymouth
All rights reserved. Printed in the United States of America.
No part of this book may be used or reproduced in any manner
whatsoever without written permission except in the case of brief
quotations embodied in critical articles and reviews. For information
address HarperCollins Children's Books, a division of HarperCollins
Publishers, 195 Broadway, New York, NY 10007.
www.epicreads.com

Library of Congress Control Number: 2017956223
ISBN 978-0-06-269688-5

Typography by Torborg Davern
19 20 21 22 23   PC/LSCH   10 9 8 7 6 5 4 3 2 1
❖
First paperback edition, 2019

For all the lost girls—
may you find your way home.

EVELYN

SEPTEMBER 1949

1

WE'RE BURYING OLD NICK IN THE BACK GARDEN. IT'S JUST Jamie and me, and it's raining, and I know he's worried because of the way he stands, head bowed, shoulders tense.

"You can cry, Ev," he says, and takes my hand in his own. No one's held my hand in such a long time, and I nearly do cry at that, because he's always so kind to me. But if I've learned anything in life, it's to choke back tears and smile.

Jamie won't meet my eyes. Instead he glares at the freshly dug earth and kicks a clod of it with one foot. The soil hits up against the corrugated iron side of our Anderson shelter, a leftover from the war, and Jamie winces. I heard him and Philippa ask Mum and Dad about having it removed once, on an evening when they thought I was caught up in a book. My brother and sister are always having worried conferences behind my back, even though I'm sixteen and only two years younger than Phil. They fuss over me worse than our parents ever have, but in spite of their best efforts the shelter removal scheme never came to pass. Planted over with daisies now, it still crouches at the garden's far end, reminding me of what once was.

I manage the smile I don't quite feel, and I think that worries my brother more than anything else. It worries him more than the fact that the family dog is gone—one of the last creatures who remembered me as I was before the shelling, when I was a child, and untouched by war. It worries him more, even, than the knowledge that next week, he's heading back to university. With Jamie at school and Philippa off in America, I'll be truly alone. For years, the three of us were never far apart, him down the road studying at St. Joseph's and Philippa across the hallway in our girls' school dormitory. Now it'll be just me, Evelyn Hapwell, a girl caught between two worlds and left, at last, to her own devices.

I know the secret fear my smile wakes in Jamie and Phil, a worry they will never acknowledge, not to each other, not even to themselves. It frightens them to see me smile through pain because it means I refuse to give up. And my brother and sister have resigned themselves to a fate I won't accept. They've written the end of our shared history—been broken by the weight of a conclusion they see as inevitable. Cracks run through them; fault lines, breakages, places where they've shattered just a little.

And they worry because I will not, cannot, be anything but whole. They think one day I'll break, too, and that I'll go off like a bomb because I've refused to let my breaking happen bit by bit. Maybe so. But every morning I wake up and watch the sun rise and listen to the birds sing and know that I will not let today be that day. My story hasn't ended yet.

Jamie's words still hang on the air as his warm fingers grasp my own. He looks at me and I look at him.

"I'm not crying till I get home," I say. The words are a prayer, a promise, and they burn my tongue with the heat of faith they require.

"Oh, Ev," Jamie mutters, and stumps back up to the house with his shoulders bent.

What he doesn't see, what he and Philippa never see, is that when my words burn, they leave ashes on my lips.

Hope doesn't make parting less bitter.

It doesn't lessen the sting of loss.

It is, in itself, a sort of pain, but one I would break without.

"Have you got everything you need for school, Ev?" Mum asks at breakfast. She and Dad and Jamie say nothing about Old Nick. All their words are careful, mouthed like razor blades that might cut me if they're not spoken just so. They needn't bother. I've never been as frail as they think.

"I've just got to pick up more socks," I say around a bite of toast. "But I'm all packed, so we can stop for more on the way to the station."

Mum sighs. "The rate at which you children go through clothes—it's a mercy clothing rationing's ended."

"I'll drive Ev to the station," Jamie volunteers. I sip my tea suspiciously. He ought to be up to college already—he's got a scholarship studying the law at Christ Church in Oxford. When I give him a hard stare, he won't meet my eyes. He knows that I know he should be elsewhere. I don't like this. I don't like being handled as if I'm made of spun glass just because a dog who followed me in from the streets died three days before term. Just because Philippa's flown off to America for school and the entirety of the Atlantic now lies between us.

At least no one knows it's my fault she's gone. The sighs and sympathy and gentle treatment would be even worse if they did.

Mum and Dad exchange a look. They were pressed from the same mold, both ordinary and brown-haired with worry-lined faces, like two fretful bookends. They hardly need speak to understand each other. I wish I could decode the meaning of Dad's raised eyebrow and the quirk of Mum's mouth that serves as a conversation between them.

"That's good, thank you, James," Dad says to my brother before reaching across the table and pressing something into my hand. "In case you want anything on the train, love."

It's a crisp five-pound note and I swallow hard. Kindness always threatens to undo me, and my parents can't afford this. It's not much, but we've never been rich and they've put everything into working for a future for Philippa and Jamie and me. I've watched them make quiet sacrifices for years to scrape together the money for expensive schools, the sort of places they think will open doorways.

I wish I wanted to open the sort of doorway they're thinking of. I wish I wanted to go somewhere other than home, to be someone other than who I was.

I take the note, because I can hardly say *I love you but I am as I am and I will never be who you want me to be*, at least not over the breakfast table when my suitcase is sitting by the door and we'll part ways in less than an hour.

Instead, I tuck the money into the pocket of my school skirt and smile. "Thanks, Dad. You're a brick."

The words come out light and normal, and a bit of the worry fades from my parents' faces. Jamie frowns down at his eggs, but keeps his counsel.

When I'm meant to be looking my room over to make sure I haven't forgotten anything, I steal back out to the garden. I only have a moment, otherwise I'll be missed, but I plod through the rain and past poor Old Nick's grave. Then I lower myself down into the bomb shelter's musty half-light.

The splintered, moth-eaten cots that once crammed the shelter's interior are gone. It's just an empty metal shell that smells vaguely of earth and rust. I press my forehead to one aluminum wall and shut my eyes, trying to fill myself with radiant Woodlands light. Light from a far world. Light from a place of myth and wonder.

"Five and a half years," I whisper to the dank, uncaring air. "That's how long it's been since you sent us back. Have I not waited long enough to come home? I swear to you, Cervus, if you cut me, I bleed Woodlander's blood. My heart beats with a Woodlander's pulse."

There's no answer, of course. There never is. The rain drums steadily on, and I hurry back to the house.

Before long, it's time to go. Mum and Dad kiss me goodbye at the door, and I climb into Jamie's car. It always takes me by surprise that Jamie has a car. We spent so long traveling on horseback or on foot that it gives me an odd, unearthly feeling when I climb into the passenger seat and he competently shifts gears.

For the most part we drive in silence, but I don't mind. None of us Hapwells have ever felt the need to fill the air with pointless chatter. We stop once, and I get my socks, and then Jamie pulls to a halt in front of the station.

"You going to be alright, Ev?" he asks while lifting my bags out of the boot. There's uncertainty in his eyes, a pleading note in his voice. He wants me to be alright. I want him to be, too, though neither of us knows how that should look for the other.

But I know what could make a start for him.

"Of course." I smile brightly, an ordinary girl with her ordinary brother, being dropped off for a term at school. He hugs me a little too tight, and ducks back into the car as if he can't bear to stay, or to see me walk into the station alone.

It's only once he's gone that I let my smile slip and fall.

I pace the platform restlessly. I've never faced the journey back to school without him or Philippa at my side, but it's past time I stood on my own, no matter the depth of the regrets I carry.

The emptiness of the bunker haunts me still. Five and a half years since we last cowered in its dark interior, listening for the low growl of approaching planes or the muffled reverberation of nearby bomb strikes. Five and a half years since something inexplicable happened in the midst of all that darkness and waiting and fear. The truth haunts my brother and sister, too, I know. Poor darling Jamie, who works so hard and never quite feels he's doing enough. Poor lovely Philippa, off in America, running from our past.

As for me, I refuse to be pitied. I refuse to be anyone but who I've always been: Evelyn Hapwell, teller of truths and walker of worlds, friend of the Woodlands and enemy of tyrants, beloved of Cervus, the Guardian of the Great Wood.

The words Cervus once spoke to me are emblazoned on my bones, writ large across every inch of my skin.

A Woodlands heart always finds its way home.

Your words, Cervus, not mine. No matter how many years pass, I plan to hold you to them.

2 ~

THIS IS HOW AN AIR RAID BEGINS: IN THE DEAD OF night, with silence and normalcy shattered by the wail of a siren.

It's February 1944, and London has been under fire for over a month. If there'd been anywhere else to send us for our half-term holiday now the shelling's started up again, Mum and Dad would have kept us out of the city. This time, though, they weren't able to find us a place.

I've been through drills before, and we've spent more time in London than most children. But we were away for the Blitz at the beginning of the war, shuffled off to distant cousins and friends of friends who were willing to house us when school was out. It's the idea of us going to strangers that Dad and Mum don't like, so we've never truly been evacuees, just schoolchildren who go somewhere other than home for holidays. When things were calmer over the last two years, we were even allowed back to London for a week.

None of the drills have prepared me for this, though—for the banshee cry of the air raid sirens that works itself up to an insistent scream. I roll out of bed and Philippa's already on her feet across from me, white-faced but holding out a hand. I grab on to it as if it's a lifeline, and we meet Jamie in the hall.

We've been taught well by our parents, and carried their instructions with us through every drill at school: Look out for your siblings. Keep together whatever happens. Wait for no one else.

Not even Mum and Dad.

So we hurry out through the back door and into the garden, where the cold wet grass nips at our feet. It's strange, being out-of-doors so late at night. Shadows loom long and make our postage-stamp lawn and frost-covered shrubs seem eerily unfamiliar. Jamie helps Philippa and me down into the shelter and stands at the entrance, staring back to the house with hunched shoulders and one foot tapping. Philippa wraps a damp blanket around me and we sit side by side, shivering in the cold.

The siren wails on. Somewhere in the distance, bombs begin to fall.

"Do you see them?" Philippa asks anxiously. Jamie shakes his head.

"No, I—wait." His voice cracks with relief. "There's Dad."

Our father looks in at the entrance, and everything's suddenly a little less dreadful than it was before. Until he frowns and looks at Jamie. "Didn't your mum come out?"

Before Jamie can answer, Dad sprints back across the lawn. The dull blast of explosions is growing louder, closer. I gnaw on my lower lip and Jamie joins Philippa and me. We put our arms around each other and wait, and I would give anything to be away from here—to leave the dark and danger and fear behind.

"Where are—?" Philippa asks, choking with worry. But a bomb falls so close that it drowns out her last word and shakes the walls of our small shelter.

"Anywhere but here," I whisper. Philippa pulls me close, as if her very presence can shield me from harm. Squeezing my eyes shut, I will away the present, picturing somewhere calm, somewhere peaceful—a haven of silence and golden light. "Anywhere but here. Anywhere but here."

And then, silence. The dark in the shelter grows, till I can make out nothing but my brother's and sister's pale faces.

After a moment a sound begins. It's neither air raid siren nor bombshell. Ringing through the air, it's low and insistent, halfway between the bellow of a bull and the bugle of an elk. It pulls at my blood and bones until I want to crawl out of my own skin to answer it. Jamie, Phil, and I stare at each other, wide-eyed.

"Hold on to me," Jamie orders, panic lacing his words. We join hands and I can barely breathe, I'm so afraid. Under that fear, though, there's something new and unexpected—anticipation.

The call grows louder and louder until at last light explodes around us. I blink and squint, eyes watering, sure I'll see only rubble and devastation when my vision clears. But the light stays constant, unlike the flash and sizzle of shelling. It resolves into afternoon sunshine and my heart leaps to find that, impossibly, we're standing in a wood.

After the confines of the bunker everything in me sings to be surrounded by sun and trees and good clean air. There's a pungent green smell all about, and a riot of birdsong undercut by the sound of running water. Wind lifts the hair from my forehead, and it's not a bitter February blast but a soft spring breeze.

Jamie and Philippa glance at each other, wide-eyed as a pair of ghosts.

"Did we—" Philippa begins, and Jamie shrugs.

Ahead of us a tall and regal shape steps from between the trees. It's a stag, his hide the color of autumn leaves, a thick red ruff of fur around his broad shoulders. He wears his branching antlers like a crown.

Instinctively, Philippa pushes me behind her, but I pull away. There is something about this place—about the earth beneath my feet and the branches above my head and the stag stepping toward us and the wild rightness of it all. A moment ago, I was afraid and broken, and now I feel as if the splintered pieces within me have begun knitting back together.

Walking forward, I meet the stag before a tumbledown, moss-covered boulder.

"Hello," I say quietly. "I'm Evelyn."

In answer, the creature steps forward. He lowers his great head and presses his velvet muzzle to my cheek. I feel a whuff of hot air that smells of grass and leaves and wildflowers. When he speaks, it's a heart-deep rumble that comes up from his chest and there's a fierce joy in his strange voice.

"Little one. Welcome to the Woodlands."

"This can't be happening," I hear Philippa mutter to Jamie behind me. "Either we're dead or there's been some sort of gas attack, something new that causes delusions."

"I don't know." Jamie sounds torn. "It looks real enough, Philippa."

"But it can't be. And even if it is, what about Mum and Dad? What's happened to them? They're still back in the middle of all that shelling."

I feel a pang of regret at Philippa's words. But the stag fixes his fathomless dark eyes on me and for the first time that I can recall I am struck by a sudden and unshakable impression that all shall be well.

Anywhere but here, I said. Somehow, I've got my wish.

"If we really have gone—someplace else—and they find us missing from the shelter, they'll think the worst. Jamie, it'll break their hearts." Though I don't look back, I know Philippa's near tears. I can hear it in her voice.

The stag brushes past me. I turn to watch him go, and see Phil standing with her arms wrapped tight around her waist, the only unhappy thing in this lovely, verdant wood. But when the stag approaches she straightens, pushes her shoulders back, raises her chin.

"Whoever and whatever you are, you've got to send us back," Philippa shakily demands. "We have family and a war going on. We can't be spared."

Guilt lodges in the pit of my stomach because I love our parents but they're nearly strangers, I've seen them so little the last four years. All I want is to stay in this place, away from the sound of falling bombs.

The stag tilts his head to one side. "I called you because you called to me first. Was there some mistake?"

Philippa and Jamie look questioningly at each other. I twine my hands together, wishing to sink into the ground. When they turn to me, I flush, hot and embarrassed.

"Evie, what—" Jamie begins.

"It was me." The words come out all at once. "When we were in the shelter I wished to be somewhere else and I thought of a peaceful place and I wanted it more than anything. I'm sorry."

"That's not possible," Philippa insists again. She stares off into the trees with her lips pressed tight together.

The stag still stands, watching us curiously.

"What do your eyes tell you?" he asks. "Your ears? Your nose? Your skin? The Woodlands are real enough, and though I've never called between the worlds before, it's within my gift."

"This is all a mistake. You'll have to send us back," Philippa says, and Jamie nods reluctantly.

Ice pours through my veins. I can't. I can't. Whatever troubles this world may hold, at least for now they're further off than the ones we left behind.

"Please, Phil," I whisper. "Couldn't we stay? Just for a little while?"

"Evie!" Philippa sounds scandalized, and it makes me feel so small. "What about Mum and Dad?"

It's the stag who saves me. He moves to my side once more and I twist my fingers into the thick fur around his shoulders.

"You may stay as long as you like, and when you are ready to return, I will send you back to the very moment you were called," he offers, lowering his head. "It will be as if you never left. But don't look to escape trouble in the Woodlands—your world may have a war already being fought, but here we live under the shadow of a war that's sure to come."

For a moment, Philippa is silent. Then she speaks. "Swear it. Swear that Mum and Dad will be alright—that they won't miss us, and that all of us will find our way home."

The stag bows his head. "On my name and my honor. I, Cervus, Guardian of the Great Wood, born at midnight to Afara the milk-white hind, keeper of the Woodlands' sacred heart, possessed of the power to call between worlds, swear this to you."

"Swear what?" Philippa presses.

"That your family will be safe. That you won't be missed."

"And that we will find our way home."

Cervus lowers his head further in assent. "And that you will find your way home."

"All of us," Philippa says sharply. "That we will all find our way home."

The stag paws at the forest floor, and I'm not sure if it's a gesture of annoyance or amusement or perhaps both. "I swear by my power and pride that you will all find your way home."

But Philippa still looks uncertain, until I cross the clearing and slip my hand into hers.

"Phil, everything's going to be alright. I believe him."

When she turns to me I smile, more brightly than I have in years. My sister pulls me close and I can feel her nod to the stag, though her hand on my shoulders trembles.

Cervus turns to Jamie, who stands watching us.

"What about you? Will you stay in the Woodlands for now? Or should I send you back?"

Jamie's wearing his serious, ever-so-responsible-eldest-brother look, but excitement lurks behind his eyes. "Well, I think Phil's covered any objections I'd have. So if you've got a war effort and you're on the right side, point me at it. I've been waiting to help out with ours long enough."

"And you, little one?" the stag asks me. "Will you stay in the Great Wood now you've seen it? Now you know what we wait for?"

I hesitate. "Can I speak to you, sir? Alone?"

In answer, Cervus leaves the clearing, slipping between the over-arching trees.

"Not too far, Ev," Philippa warns, and I raise a hand in acknowl-edgment as I follow after the stag. He waits patiently, just far enough *from my brother and sister that if I pitch my voice low, we won't be heard.*

Biting my lip, I stare down at my bare feet, still grimed with mud from our back garden in London. "How did this happen? How could I possibly have called to you when we've never met? When I never knew there was such a place as this wood?"

Cervus watches me unblinkingly, and I look up to meet his gaze.

"Child, in the Great Wood we have a saying—a Woodlands heart always finds its way home. We speak it over our newborn. We speak it over our dead. We speak it to one another as we live. I may be the forest's Guardian, but it's not for me to question into which bodies Woodlands hearts are placed, or when they call out for home.

"And I wish I could offer you a world without war, but here are the Woodlands, such as they are. We are not at peace in the Great Wood, but there is still a measure of it to be found under these trees for those who are willing to look. Will you search for it with me?"

"I was afraid of our war," I confess. "And I expect I'll be afraid of another, but being here—it's like everything's turned right-side up when I never knew I'd been living upside down. I think—I know— I'd follow you anywhere, and into anything."

"Then step lightly, and tread where I tread," Cervus says, loud enough so Philippa and Jamie will hear. "I have an appointment to keep, and we have far to go."

3

A BOY JOINS ME AT THE MAGAZINE STAND ON THE railway platform. It's a relief to have someone to take my mind off things—off the fact that not only am I out of place, in the absence of Jamie and Philippa, I'm also alone. The boy is ginger-haired and freckled, with big hands and too-long, awkward limbs. I like him before he even speaks. I like his honest smile and his ears that stick out a bit. Despite his height, he reminds me of a Woodlands people called stonewardens. When he speaks, it's in a Yorkshire accent, and my toes curl in my school shoes. He even sounds like a stonewarden.

"I'm Tom." The boy holds out one of his preposterous hands and I shake it, my own swallowed up in his grip. "Tom Harper. I've seen you on the train before, I think, and when St. Agatha's takes day trips. I go to St. Joseph's. I know your brother, Jamie—good lad, he is. He asked me to have a chat with you if I saw you on the way up to school, so I'm glad we ran into each other."

I wrinkle my nose. "He needn't have worried. I'm not a child."

Tom smiles broadly. "'Course you're not, but nobody's ever had too many friends, have they?"

I could take offense over the fact that after all our years, Jamie still thinks I need looking after, but instead I laugh, because Tom Harper can have no idea of the depth of meaning behind the words *I'm not a child*, and of how many years I've lived.

To his credit, Tom grins, then pulls a bag of toffees out of one pocket and offers them to me. I take one, because you should never turn down a toffee, and quite suddenly we appear to be friends, just as he promised.

Tom makes for an excellent traveling companion, who doesn't try to talk when I want to look out the window at the passing view. If I squint, I can imagine the trees are waving as the train rushes past. The beeches are going gold early this year, and that's just how their spirits looked, back home—they were restless golden things, who carried themselves like queens.

"Sandwich?" Tom asks when the meal cart goes by.

"Please."

They're ham and cheese, the bread ever so slightly stale already, and I watch as Tom tears through three in quick succession. He catches me at it and goes red to the roots of his ginger hair.

"Mum always says I cost as much as a horse to feed," he says around a mouthful of crumbs. "I've only got a pair of sisters at home, little things like you."

I smile. I can't help it. This boy on this journey is a gift. I'd expected to spend the trip staving off loneliness through sheer force of will, but instead I'm sitting across from Tom Harper with his

Yorkshire accent and his big hands as he unwraps a fourth sandwich. Here is why I never lose hope—because this boy is a breath of fresh air and a reminder of home.

Which is rather remarkable, given that home is worlds away.

Tom grins back at me. "So, St. Agatha's. You glad to be getting back, or would you rather have the hols stretch on a bit?"

"I'm glad to be getting away from London." I brush stray bread crumbs from my school skirt and smooth out the pleats. "Not glad to leave my family, though. But happy I'll be seeing friends. In answer to your question, both, I suppose."

Tom's grin has softened, and one of his big hands sits on his lap, holding the last bit of his final sandwich. "Torn between two places, eh?"

I trace a finger across the window as a green valley slides by us. A silver pool lies at its heart, surrounded by birch trees. What a lovely place that would be for water spirits.

"Yes," I say, trying not to put too much weight behind the words. "I certainly am."

Tom scoots forward and presses something into my hand. I don't have to look away from the view to know what it is. The feel of rumpled brown paper and the smell of sugar tell me all I need to know.

"Have a toffee," Tom says. "And buck up. Everything gets better after the first week back. You just need to settle in again."

He takes out a book and lets me be. I pop a toffee into my mouth.

Outside, the beeches shiver and wave.

Tom nods off on the seat opposite mine. He snores a little, but not enough to bother. I smile and take out a book of poetry, losing myself in words and memory.

The meal cart comes round one last time, to clear away our rubbish. Tom stirs and yawns and hands over his sandwich wrappers with a thank-you. We're nearly to the station now, nearly to the end of this journey and on to the next.

I peer out the window, taking one more look at the beeches to steady my nerves and strengthen my resolve. This year will be different. This year, I will try to put down roots in the world I was born to.

Wherever I am, wherever my feet are planted, that is where I will make my life. I won't withdraw or put up walls. Every day is a treasure, every chance meeting a gift, and I will treat them as such until at last, my Woodlands heart finds its way home.

Tom is looking at me, red-faced. "I know you're allowed visitors on weekends. Do you think on Saturday I could bike over? Or not, you can say if you'd rather I didn't."

A gift. A journey. And it's true—one can never have too many friends.

"Yes." I smile. "I'd like it if you came."

4

WE'RE BOUND FOR THE HEART OF THE GREAT WOOD
to meet a tyrant, or so Cervus says. But he'll tell us no more, and Jamie
and Philippa look worried as we go deeper into the forest.

For two weeks, we travel through the Woodlands in Cervus's company, and despite the meeting that lies ahead I feel myself falling in
love, perhaps a little with the stag himself, but mostly with the Wood.
Only eleven and desperate for a sense of peace and belonging, I can't
imagine a more beautiful place. The forest itself is a cathedral; the little
rivers and songbirds are its choristers; the filtered and shifting sunshine,
candlelight; the smell of earth and moss, incense. Each day as we walk,
I lose myself in numinous calm.

We catch glimpses of the Woodlands people: a short, stocky form
vanishing around a boulder, leaves swirling through the air in a wind-
less clearing, dappled faces peering from the boughs overhead. We pass
by houses built around the bases of trees, too, and clearings laid to crops
or fenced in to keep grazing sheep from straying. Cervus never slows his
pace, just hurries us along toward an unknown destination. We stop
only at night, or to gather berries and fish in the streams.

Philippa's still anxious, her nails bitten to the bloody quick. She hardly speaks except to fuss over me before we sleep or when we eat. Jamie does his best to cheer her up.

"Come on then," he says each morning when we wake cold and stiff from sleeping on the ground. "It's still better than school, isn't it? You can't possibly want to go back until we've seen a bit more of this place."

But we never talk about the air raid. We never bring up the fact that we left without knowing what had happened to Mum and Dad. I know it's eating at my elder sister, yet I can't help being secretly relieved. I am happy to be here, and happy to trust Cervus, believing that somehow, someday, in spite of everything, all shall be well.

On our second week in the forest, we come to a place that feels different from the others. Everything has been lovely since the moment we were torn from the darkness and clamor of the bunker. But Cervus leads us into a ring of white birches and I know this place must be the very heart of the Great Wood.

A hush hangs on the air. Golden sun filters through the shifting leaves overhead, which move with barely a whisper. Motes of dust and the little wishes from full-blown dandelions dance in the shifting light. The grass beneath our bare feet is the color of spring itself.

Cervus steps into a pool of sunshine at the center of the clearing. His rust-red hide flames and he raises his head, scenting the air before sounding his clarion call.

The stag lowers himself onto the grass, legs folding gracefully beneath him, and waits.

Philippa and Jamie wander about the clearing, speaking in low voices and stopping occasionally to look at one of the ancient stone figures ringing the open space. The statues are so old their shapes are impossible to determine—only a carved line here and there, peering out between patches of moss, indicates that they were once more than plain standing stones.

I trail after my brother and sister for a while, but am drawn back toward Cervus. He might be a stone figure himself, he's so motionless, but when I crouch down to sit at his side, his ears flick back. Tentatively, I let one hand drop onto his shoulders. For a long while we just sit, but at last he lowers his great head and rests it in my lap.

I think this is where I was born to be—in the center of a clearing in another world, with this strange, wild creature at my side.

Philippa looks over one shoulder and something crosses her face at the sight of us. Fear, I think, or maybe grief. I can't bear to see her unhappy in this glad, bright place. I smile, not just with my eyes and my mouth but with everything in me, until I feel incandescent. Phil smiles wistfully back.

At the edge of the clearing, the undergrowth stirs. Cervus stands in a single, fluid motion.

"Come, children," he says, and we cluster about him. I keep my hand on his shoulder, fingers buried in thick, coarse fur.

The Woodlanders have arrived. They step out of the trees silently, all of them barefooted or barehooved, like my brother and sister and me. There are half a dozen bay and dun centaurs, a group of short, stocky folk I'll come to know as stonewardens, and tree spirits who swirl into the clearing as a drift of leaves before taking human shape. Water spirits and winged girls come, too, and other creatures who have no names besides the ones each individual bears. When they've all assembled, I marvel at how silent the clearing remains.

But muffled hoofbeats sound in the distance, and armor flashes through the trees. A white flag gleams in the sun and suddenly armed soldiers are dismounting just outside the clearing. They leave their horses and push past the gathered Woodlanders, trampling the green grass of the clearing beneath their booted feet.

At the head of the procession is a pale and haughty young man, who must be four or five years older than Jamie's fifteen. A thin circlet of steel rests on his golden hair, and when he reaches the place where Cervus waits, he stands proudly before the stag. His eyes flicker, red then orange, as if a fire burns inside him.

A rustle breaks the calm. I glance up and see that all the Woodlanders have taken a knee. A muscle works in the armored young man's jaw and anger sparks in his uncanny eyes. It's not him the Woodlanders bow to, then, but the stag. Cervus, in turn, bows back.

"Venndarien Tarsin, heir to the Empire's throne," Cervus says as he straightens. "Welcome to the heart of the Great Wood. None of your line has ever set foot here before."

Venndarien casts about him, taking in the gathered Woodlanders and the ring of birch trees. "Your rustic shrines hold no interest for those of my country. Tell me you've called on me to offer up your surrender, Cervus, and that you're not wasting the Empire's time yet again."

"There will be no surrender," Cervus answers. "And I will use as little of your time as I can. I've brought you here to ask for a stay of battle once more."

"Unless you're ready with the timber we demand and every last one of you takes a knee before the Imperial crest, you'll find us impossible to sway," the pale young man says.

A low rumble of discontent rises from the people gathered.

"We will never bow to Tarsa," one of the Woodlanders calls. "Much less fell trees to fuel your wars."

Venndarien raises an eyebrow, as if the protests coming from the Woodlanders are nothing more than the buzzing of gnats.

"The Empire does not hear you," he says.

Cervus throws back his head and bellows. By the time the echoes of his call have stopped resounding from the trees, the Woodlanders are silent again, regarding the Tarsin delegates with barely subdued anger.

Venndarien turns his attention to us, and Philippa meets his gaze stonily as his eyes linger on her.

"Who are these ragged upstarts?" the Tarsin heir asks Cervus. It's true we hardly look our best, still in our nightclothes after two weeks of walking through the Woodlands. "They're not forest dwellers. What hovel in a back corner of the Empire did you steal them from?"

Cervus leaves my side and stands beside my sister. Venndarien falters beneath the combined force of their stares.

"They come from elsewhere," Cervus says. "They were born beyond this world, just as the first of your Tarsin line were."

Whispers ripple between the Imperial soldiers, like the sound of an uncertain breeze. They are all alike, as paper white as their leader, with the same balefire gleaming in their eyes.

Venndarien stiffens. "Impossible. No one has walked between the worlds since my forefathers first came to this place from Heraklea and founded the fledgling Empire."

Cervus shakes his great head. "I assure you, I speak the truth."

"Bastion, a dagger," Venndarien snaps. One of the lackeys behind him hurries away to the horses and returns bearing a knife set with crimson gems. "Which of these pretenders will offer up blood, to prove that it still calls to another world?"

Jamie steps forward at once, before Philippa or I can even consider it. He doesn't flinch as Venndarien pulls the dagger across his palm. When Jamie's blood drops to the clearing's green-clad floor, a cloud of smoke rises from where it fell. The whispers coming from the Tarsin delegation grow to a dull murmur.

"And yet you deny a Guardian's power," Cervus says quietly.

Venndarien scoffs. "There must be some trickery or witchcraft at play here."

Philippa holds out her hand. Even at thirteen, it never takes her long to find a way to master a bad situation. "There is no lie in what Cervus says. Test my blood. Test my sister's. You will find another world singing through the veins of all three of us."

"And you mean to stay in the Great Wood?" Venndarien asks in disbelief.

Jamie, Philippa, and I nod in unison.

The Tarsin heir's eyes narrow. "Do you know what we could offer you in the Empire? Lands. Titles. Riches beyond compare. And more than that—safety. Come with me, and give Tarsa the secrets of your world. Leave this little forest, and I will show you wonders."

Philippa swallows, but Jamie's mouth twists. "No fear of that. We may be from elsewhere, but we know what a devil's bargain looks like."

Venndarien scowls. Before he can speak, Cervus cuts him off.

"Kneel, children," the stag commands.

Philippa, Jamie, and I look at each other. There's a tightness in my chest and my brother and sister seem uncertain, but I turn to Cervus. He's waiting expectantly, his wild face a careful blank, and something in me still calls to him just as it did a world ago in the midst of all that darkness and panic. When I drop to my knees, he lowers his head almost imperceptibly.

Philippa and Jamie do as I've done. From her place in the middle, Phil slips her hands into both of ours and squeezes.

Cervus speaks the words of an oath, but never looks down. He stares past us, at the Tarsin heir. "Children from another world, do you swear to serve the people of the Great Wood faithfully for as long as you remain here?"

"Yes, sir."

"Do you swear to withstand the enemies of the Great Wood in whatever way will safeguard its people best?"

"Yes, sir."

"And do you swear to hear your fellow Woodlanders, holding their thoughts and words in the same high regard you would your own?"

Cervus's stare is all but a weapon, and I don't know how Venndarien can possibly hold up beneath it.

"Yes, sir," I murmur, in concert with my brother and sister.

"Then as Guardian of the Great Wood, I bind you to our cause. Rise, and face our people."

We stand and turn. The gathered Woodlanders are absolutely silent. They watch us without moving, their faces unreadable. But Venndarien Tarsin's thoughts are etched clear in every angry line of him.

Two weeks in the Great Wood, and we've already made an enemy.

5

THE DORMITORY AT ST. AGATHA'S IS A BEEHIVE OF activity. Girls buzz every which way, shouting names and laughing. Suitcases make a minefield of the hall and when I step into the room that's been mine since I first arrived here six years ago, Georgie's already sitting on her bed.

Georgia Maxton and I were assigned to one another as roommates the day we began at school, less than a year before I found my way home to the Great Wood. She's short and clever, with deep-brown skin and curling black hair, and it didn't take long for the two of us to discover a shared fascination for the written word.

"Oh, thank heaven you're here," she says when I step over the threshold of our shared space. "That racket's been going straight through my head for the past hour. Shut the door, won't you? When I do, Penwallis says I'm being unsociable."

I shut the door slowly, ensuring several of Lizzie Penwallis's underlings see me in the act.

"Best verse of summer," Georgie says from where she sits, still looking down at her book with her chin propped on her hands.

"Let's get yours out of the way, because I *know* it'll only be Dickinson or Teasdale."

I don't mind Georgie's teasing. She's right—I go back to my favorites again and again while she reads voraciously, forever seeking out new words.

"This won out for me," I tell her. "It fits for start of term, too—

> "I have no heart for any other joy,
> The drenched September day turns to depart,
> And I have said good-bye to what I love;
> With my own will I vanquished my own heart.
>
> On the long wind I hear the winter coming—
> The window panes are cold and blind with rain;
> With my own will I turned the summer from me
> And summer will not come to me again."

"Teasdale, isn't it?" Georgie asks, and rolls her eyes good-naturedly when I nod. "Evelyn Hapwell, you've got to expand your mind. Listen to this—it's Frances Harper, and rather brilliant . . .

> 'Light! more light! the shadows deepen,
> And my life is ebbing low,
> Throw the windows widely open:
> Light! more light! before I go.
>
> 'Softly let the balmy sunshine
> Play around my dying bed,

E'er the dimly lighted valley
I with lonely feet must tread.

'Light! more light! for Death is weaving
Shadows 'round my waning sight,
And I fain would gaze upon him
Through a stream of earthly light.'"

I take a slow, measured breath. They're starting early this year,
my memories of the Woodlands. Pushing back at the recollection
of a moonlit valley, and a haunting voice singing of *light unto light*,
I open my school trunk.

When I say nothing about the poem, Georgie glances up for the
first time. "You look like you've just come from a funeral. What
happened?"

Unpacking at least affords my hands something to do. School
sweaters, navy with St. Agatha's gold crest on one pocket. Wool
socks for the colder months. Handkerchiefs and bars of pink soap.

"Old Nick died," I tell her. "And I've been writing to Philippa,
but she never writes back. I'm afraid I might have ruined things for
good between us."

"Oh, Ev, I'm sorry." Georgie shuts her book with a snap. "But
sisters fight, and she'll come round eventually. Leave the unpacking
for now—we'll have plenty of time this evening. If you're having
trouble with your own sister, why don't we go find mine and get
you a cup of tea?"

The clamor in the hall hits us like a freight train when Georgie opens the door. We wander through the crowded and noisy

dormitory corridors, and I'm happy to let Georgie lead. Now that I'm here, I feel deflated, as if I've come to the end of something and nothing new has begun. I'm just . . . waiting. But I smile and nod with false good humor to all the girls who greet us.

The truth is, I'm not at home here. My sister, Philippa, was. When we were sent back from the Woodlands, Phil began making this world hers in earnest. Powder and pumps, nylons and cinema and boys took the place of tree spirits and stonewardens and wooded glades. She was a radiant star in constant motion, all the rest of us caught up by her inescapable gravity.

And then she left me behind. Although she's still in this world, she's an ocean away and the distance feels unbearable.

I miss you, Philippa. I wish you were here.

Now there's just me, following Georgie, and how can I tell her that the last time I was sixteen, I danced in grassy clearings, visited centaurs, and chatted with talking beasts? I can't speak of it, but there's still too much of me left behind not to think about it.

Just like that, in the noise and rush of start of term, a crack forms inside me. The first hairline fracture. I've made it through the summer hale and whole, with a faith like the burning sun, and now loneliness has started the breaking.

Five and a half years I spent in the Woodlands with my brother and sister. Five and a half years I was always with one of them. Yet here I stand, separated from both home and family, and it's all come rushing in on me.

Georgie stops at the door closest to the dorm's front entry, which bears a small plaque inscribed with the words *Josephine Maxton,*

English Literature Supervisor. Knocking half a dozen times, she raises her voice to be heard. "Josie, are you in there? We want a cup of tea."

Music billows from Max's rooms—a new jazz standard, something loud enough to drown out the noise from the hall. It cuts off abruptly and the door swings open. Max stands there in fashionable slacks and a paint-spattered blouse, a scarf holding back the tight curls of her hair. She beckons to us to hurry inside, and once we're in, all but slams the door.

"Sorry, I'm trying to keep the clamor out by making my own. And I'm repainting. The Curmudgeon gave me permission, after five years of stubbornness. Tea, you said?"

Max throws one arm around Georgie and one around me, sweeping us into her tiny kitchen. She's the English Lit teacher, and the youngest faculty member, which makes her our dorm supervisor by default. Max sets the kettle on, wipes a smudge of paint off her chin, and looks us up and down.

"Georgie, my love. Evie. What's wrong?"

"Still fighting with Philippa," Georgie says. She and Max know me better than my own parents do, and let it rest at that. I've never liked to say much about my troubles—even if I wanted to, how would I find the words? I prefer good tea and sympathetic company, and no one pressing me to speak.

I steal glances around the room as we sip cups of tea and Max and Georgie talk quietly. It was drab in here before—Max used to joke the color ought to be named Funeral Parlor Foundation—but it'll be drab no longer now she's finally worn the Curmudgeon down. A first coat of hyacinth purple is already up on the walls, and there's a box on the counter with blue shot silk curtains peeking out of it.

I had a gown that shade of blue, which was made for me during our fourth year in the Woodlands. I used to wear it on the beach below Palace Beautiful, out at the very Wood's edge. Philippa scolded me for spoiling my hem, but I liked to sit and watch the water, wrapped in something the color of waves. Jamie used to sit on the sand, too, when he was home from the front, and whenever I saw him there I'd go down. We'd talk until the ugly things he'd seen faded to distant memory and he laughed instead of frowning. I always had enough laughter for him, enough faith for Philippa—or so I thought.

Now I'm left wondering what I have for me.

The dinner gong rings out across the quad, and Max looks up. "Alright, Evie?"

When I nod, she reaches across the table to squeeze my hand. "Check the fern after lights-out, if you need to."

Georgie and I clear away our teacups and brave the hallway once more, where we're swept up in the rush of girls heading out of the dorm and across the quad. I hear someone shout Georgie's name, and she bites her lip, twisting the end of her thick braid around one finger.

"Ugh, it's Penwallis. Can't I just have one evening of peace?"

I wrinkle my nose. "Apparently not."

"Remind me again why I put up with her."

"Her father's a Cambridge dean, and that's where you're headed next year. So you've decided it's better to make her a friend." The words come out like a piece of recitation, I've said them so many times before.

"I'm not her friend, I'm her project," Georgie answers drily. "And I *hope* I'm headed to Cambridge."

"They'd be fools not to take you."

Giving my arm a quick squeeze, Georgie disappears into the crowd, following the sound of Penwallis's voice. I realize, surrounded by this press of girls I've known for ages, that without Philippa I'm a stranger in their little world. I don't belong. I've grown into a shape that cannot bend, and Cervus help me, though I've been trying to change it for five years, it's a Woodlands shape.

Dinner is tough, fat-marbled beef with scant gravy and boiled potatoes. The Curmudgeon gives the same start-of-term speech she does every year—excellence, dignity, the good of the nation, that sort of thing. It's stuffy in the refectory, the food is dreadful, and the wool collar of my school sweater itches terribly. When the Curmudgeon finishes, it's a relief to be sent back to the dorm.

Georgie's gone over to someone else's room to compare notes on the summer reading list. It's just me, and to be honest, I don't mind. I've felt alone since the day began and now I truly am. So I sit down on my bed next to the window, because Georgie's never much cared about the view, and throw open the leaded glass casement.

The sun went down in its blaze of glory while we were at dinner, listening to the Curmudgeon drone on. Now the moon is up, casting quiet and friendly light across the sheep fields and wooded copses behind St. Agatha's. I sit and look and breathe. For the first time today, I'm myself—Evelyn Hapwell, a girl caught between two worlds. But the moon looked the same in the Great Wood as it does in England, and so did the sheep and the tree-cloaked hills. The sight of the silent, dreaming countryside knits the crack inside me back together.

The far, white moon is the curve of a smile, and for all my loneliness, I can't help but smile back.

6

WIND SIGHS IN THE BRANCHES ABOVE, AND SOME-
where, a lark breaks into song. We still stand beside Cervus in the birch
ring watching the gathered Woodlanders, who silently watch us, too.

Cervus steps past my brother and sister and me, careful on his cloven
hooves. He stops in the middle of the Tarsin delegation, his velvet muzzle only inches from Venndarien Tarsin's face. "Go back to the Emperor
and his armies. Tell him the Woodlands offers no surrender."

Venndarien's eyes blaze and sparks snap between his fingers. "If the
Empire had no need of fuel for its siege fires, I would burn this little
wood to the ground."

Cervus says nothing, merely twitches an ear as if troubled by a fly.
For a moment, it looks as if Venndarien will speak again. Instead, he
turns and stalks out of the birch ring, beckoning to his retinue to follow.

The Woodlanders remain still as stone until the last muffled sounds
of hooves and tack die away. Then they all begin to shout at once.

"Cervus, what were you thinking, calling those three?"

"It's been centuries since a Guardian called beyond."

"Where did they come from?"

"Are you sure of them?"

Cervus swings round to look at us, for all the world as if the clearing still remains silent.

"Children, welcome again to the Woodlands," he says, and his eyes are kind.

Philippa presses her lips together and Jamie shifts his weight.

"Perhaps they could be of use," a voice I recognize says.

The Woodlander who spoke against the Tarsin heir steps out into the middle of the clearing. He's tall and sparely built, with dappled copper-brown skin, the loose curls of his black hair cut short. Leather straps hold twin scabbards secure against his back, and his clothing is simple—tan breeches, and an unbleached linen tunic. Like everyone else I've glimpsed in the Great Wood, his feet are bare. The rest of the Woodlanders are silent, eager to hear what he has to say, though he seems young—certainly no older than the haughty Tarsin heir.

"We all know the Tarsin Imperials are creatures of ambition and intrigue, and they'll want a measure of these children. The Empire never destroys a thing if it can be bought, or used. Let the young ones convince the Emperor that they might be persuaded to become oathbreakers—that the Empire has a chance to steal them away from us. It will take time for him to realize that will never come to pass, and that time can be spent preparing ourselves for the war to come."

"How can you be so sure of us?" Philippa asks.

The Woodlander shrugs. "I can't be sure of you, but I'm sure of Cervus. Break your oaths, and he'll simply send you back to the world you came from."

"Perhaps we don't want to be of use," Philippa says. "There was enough danger at home. Perhaps we don't want any more of it, and we'd rather be sent back now."

The Woodlander gives her a long, inscrutable look. "No one will hold you against your will. You're free to return home if you wish."

I can't breathe. I won't go—not back to the dark and the bombs and the gunmetal smell of our frigid shelter, and after that (if there is an after) the endless parade of strange houses and strange beds, and never knowing where I belong.

"No. Thank you," Jamie cuts in. "We swore to help, Phil. We've got to stay, at least for a little while—until we've done what we said we'd do."

The forest dwellers break into conversation again. I watch them quietly, wondering what it will be like to live among them.

Jamie's already deep in conversation with a stonewarden when I notice Philippa walking across the clearing alone. I drift after her, but hang back when I see Cervus following, too.

"How long will it take to honor our oaths?" she asks when he joins her. "It's not—it doesn't seem clear-cut. There's no real end to it, and no way for me to hurry things along."

"I don't know," Cervus confesses, and his head droops. "I'm sorry, little one. Perhaps I did wrongly in calling you."

Philippa wraps her arms around herself. "No. We're here now. And Ev—well, I haven't seen her look so happy in years."

"What about you?" Cervus swings his head round to look at her. "I could send you back alone. You'd never know the time without your brother and sister had gone by."

Please, I beg silently as bombs go off within me. Please, Philippa. Stay.

She's quiet for a long while. Then she turns to Cervus, and I can see tears on her face. "I couldn't leave either of them, but especially not Ev. Do you know what my parents told me, the first time we were sent away at the start of our war? 'Look after your little sister, Philippa. She's yours to take care of now.' And I've tried. I made a promise to them, and it's binding me here as much as the promise I just made to you. So if you want someone to dangle as a prize for the Empire to snatch at, let it be me, but there's something I want in return. An oath that Evie will come to no harm."

"I'm only a Guardian," Cervus says. "I am here when a Woodlander's journey begins and when it ends, but I have no control over what lies in between."

Philippa stills. Her shoulders set. "If that's true, what did you mean when you promised we'd find our way home?"

"What all Woodlanders mean when we speak of homegoing. That if not in life, then at last in death, your heart will find its true resting place."

I watch as Philippa balls her hands into fists at her sides. "That's not what I meant when I made you swear. I wanted to know that my brother and sister and I will all return safe and well to our own world."

"I could not promise such a thing." Cervus lets out a sharp breath. "I will do everything I can to ensure the three of you stay safe and return to your world. No Woodlander will do less. But swearing to do anything more would be dishonest. I don't control your fate, little one."

Philippa takes a step away. She's quiet for a while before answering, and when she speaks, her voice is colorless. "Even if you can't promise to keep Evie safe, I did. So I suppose it'll be up to me as always, to look after her and to get her home. If that means helping to hold off your war until you're ready, then so be it."

Cervus rests his head on her shoulder, and at last she turns, throwing her arms around his neck and burying her face in that ruff of rust-red fur. I creep away, knowing she's said things she wouldn't want me to overhear.

7

"—EV. EV, ARE YOU LISTENING?"

Georgie's voice and the clamor and chatter of girls leaving English Lit comes into focus. I blink a few times, shedding remembered Woodlands sights and sounds like so many dried leaves. The corners of Georgie's mouth tuck in, and she rubs the back of one hand against her forehead.

"Ev. The bell's rung. It's time for Latin."

No one's left in the room but us and Max, who sits behind her desk watching our conversation. I push my chair back with a scraping noise and gather up my books carelessly. "Thank you, Georgie."

I don't mean to be ungrateful, but it wears on me, always having people take such care, always having them watch and worry. I'm *fine*, and I don't need help.

Philippa obviously thought so or she wouldn't have left, even after the things I said.

The truth is, my sister may have gone, but she's still everywhere in this place. As I trail down the hall to Latin, following Georgie, who pretends she's not waiting for me, I can't help but notice a dozen places haunted by Philippa's ghost. The Woodlands have plagued me for years, but this is new.

Across the corridor is the Science Room, where Phil held meetings for the school's Aid Committee. It wasn't a particularly glamorous club, but it was her favorite, and she made it popular just by her presence. There was always something or other they were fund-raising for by baking or canvassing or hosting concerts. They started out sending books to soldiers in hospital, during the war, and moved on to knitting hats and mittens for those left homeless on the Continent.

Next to the Science Room is an urn of imitation flowers, and they were Philippa's doing, too—part of her successful but short-lived School Beautification Scheme. The refectory's not safe because she held court there, ruling benevolently from a table beneath the windows. The library's a minefield because it's where she took me to deliver her lectures—Buck Up, Ev, Just Keep Busy, There's Plenty of Good in This World If You Only Look for It.

I never expected I'd miss her so much, though I'm the one who drove her away.

Georgie's standing in the doorway to Latin, having given up pretending she's not waiting for me. I duck my head and hurry along, sliding into my desk just as Foyle, our stern and pinch-faced Latin magistra, begins to speak. She peers at me, but says nothing about my tardiness.

Even Latin's thick with memory, though. I've never been a good student, but Philippa, the diplomat and negotiator of our family, loved old languages. Even in the Woodlands I'd catch her muttering under her breath, *"aut viam inveniam aut faciam"* or quipping "*asinus asinum fricat*" when a letter from the Empire contained a little too much flattery.

I sit in Latin and bide my time, badly translating the texts I'm given and waiting for the bell. When it rings, I hear it without a reminder from Georgie, and am first out the door, hurrying through hallways and past rooms that all serve as reminders of my sister. Haunted by her on the outside, haunted by the Woodlands on the inside, haunted, haunted, haunted.

Maths would be intolerable. All those numbers are bad enough on their own, but now all I see when I look at them is Philippa. She and Alfreya spent hours bent over a ledger at Palace Beautiful, keeping careful track of the farmstead's produce. And afterward, when we'd been sent back here, she tried to make a game of algebra for me, teasing me into laughter rather than tears when an equation wouldn't come out right.

I push through the press of girls and bolt down a back corridor.

The outside air reminds me how to breathe. It's crisp and already cool with the promise of autumn. I skirt the back of the school building, keeping close to the walls and out of sight, then sprint for the relative security of the gardener's cottage. No one calls after me—there's no indignant shout from any of the classroom windows. This time, I've escaped notice.

I stick to the narrow trail left by my own two feet as I cross the overgrown back field. Then through the gate to freedom. The tame woods of this world close around me, with their familiar scents and songs.

I cut through the forest to a place where the River Went runs dark and swift through the trees. With the noise of water to drown out my memories, I perch on a river rock and try to write a letter to my sister. I gnaw the end of a pencil and stare down at the blank page on my lap, wishing I could make a magic out of letters strung together. If I could—if some power commuted my words to an undeniable summons—I'm not sure who I'd call.

I miss you, Philippa. It's sharp as a toothache, this missing—new and fresh and undeniable.

I miss you, Cervus, like broken bones set the wrong way, a deep and abiding ache that never leaves me, a constant reminder of how far I am from home.

I sit by the rushing water, a patchwork girl, pieced together from bits of pain, all of them a different shape, a different color, a different sort of unhappiness. And the paper stays blank before me, because I don't know what to write. I don't know how to take back the things I've said and done, or to bridge the spaces that lie between us.

8 ⤴

WE JOURNEY THREE DAYS FROM THE BIRCH RING
with Cervus and a group of Woodlanders. There's Hector, whose
idea it was to put us to use against the Empire, and who's taken up
the leadership of our party. He travels without speaking for the most
part, and looks over his swords carefully every night when we make
camp.

A stonewarden joins us, too. His name is Dorien, and he stands
a foot shorter than I. He has a weather-lined white face, a thatch of
brown hair, and a friendly way of looking at the world. He and Jamie
walk together often, Jamie asking earnest questions about this strange
land we've come to, and Dorien answering patiently.

My favorite is Vaya, who's come on behalf of the tree spirits. She's
a tricky, lissome thing, made all of wind-tossed leaves that take the
shape of a girl with bark-brown skin and a fall of russet hair during
her quieter moments. I think she must be young, like my siblings and
me. She has an easy laugh like the bright chiming of bells, and leaves
the path often to venture into the woods. When she returns, she brings

gifts—a broken eggshell for Hector, who cups it in surprisingly gentle hands, or a crown of daisies for Dorien, who sets it on his head as if it's spun from gold.

On our third night out from the birch ring, I'm given a gift, too. I wake to find Vaya hovering at my side, the touch of soft leaves still lingering on my skin. She swirls into her girl shape and holds a finger up to quiet me, then beckons with her other hand. With a glance back at Jamie and Philippa, sleeping near the dying embers of our fire, I throw back my blanket and follow.

Vaya leads me deep into the woods, over mossy logs and boulder-strewn trails, past little clearings and over icy streams. Occasionally, when I have to stop and catch my breath, I call out to her. "Vaya, wait."

Every time she comes dancing back, laughing like a run of music and chiming in her bell-like voice, "Keep up, little one!"

The ground begins to slope upward and I pick my way between fallen branches and drifts of dead leaves. At last, I see that Vaya has stopped between the trees ahead. When I reach her, I stand and stare.

Beneath us lies a valley carpeted with green grass and spangled with white daisies. At its heart, a tree stretches its bony hands skyward. The girth of its trunk speaks of centuries growing in rich Woodlands soil, but though the spring air is warm even after nightfall, few of the tree's limbs bear leaves. Instead, small lights wink and glow from its naked branches, like stars pulled down from the sky.

Woodlanders move about below the tree, their shadowy forms still unfamiliar to me, but as Vaya and I watch, a silhouette I recognize appears. Cervus crosses the valley floor and walks through the assembled Woodlanders until he reaches the base of the tree. Once there, he lowers his head to rest it against the thick trunk, antlers and muzzle brushing rough bark.

A gust of leaves takes the shape of a woman with skin the same faded grey as the tree itself. Her face is lined with age, her head smooth and hairless. She turns her face toward the overhanging branches, and begins to sing.

The woman's voice rises, cold and clear and jubilant, to the sky, and I think when I listen hard enough, I can hear the stars answer back. Notes and words rise and fall, intertwining, soaking through my pores and spreading under my skin.

> "When the night breaks
> And the sun shines in
> I answer back
> Light unto light.
> May I be borne on
> Beyond the morning
> Beyond the stars
> Light unto light.
> Let the last of me
> Be given to flame
> Sparks flying upward
> Light unto light."

This world turns on its axis. Beneath me, the soil sings. Above me, the sky sings. Within me, my blood sings.

As the song swells and its highest note rises to fill all the Great Wood's empty spaces, Cervus throws his head back and bellows. The sound splits me apart and shakes the ground, ringing louder and louder until I can hardly stand it.

Then all falls abruptly silent.

Into the silence, Cervus speaks. He brushes his muzzle once more against the barren tree, then steps back and bows gracefully to the singer. Somehow, his words are harder to bear than even the singing, or the great stag's clarion call.

Cervus's voice rings out across the valley. "A Woodlands heart always finds its way home."

He drifts back through the gathered Woodlanders, heading away from us and into the trackless depths of the wood. I drop to the ground, wrapping my arms around my knees and letting what I have seen and heard sink further into me, fixing it forever in my heart and mind until I've reoriented myself, like a spinning compass that finally finds north.

"The singer is one of the great trees that were planted when the Wood was founded," Vaya chimes softly. I don't know how much time has passed, but away eastward the sky is growing grey. "There are very few of them left, and this is her last year. She won't live to see another summer. When winter comes, she will drop the few leaves she has and die, and be felled to warm Woodlanders who have blood and not sap in their veins."

"I'm sorry," I whisper.

Vaya rustles, the edges of her scattering into leaves once more. "Don't be sorry. Don't ever be sorry. Be bold, and remember—a Woodlands heart always finds its way home."

I swallow and look down into the valley.

"What is it?" Vaya asks.

49

"Were they from my world? The first of the Tarsin Imperials, who founded the Empire?"

"No."

Relief warms me from my head to my toes at that simple word.

"They were the last left living on their world, Heraklea, after a thousand years of war turned it to ash and ruin. When there was nothing left, they came here, to begin that war again."

I pick up a mossy pebble from where it lies, nestled in the undergrowth, and weigh it in my hand. "Their world sounds like mine. Terrible things are happening where I came from."

With a gust of wind, Vaya bursts apart into a joyous swirl of leaves. Taking shape again, she leans in close to me.

"Terrible things happen in all worlds, little one. But every tree and every leaf in the Great Wood would have to burn before we allowed such things to break us."

9

ON SATURDAY IT RAINS, AND MY MOOD IMPROVES. I'VE always loved the rain—the way it sang against the leaded glass windows of Palace Beautiful, the way the beach and the sea and the sky went grey, until the whole world was a blank canvas waiting for color.

I wade out to the gardener's hut in my galoshes and borrow an oversized mackintosh. Though I'd never say it and risk hurting his feelings, St. Agatha's groundsman, Hobb, really ought to take on help. He must have fallen behind on things the week after I went home.

Weeds choke the school gardens, grown up in my absence over the summer and reluctant to surrender their place. It was Philippa who first suggested garden work here at school might do me good—in the Woodlands I liked nothing better than working on the castle's farmstead with Dorien.

The smell of damp earth and green things growing reminds me overwhelmingly of home. The Great Wood is so near to me, in the sound of wind whispering by, and the chill taste of rain running down to the corners of my mouth. If I could shut my eyes and open them just so, I know I'd be back. St. Agatha's would vanish, replaced by a birch ring at the heart of the place I love best.

I spend an hour on my hands and knees with a trowel before reaching a patch of nettles. Rocking back on my heels, I swallow, setting the trowel down.

I shouldn't. I shouldn't. Philippa would be so disappointed. She'd fuss and cluck and lecture. She'd tell me we all have to do better, we all have to cope.

Glancing over one shoulder to ensure the quad is empty, I peel off my gloves. Just a touch. Just one more memory of home.

I take a saw-edged leaf between my thumb and forefinger and draw in a breath at the sharp, stinging pain. Pulling my hand back, I look at the place where the nettle kissed it. Red welts are already forming—the very skin of me is angry at what I've done.

Stop, Evelyn. Stop now.

But I am greedy for pain that hurts my hands more than my heart. With another furtive look over my shoulder, I reach out and tear up a fistful of nettles, then another, dragging them from the earth in great bunches.

When they all lie on the heap of weeds next to me, I bury my hands in the mud, not to dull the fierce burning but to hide what I've done. I don't want anyone to see, but at the same time I'm calmer now than I have been all week. Taking a deep breath, I straighten out the kinks in my neck and relax into the pain.

I don't know how long I crouch there in the downpour, languidly thinking of the day I burned my hands on priest's thistles in the Great Wood. Finally, a voice cuts through my reverie.

"Evelyn Hapwell?"

I turn as best I can and blink raindrops out of my eyelashes. Oh dear. I'd forgotten I was expecting a visitor. Tom Harper stands a few feet away, properly equipped for the weather in a mackintosh that nearly matches mine, but with the sensible addition of an umbrella. I realize for the first time that my skirt and wool stockings are soaked and muddy. The mound of weeds beside me is as high as Tom's knees.

"What are you doing?" he asks. His eyebrows are pulled together and he's squinting because of the rain. In spite of his height, he reminds me so strongly of a puzzled stonewarden that I purse my lips to keep from smiling. I want to be angry with him for intruding, but I can't—not when I gave him permission and when he looks so befuddled.

"What does it look like? Pulling weeds. Sorry, I forgot you were coming."

Tom folds up his umbrella and kneels beside me. "That's not very flattering, but how can I help?"

I turn back to a stubborn mess of roots and snip away at the worst of them with a pair of clippers, still trying not to smile. "There's a thistle over there that needs digging out. The spade's leaning up against the wall, just around the corner."

"Of course it's a thistle," Tom complains good-naturedly as he gets to his feet. "You would save the worst of the work for me."

I scrunch up my face at him in a way that says *don't you think you're funny*, but half of that waiting smile slips out, tugging at the corners of my mouth. It's only once he's gone round the corner for the spade that I sigh and set the clippers down. Stuffing my gloves into one pocket so they can't be seen, I shove the nettles down to the bottom of the pile of weeds.

"Blast," Tom grunts, yanking on the thistle a dozen or so yards down the main building's long stone wall. It comes loose all of a sudden and he topples over backward, sitting down hard in a puddle with a shocked expression on his face.

Laughter wells up out of me for the first time since school began, and Tom flashes me a wry grin from where he sits. "Am I impressing you with my competence? I'm born and bred on a Yorkshire farm, though you wouldn't know it to look at me just now."

Holding out a muddy hand, I help him to his feet, trying not to wince at the sting of my burns or to blush because my skin, damaged as it may be, is touching his.

"I think we've put in a good morning's work," I say. "Tea in the library?"

It's Max's doing that we can have visitors apart from family members. Philippa told me there had been a rule against it until Max informed the Curmudgeon that given the proximity of St. Agatha's and St. Joseph's, students were bound to be meeting anyway, so they might as well be supervised. Accordingly, we're allowed boys once a week in the library and the refectory. When Philippa was here she spent every Saturday presiding over a circle of lovestruck swains, though there was never a spark of hope for any of them.

This is the first time I've entertained a Saturday caller. We get cups of tea and plates of hot buttered toast and sneak them into the library when ancient Mrs. Everhart's back is turned. Georgie's at one of the study carrels, and I feel her eyes boring into the back of my head after we pass. I lead Tom to a quiet corner where a pair of armchairs are drawn up to a rain-spattered window.

Once he's settled, I excuse myself and hurry to the lav to wash up. There's no help for the fact that my stockings and skirt are filthy, but Tom's happily munching toast and leaving a damp patch on the library floor beneath his chair, so it's no matter. My hands are worse than I'd thought, covered in raised blisters up to the wrists. There'll be no hiding what I've done.

I hurry out of the lav and ignore Georgie's frantic waving as I weave back through the library shelves. At the edge of the last shelf, I stop short.

There's a girl leaning over the back of Tom's chair, chatting with him in that easy, familiar way all of Philippa's courtiers had. I don't know her name, but she was part of the outer circle, one of the girls who orbited Phil like slender, well-groomed moons, desperate to catch a bit of my sister's reflected glory.

I step out from behind the shelf and tuck my hands behind my back. The girl straightens and shakes a fall of flaxen hair back from her rose-pink face, fixing me with cornflower-blue eyes.

"Hello, Mad Hapwell," she says lightly, almost disguising the edge to her words. "Have you heard from Philippa? We're all longing for news."

"No." The word comes out terse and unpleasant. I'm slipping, losing the careful manners Philippa taught me in the Woodlands, but that question rattles me. I haven't heard from Phil, and I'm not likely to. But in spite of my bitter words before she left, I miss her like I'd miss a piece of my very own self; a limb perhaps, or a fragment of my soul.

The girl only laughs. She's uncaring as a water spirit, and casts a last inviting glance back at Tom as she walks down the rows of bookshelves, her school skirt swinging.

Jealousy bites at me, but I look at Tom Harper and he's not watching the girl go. He's taken no notice of her at all. Instead, he smiles up at me, his face open and honest, and holds out a paper bag that smells faintly of toffee.

The jealousy inside me twists, turning to shame. Tom's better than I am. And I know I'll lie to him if he asks about my hands, because I can't see a way around it.

Tom's smile vanishes as he catches sight of my burns. He reaches out, then draws his own hand back, reluctant to touch me, as if he knows it will hurt.

Oh, Tom Harper, if you only knew. I'd shy away from this whole world if I refused to touch things just because they hurt.

Rolling my eyes, I heave a sigh. "I tore through a patch of nettles without gloves. That'll teach me not to pay attention next time I'm weeding."

I wait anxiously to see if he'll catch me in the lie, but straightforward Tom only shifts in his chair, all worry and concern. "Should I go, so you can see the school nurse?"

"No, please don't!" The words come out so quickly I blush and glance down at my muddy boots. "I'm fine, and you came all this way. I'd hate for you to leave."

When I look up, Tom's smile is back. He offers the bag of toffee once more and I take a piece, embarrassed by my blistered hands. But Tom's smile never falters. "Do you always pull the weeds at St. Agatha's, Evelyn Hapwell?"

I nibble at the edge of my toffee. "Only on days when it pours."

We sit and watch rain sluice down the windows. I slide my boots off, pull my knees up to my chest, and let my eyes unfocus. Our surroundings go fuzzy, and this might be any window. The water sheeting over it might be Woodlands rain.

Tom's voice pulls me back to the present, quietly quoting a bit of verse. He's sitting forward, staring out at the rain, and his eyes are as far away as the Great Wood itself. There's something wistful and almost lovely about his ordinary face.

> *"There will come soft rains and the smell of the ground,*
> *And swallows circling with their shimmering sound;*
>
> *And frogs in the pools singing at night,*
> *And wild plum trees in tremulous white,*
>
> *Robins will wear their feathery fire*
> *Whistling their whims on a low fence-wire."*

I know these words. I've known two worlds' worth of songs and stories and poems, but these lines I hold very close. Tom's voice trails off as I pick up the last three verses.

> *"And not one will know of the war, not one*
> *Will care at last when it is done.*
>
> *Not one would mind, neither bird nor tree*
> *If mankind perished utterly;*

And Spring herself, when she woke at dawn,
Would scarcely know that we were gone."

We sit for a long time without talking and watch the rain until our tea goes cold, and I am enormously, unspeakably glad to have found someone I can be silent with.

That night, long after Tom has gone back to St. Joseph's and I've been subjected to merciless questioning from Georgie, I lie in the dark and fall into a dream that is half remembering.

Grey sand. Grey sea. Grey sky.

The entire world has been washed clean of any color, and the waves beside me sigh a melancholy song.

I stare out across the fathomless expanse of the sea, to the invisible point where it ends and the sky begins, and when I look back, there he is, coming along the beach. In dreams he's always more, somehow, than he was when I knew him. His split hooves leave deep impressions in the sand that fill with salt water, and he is everything bright and good distilled into a single point of intolerable light. A storm is not fiercer; an avalanche is not wilder; when he fixes his eyes upon me, I drop to my knees.

Words rumble up from his rust-red chest. The sea grows louder and his voice is overcome by the sound of waves and rain.

I wake filled with loss and longing. There is a grey ocean inside me that weeps and sighs. But when I turn my head, moonlight streams through the crack in my curtains.

For now, at least, the rain has moved on.

10

AT LONG LAST, WE'VE COME TO THE END OF OUR *journey through the Great Wood. A thin rain is falling the day Hector stops in a grove of pines, at the lead since Cervus left us following the lighting ceremony in the valley.*

"We're nearly there," he says.

I nod solemnly, as does Jamie. Philippa only sneezes—she's caught a cold, and looks worse off than the rest of us. Hector leads us through the pines until the soil grows sandy beneath our feet, and beach grass sprouts between the pine roots. Suddenly, the trees stop, and we step out onto a spit of sand.

Before us is the wide and restless sea, stretching to the horizon, and a long beach runs away to the north and south. Waves murmur against the shore, and rain sighs onto the sand. Philippa pulls her blanket up over her head and coughs.

Southward, perhaps a mile down the beach, a sheer grey cliff rises from the forest. A castle perches at the summit, grey, too, with vines softening its edges. Trees grow up between the curtain walls and the keep, and a pennant flies from the highest point, stitched in green and brown and blue.

I've seen castles in our world surrounded by barbed wire, with tanks and armed men in their courtyards. I watched them from train windows while speeding past on my way to yet another term of school, or another unfamiliar house with its own strange smells and rules. To see this place, alive and inviting, with its proud flag flying and smoke curling up from its many chimneys, makes me so glad I ache.

"Palace Beautiful," Dorien says as Hector leads the way toward it across the shell-strewn beach. "It was built long ages ago, in the years before the Wood. We use it as a meeting place now, when all the councils come together or on high days. Between times, Alfreya and I run it as an inn, so that those on their way through the forest can be sure of a warm bed to sleep in at least once along their way. It's as close a thing as we've got to a capital."

"A warm bed sounds like heaven," Philippa croaks, and I have to agree. These woods may be magic, but I'd love a chance to be clean and dry, with a roof over my head to keep off the rain.

Vaya appears in the shape of a girl. She hurries on ahead, taunting me with that chiming laugh of hers, and I can't help it. I grin and race after her across the sand, the sodden blanket around my shoulders flapping like another small standard.

A narrow stone stairway runs up from the base of the cliff, curving around through the woods, so that it's as if we're climbing among the treetops. By the time we come out into a wildflower meadow at the pinnacle of the cliff, I'm breathless, both from my run and from excitement.

The main gate stands open. Inviting smells drift out to us along with the wood smoke—roasting herbs and something warm and gamey.

"Well, praises be," Philippa murmurs at my side.

But we aren't meant to have a reprieve. I barely have time to glimpse gardens laid out between the walls and the keep, with thatch-roofed shelters for livestock. A tall woman with leaf-green eyes and dappled skin that runs the gamut from golden brown to snow white hurries out of the keep and over to Hector.

"Is Cervus with you?" she asks.

Hector shakes his head. "He left us after Mira's lighting ceremony. I don't know when he'll be back. Is there trouble, Alfreya?"

"The Tarsin delegation's here," the woman says, pushing the long braid of her auburn hair back over one shoulder. "They arrived just this morning, apparently at your request. That boy"—her mouth twists—"said he wanted a few words with the Children from Beyond before he carried on southward. I'd already heard rumors that Cervus had called between the worlds, or I'd have thought the Tarsin prince had taken leave of his senses. What shall I tell him?"

Hector looks at us, and there's a challenge in his eyes. "Can you be ready in an hour?"

Philippa sniffs. "Half, if need be."

For the first time that I've seen, Hector smiles. "An hour will do."

When Jamie, Phil, and I have been hurried upstairs, scrubbed clean and clothed in whatever Alfreya could find that fit, we're left alone together for the first time since coming to the Great Wood.

The room we're in on the fourth floor of the keep is large and blissfully warm, with a roaring fire and thick rugs to cover the stone beneath our feet. Jamie stands in front of the hearth in fitted breeches and a long tunic belted at the waist. It gives me a strange sense of nostalgia to see him this way—as if I'm recalling something that's happened before.

Philippa and I sit on a long carven couch mounded with pillows and I lean back against her, breathing in the clean smell of her hair. I'm dressed like Jamie, in clothes I suspect came from a stonewarden, and Alfreya kindly pulled my hair back into a braid. But Philippa wears one of Alfreya's own woolen kirtles, dyed the deep green of a pine copse in winter. Her hair hangs loose and curls at the ends as it dries and I can't help but shift closer, until she looks down at me and smiles. She's always been beautiful, our Philippa, but at home it was just in the usual way of pretty girls. Here there's something different—she's grown pensive over the last few weeks, and in spite of her head cold, once you've taken a look at her, it's hard to turn away.

We're all quiet for a while, listening to the snap and hiss of the fire and the fitful drumming of rain against the narrow windows, which are thankfully fitted with glass. Finally, Jamie speaks, his eyes fixed on the leaping flames. "This can't be a game to us."

I know his words are for me, and I stiffen.

"It's not just an adventure, or a fairy story," he says. "There's life and death hanging in the balance here, same as at home, and if anything our choices mean more now than they did before. What we do matters."

Pulling away from Philippa, I get up and walk over to one of the windows, watching rain trickle down its surface.

"Ev, did you hear me?" Jamie asks.

"Yes," I tell him. "I heard you. And you don't need to lecture."

"Are you sure?"

I turn to face him. "Of course I'm sure. I know what a war is like, Jamie. I've been living through it, same as anybody."

"Are you in this, too, Phil?" Jamie asks. I look over one shoulder and he's facing her. "Because at first it seemed like you were unsure."

Philippa stares down at her hands, neatly folded on her lap. "I gave my word to Cervus, Jamie, and when I do, I keep it."

A knock sounds at the door. Jamie squares his shoulders and I take in a breath. Philippa gets to her feet.

"Right," Jamie says. "Here we go. Time to play at being turncoats."

II ⚘

ON SUNDAY AFTERNOON, ONCE WE'VE GONE TO THE
little chapel in Hardwick and come back, I retreat to my own cathedral in the forest behind St. Agatha's.

I found it years ago—a birch ring, gleaming white in the wooded shade. There's no other place in this world that reminds me so strongly of home, so I lie on soft grass surrounded by the whispering birches and pretend that if I wanted to, I could wake them. I could set my book aside and run my fingers along smooth white bark only to have it turn to smoother white skin, and a birch girl step out to join me, tall and slender, with hair the color of new leaves.

Instead I turn a page, fumbling with swollen hands. When I glance up no tree spirit has appeared but Max is picking her way down the path, with a green scarf wrapped around her hair.

She drops onto the grass and peers at my book. "Dickinson. I should have guessed. What happened to your hands, Hapwell?"

"Nettles." I shrug. "When I was weeding yesterday morning."

"Yes, in the middle of a downpour. I saw." Max fixes me with her keen brown eyes, one leg tucked under her, the other drawn up to her chest. She rests her chin on her raised knee. "Why didn't you wear gloves?"

"Forgot." I stare down at the pages of poetry before me.

There's a long pause, and then—"Did you do it on purpose?"

I blink twice. "Of course not."

But the itch and burn of my hands is pulsing a reminder through my veins, of the dark wood and Cervus and how he moved through the trees, alone and wild and utterly free.

"I'll take you at your word." Max fiddles with a bangle wrapped around one of her wrists before speaking again. "Did you know I used to come out here to the woods, Ev? When I was a student at St. Agatha's?"

I roll over onto my side to look at her. "No, you've never said."

"Well, I did. The first few years were very hard—I felt worlds away from London, and most of the girls were unkind, thinking I didn't belong here. Whenever things got especially lonely, I'd walk to the woods. It didn't make things better, but it seemed more natural—to be alone by myself, rather than surrounded by people."

"Why did you stay?" I ask, not bothering to hide the desperation behind my words. "You could have left. What made you keep going?"

Max looks off into the forest's dim green depths. "If I'd left, it would've felt too much like other people made the choice for me. For some girls, it might've been better to go. For me, I knew I'd always regret it if I did."

"What if you could leave altogether?" I ask. "Not just St.

Agatha's, but England. What if you could go somewhere fairer? Would you?"

Max smiles and pats my hand. "Oh, Evie. I'd have to leave our world entirely to find such a place."

We sit in silence for a while, before she stands and brushes off her trousers.

"This wood does have its way with you once you walk in," Max says with a shake of her head. "I only came out here to ask if you'd recite at the winter concert."

I frown up at her in dismay. "Oh, Max, I'd rather not. I—"

She raises a hand to stop me. "Think about it. Don't make up your mind yet. You needn't choose something long, but it would be good for you, Ev. Give you a chance to show everyone else a glimpse of that mysterious soul of yours. There's months before I need an answer, so just sit with the idea."

I nod, because there's very little I wouldn't do for Max. The kindness she and Georgie have shown to me for years is so often more than I deserve.

"Anyway, I won't intrude any longer in your sanctum sanctorum," Max says. "But Georgie was looking for you, too. She says your brother rang, and he wants you to phone him back when you can. I'm going out—use the telephone in my room if you don't want the Curmudgeon listening in."

"Max."

She stops at the edge of the clearing and looks back at me.

"Thank you."

A crease forms between her eyebrows, the barest suggestion of worry. "Of course, Ev. We care about you here. You know that, don't you?"

I swallow back a tightness in my throat and nod. I do know, but sometimes things would be easier if no one cared. Simpler.

Max melts into the forest shadows and I roll onto my back, staring at the shifting latticework of birch branches and the sun and sky beyond. The day is warm, the ground still slightly damp from yesterday's rain, and a pungent, earthy scent rises from the woods around me. I suck in a breath of that agonizingly familiar smell, holding it to me the way I hold the discomfort in my hands. Memory is a sharp-edged knife I can't help but cut myself on, no matter how carefully I wield it.

The wind shifts as I squeeze my eyes shut. It brushes against the side of my face. The good earth holds me up. Light and shadow play across my closed eyelids. Beneath me, I can almost feel the world turn. Around me, I can almost hear the trees whisper.

"Cervus," I breathe. "I'm waiting. Come take me home."

When I open my eyes, the birch ring hasn't changed. My thin volume of poetry lies nearby, its pages rustling in the breeze. I still them with a blistered hand, and the words stand out, printed stark and black against white paper.

> *"I lost a world the other day.*
> *Has anybody found?*
> *You'll know it by the row of stars*
> *Around its forehead bound.*

A rich man might not notice it;
Yet to my frugal eye
Of more esteem than ducats.
Oh, find it, sir, for me!"

I hug the book to my chest and get to my feet. As I leave the birch ring, I brush one longing finger against the nearest tree's smooth, pale skin.

Wake up.

She sleeps on.

Max has finished her redecorating, though I can't imagine when she found the time during the rush of the first week back. The walls of her rooms are the color of lilacs, and all the windows are thrown open to catch the autumn breeze. Blue silk curtains billow on the wind like waves.

The phone rings half a dozen times before Jamie picks up, and when he does, he sounds breathless and happy. "Hello?"

"Jamie. It's Ev."

The happiness in his voice vanishes, fading as quickly as a shred of cloud on a hot summer day.

"Evie. I'm glad you phoned me back. How are you?"

He hesitates so briefly before asking the question that I wouldn't have noticed the pause if I hadn't known to listen for it.

"I'm well." I smile so he'll hear the expression in my voice, and shift the telephone receiver from one hand to the other. "It's good to be back, actually. And I met a friend of yours on the train—Tom Harper."

"Did you!" Jamie exclaims, as if he hadn't asked Tom to look out for me. He's not quite happy again, not the way he was before he knew it was me on the line, but I think he's relieved. "And what do you think of old Tom?"

I weigh my words. "He's nice. I like him. He came by yesterday morning, during visiting hours. We pulled weeds and had tea."

"Is that so?" Jamie's satisfied now, and I'll take that. "I thought he'd be good for you, Ev. I'm happy to hear the two of you are getting on."

"We are. For now," I say.

Jamie's quiet for a moment.

"I spoke with Philippa," he says after a long pause.

Everything in me freezes. "And?"

"She's met half the people in New Hampshire, from the sound of it, but that's just our Phil. Says she loves her classes, loves the countryside there. She said—"

I wrap the telephone cord around my wrist, just where the line of nettle welts begins. "What does she say, Jamie? Tell me."

"She said the woods there remind her of you."

I keep very still, not knowing what that means—whether my sister misses me, or hates that she can't escape the memories of all we've shared.

"Ev," Jamie asks, "did the two of you have a falling out before Philippa left? I know I wasn't home much over the summer, but when I was, you both seemed a little off center. And she made it sound as if she hasn't heard from you."

"I've written," I answer truthfully, though I've sent her nothing but line after line of poetry, copied out in my own hand. I can't find the right words for her, not anymore. "She never writes back."

"What happened?" Jamie asks.

Heat rushes into my face and pricks behind my eyes. I don't want to lie again. I've built myself a castle of lies since getting back to school, and I never used to be that way. My word was my bond, back home in the Woodlands. Now it's just a thing I use to hide who I really am, and how I really feel.

"Please don't make me tell," I say softly. "I can't talk about it, Jamie. I just can't."

"Evie, are you sure you're doing alright? Do you want me to come out there? I can be at St. Agatha's in two hours if need be."

"No!" I'm horrified at the thought. The last thing I need is Jamie catching a glimpse of my blistered hands. "I'm fine, I promise. I'll be fine."

"If you're sure . . ."

"I'm sure. Don't worry so much. You and Philippa are always fretting about me, but I'm not a child, Jamie. None of us have been, not for years."

I can hear his gusty sigh. It travels all the way from Oxford to Hardwick. "Isn't that the truth? Ring me if you need anything, though, Evie. Promise?"

"Promise."

"Bye, Ev."

"Bye, Jamie."

I hang up the phone and stand for a moment in the middle of Max's lovely rooms. She's strung a twist of wire from one of the curtain rods and bits of colored glass dangle from it on strings. They chime together when the wind blows, making a sweet, fey sort of sound. Like Philippa, Max builds her kingdom wherever she is, no matter how difficult it may be.

And me? I'm trying. But most days I'm just an exile with Latin homework waiting to be done.

12 ⌐

"*HERE'S HOW YOU'LL CONDUCT YOURSELVES TONIGHT,* *if you wish to help us,*" Hector warns when we open the door of the room we've been given and stand in front of him, clean and presentable and waiting to meet with Venndarien Tarsin again. "*Should the Tarsin heir angle for information about the Woodlands or our plans, deflect him or change the subject. You won't be able to answer anyway—you know nothing of the Great Wood yet. If he tries to strike up an alliance with you, seem interested but undecided. If he threatens, don't be concerned—you're in the care of the Woodlands now and we'll keep you safe. Try to ensure his attention stays on the three of you after he's left the Great Wood, rather than drifting elsewhere.*"

With those words still ringing in our ears, Hector shepherds us down to the castle's great hall. It's a long, cavernous room with two huge hearths at either end, both sending out waves of dry heat. Torchlight illumines the corners, and catches at gold threads in the tapestries. Venndarien Tarsin and his retinue are already seated at an enormous table.

The Tarsin heir slouches as we enter. He stays in his seat, eyeing Hector, who nods to Venndarien with more courtesy than he deserves.

"Venndarien Tarsin, First Son of Heraklea. The Great Wood greets you."

"The Empire does not hear you," Venndarien says. He snaps a finger and the skin stretched thin across the back of his hand begins to glow. Making a fist, he waits a moment before opening his hand. A ball of fire rests on his palm, perfectly round and apparently doing him no harm. Venndarien stares moodily into the flames, his strange eyes lit by their own internal fire.

As we sit, Dorien and Alfreya appear bearing enticing platters of mutton roasted with root vegetables and unfamiliar herbs. They set the platters down at the center of the table and sit, and once they're seated, the gathered Woodlanders help themselves. There's a party of stonewardens staying at the castle—olive-skinned and black-haired traders come in from a sea voyage to Illyria. A pair of centaurs, one with a copper-brown complexion and another with sunburned white skin, are passing by on their way to the singers' school in the south. The last to join us are a family of aelflings, as Hector and Alfreya's folk are called. I'm not sure who belongs to who—there are half a dozen adults who all have a familiar, comfortable way with each other, and at least twice as many children. The children eat quickly, or not at all, then play about under the table or at the far end of the room. They hardly seem to notice the tension in the air, and it does nothing to dampen their holiday spirits.

Hector joins one of the children in rolling a ball back and forth across the floor, but his swords are close to hand, and he glances at the table often.

For a time, those of us seated eat in silence. Philippa, Jamie, and I are so relieved to have a proper meal at last that it takes a few minutes before we notice the Tarsin heir hasn't touched his plate.

"Is there something wrong with the food?" Philippa asks icily.

My face heats as I glance over to her. I'm not sure this is how we're meant to behave. Alfreya and Dorien stiffen, and Hector watches from a distance, his eyes alight with interest.

"It's a little . . . simple for my liking," Venndarien Tarsin says. He still slouches in his chair and toys with his conjured fire. "It would be peasant's fare in my father's Empire. And the lack of respect the Woodlands continues to show for me as the Emperor's son and heir is an insult to Tarsa's power. Nowhere else would I be expected to eat with this rabble. If you and your brother and sister truly wish to become a force to be reckoned with—to use your knowledge of another world to your own advantage—you'll leave this backwater at the first opportunity."

Philippa presses her napkin to her lips and sets it down carefully. I know my sister. I've lived with her and fought with her and loved her all my life. When Philippa is careful, danger lies ahead.

"Sir," she says with a smile. "Not a month ago my brother and sister and I left behind a world of unimaginable violence and slaughter. We have traveled the length of the Great Wood since then, won the trust of its Guardian, sworn oaths at the heart of the forest, and now sit at table with you in this castle. Don't presume to lecture me on what's necessary to become a force you'll have to reckon with."

Venndarien sits forward as if he's about to speak, but Philippa raises a dismissive hand. "Convince us that an alliance with you would serve our interests better than staying in this backwater, as you call it. Convince me. That's why we're really here, isn't it? Because you want to bring us and the secrets you think we hold back to your father as a gift."

"My lady—" The Tarsin heir's eyes spark crimson, but Philippa cuts him off once more.

"The stories I could tell you, Venndarien Tarsin, of the world to which I was born. Stories of machines made for war, that rain fire and death from the sky, or spit it like hailstones from a thousand yards away. Your dreams of conquest are idle fancies compared to the things I have seen."

"Come with me," Venndarien rasps greedily. "Whisper your tales in the Emperor's ear, and I will make you a queen."

"No." Philippa waves a hand as if to dismiss him. "I've tired of you already. Anything else you wish to say may be said to my brother or sister. And I expect to wake in the morning and find you've gone. You're not welcome in this country, and we are, so you'll have to win us over by letter if you wish to present us as a prize in Tarsa. Good night."

She sweeps out of the room and the Tarsin retinue all begin speaking at once. It's only because I'm listening that I hear, muffled by the thick oak of the door Philippa shut behind her, a string of painfully hoarse sneezes.

For the rest of the evening, Jamie asks leading questions. He sounds reasonable and considerate, as if what he hears about the Empire's size and splendor and manifold resources are enough to impress. But at the end of the night, Venndarien parts ways with us and we've made no commitment.

Later, I lie in the room Philippa and I insisted on sharing, and listen to her coughing fitfully. The way Venndarien Tarsin watched her when she left the room turns my stomach. The hunger in his fiery eyes, as if she's something to be owned or conquered. It's the same way he looks at the Great Wood, and everyone who lives within it.

I may be young, but I've lived for years in a world where the language of force is the one used most readily. I don't like the shape of its words. I don't like the way it tastes on my tongue. Nevertheless, I will use it too, if I must.

I slip out to the stables in the dim light before dawn and watch the Tarsin delegation readying their horses for the long journey south.

"You'll have to come visit the capital one day, little fawn," Venndarien Tarsin says to me, with almost a laugh in his voice. "When we're allied, and your sister and I rule all this world together."

In answer, I take out the knife I've borrowed from the kitchen. I set its blade to my palm and draw it hard across my skin, just as I saw Jamie do in the birch ring. Blood drips from my hand to the ground and smokes, a reminder that I've walked between the worlds.

Venndarien's dead-white face grows whiter. "What are you playing at, girl?"

I stare at him until he's trapped by my attention and can't look away. "I swear to you, by my breath and bones and whatever power rests in my blood, that allies or not, if you touch my sister I will kill you."

There's a shocked silence before the first nervous chuckle breaks out. It's not long before all the men are laughing. They mount up and ride past me and I watch them go.

Let them laugh. I meant every word of my oath, though it turned my stomach even to speak it. Leaving the castle, I walk, losing myself in the glory of the Great Wood at dawn, letting my darkness burn away in its light.

13

MY HANDS KEEP ME AWAKE LONG AFTER LIGHTS-OUT.
Max was right. Tom was right. I should have worn gloves. I haven't
got Philippa to look after me anymore, and I need to start taking
care of myself. I can't go down this road again.

The sensible thing to do would be to visit the school nurse.
Instead, I slip into the shadowy hallway and down the dormitory's
wide front stairs. Faint music drifts from Max's rooms, and when I
feel around the base of the potted fern, the cold metal of the key she
keeps hidden for me offers itself up to my fingers.

I slide out into the waiting dark. The night air soothes my troubled spirit and as I walk across the gravel quad, toward Hobb's hut
and the back field and the gate beyond, a trio of cats flits along
behind me. They're grey, ghostly things—wild creatures that won't
let anyone near them, but I've been feeding them for years and they
know the sound of my footsteps. The three of them trail after me
like little wraiths, and I walk backward to watch them. I may be
worlds away from where I belong, but they neither know nor care.

I stop at the back gate and turn my face up to the star-bright sky, just breathing. Here I am. Here's the Evelyn I lose during the day, in among other people. Evelyn of the Woodlands, who knew where she belonged. I catch at that other self and bid her come to me, to make me whole and brave.

And because I'm emboldened, I take the familiar path to St. Joseph's. Before Jamie left for college, on nights like this I'd have dragged him out for a wander. While he'd have had better things to do and said so, he'd still have indulged me. Jamie was always more of a one for this sort of thing than Philippa, who'd pat me on the head and tell me to enjoy myself. If she snuck out, it was to thumb a ride into town to go to the makeshift cinema in Hardwick with her courtiers.

The crumbling stone building of the boys' school looms in front of me, and I nearly bump into someone hidden in the shadows beneath a spreading oak. It's Gorsley—I know all of the school's smokers by now, having come after curfew so many times. He's one of St. Joe's scholarship boys, and his face gleams pale beneath the moon, devoid of summer color. His classmates may have spent their holidays enjoying the sun, but Gorsley passed his cooped up in a woolen mill working alongside his parents and older sister. I suppose it's why he can't get enough of the country air during terms.

"Hello, Hapwell. Fancy a smoke?"

"No, thank you," I say with a smile. There's still a cat behind me, one last straggler peering out from behind a tree with eerie eyes. Gorsley scratches the back of his head and gives the cat an uncertain look.

"Is that your familiar, then? You out here communing with the devil, Haps?"

I cross my arms. "Don't be ridiculous. I would like to commune with Tom Harper, though."

Gorsley raises both eyebrows and stubs out his cigarette against a tree trunk. "Is that what they're calling it now? You and Tom, eh? I never thought I'd see the day."

"Oh, shut up," I grumble. "Are you going to get him or not?"

"Depends." Gorsley shrugs, inspecting his fingernails. "What's in it for me?"

"Packet of peppermints to keep you from smelling like an ashtray."

He holds out a hand. "Make it lemon drops and you've got a deal."

"I always knew you were sour." We shake on it, and Gorsley disappears inside. I crouch down and coax the cat out with a gentle voice.

"Come on. I'm not going to hurt you."

The little creature creeps up, wide-eyed and skittish, and butts its head against my knee before the creak of the dormitory door sends it flying back into the undergrowth. I straighten and turn, and there's Tom, grinning in the moonlight.

"Walk with me?" I ask. He nods.

I take him to the hills overlooking the sheep fields. A part of me wants to take him to the birch ring, but I can't, not just yet. There's too much of who I am there, and tonight is about who I'm trying to become.

We sit together on a hillside, and I keep my hands out of sight. The skin stretched across my palms and fingers is blistered and unlovely, even under the silver moon.

Tom leans back and surveys the view with a contented sigh. "Isn't that a picture?"

I hug my knees to my chest and rest my chin on them. It is. It's beautiful, even though the trees are voiceless and there's no water spirit in this happy little brook. The sheep below are just mute animals, and the dogs that guard them are clever but not clever enough to speak. This world is asleep, and no matter how many times I've wandered and wondered and spoken and sung, I've never been able to wake a single thing.

Sometimes I feel as if I'm asleep, too, lost in a dream I can't escape from.

But at the same time, there's a piercing beauty to this, to being out in the cool night air surrounded by the smell of meadow grass and the sound of the brook. The moon that shines here looks just like the moon did in the Great Wood, after all, and I have a friend beside me. This is a good dream.

Be bold, I tell myself, even as I feel my courage begin to flag. I snatch the last threads of it and speak before I can lose my nerve.

"I pulled the nettles up on purpose," I say, wishing the words back almost before I've spoken them. "I knew what they were and I was paying attention and I should have worn gloves, but I did it anyway."

I stare out across the sheep fields. It isn't the first time I've done something of this sort, and it probably won't be the last. Now Tom knows, I'm not sure what he'll do.

"I don't always like who I am." I steal a glance at him. "I don't expect you to either, but I wanted you to know."

Tom shifts in place. I'm drawn to this thoughtful, quiet boy, and to the calm at his very center. I'm still studying his profile when he turns to me, his freckled face serious. "I don't think anything could stop me liking you, Evelyn. And we're all a bit frayed around the edges, aren't we? It doesn't surprise me and it doesn't frighten me, finding out you're only human like the rest of us."

He reaches out and takes my stinging hand in his own, twining his fingers through mine.

I will never move again.

I will live and die here, content for once in this world to which I don't belong.

It's nearly midnight by the time I return to St. Agatha's and slip through the back gate. When a dark shape looms up before me, my hand reaches for a knife I no longer wear. I can never shake that instinctual motion, and it's a wrench every time I discover how helpless I am in this place, how spineless and biteless and unsure.

"Nah then, Miss Evelyn, I only waited up to make sure you got back safe and sound."

Hobb stands stooped in the shadows with a steaming thermos in one hand and a pipe in his mouth, wrinkles seaming his age-spotted white skin. I shake my head as my heartbeat slows and steadies. "Hobb, you scared the wits out of me. You should be in bed."

"Says the pot to the kettle, Miss."

I roll my eyes and he chuckles like an elderly and mischievous owl before handing me the thermos. Expecting tea, I swallow without hesitation, only to have the honey sweetness and whiskey kick of a strong hot toddy burn down my throat. I muffle a cough in my sleeve and elbow Hobb in the ribs—gently, because he's grown frail and slow in the last few years.

"If the Curmudgeon ever caught you plying students with your home brews, you'd be out on your ear." But I take another sip of the potent concoction, slowly this time, letting it linger on my tongue until I taste lemon and cinnamon.

Once we'd settled into the Woodlands, Jamie and Philippa and I used to drink spiced mead on winter evenings, next to one of the enormous fireplaces in the great hall. We'd listen to Dorien, Alfreya, and Hector go over briefings or battle plans or budgets, though on rare nights they'd set aside their work and just talk. I loved those nights best—the ones on which we'd speak of a future that might never come. We'd plan journeys to the singers' school or the western mountains, and expansions to the beach market that drew ships from across the world to the spit of sand below Palace Beautiful every summer. Hobb's hot toddy tastes like those long ago, faraway evenings.

I tuck my arm through his, and we walk back across the overgrown field to the tiny, tumbledown cottage. When we've said good night, I watch Hobb totter in through the door and the breath catches in my chest. I never had a chance to watch Dorien grow old. I didn't get to grow old myself in the company of Vaya, who'd still be young and lithe long after I'd gone grey. We were taken away too soon, thrown back into this world where I was barely more than a child again, caged in an unfamiliar body.

I can't. I can't think of this. I mustn't. I need to be present, be in this world. Though years have passed since we were called, I've never yet learned the trick of life here. But I've fought every day, in this battle that's taken more from me than any war.

The truth is, I'm tired. I'm so very tired of the fight. I slip in through the front door of the dormitory and return the key to its hiding place under the fern. It's late—no light gleams from Max's room. I ghost up the stairs in my stocking feet and slide into bed fully dressed, where I fall into a sleep plagued by dreams.

Grey sand. Grey sea. Grey sky.

Cervus comes toward me on the beach.

14

"DON'T TOUCH THOSE," DORIEN WARNS.

I glance up and wipe a hand across my face, leaving tracks of dirt. Jamie and I are Downhill, as the Woodlanders refer to the group of clearings on the woodward side of Palace Beautiful's rise. Each clearing is planted or set to pasture so that as you walk through the tangle of the forest, you'll come suddenly upon neat wattle fences, a shed, and half a dozen goats. Or a network of raised beds, with scarlet berries ripening on the vine. Or a field of leafy mounds, promising vegetables come autumn. At the center of each clearing is a little stone well tapping into the groundwater beneath the Great Wood's floor. It's very charming, and Dorien nearly bursts with pride each time I tell him so.

At the moment he stands nearby, planting berry canes and keeping a watchful eye on Jamie and me as we pull weeds. I've come to a patch of small green thistles at the clearing's edge and Dorien shakes his head.

"Mark those well, Evelyn. They're priest's thistles, and they have a nasty sting. You'll need thick gloves to pull those. There should be some in the barrow."

The sun shines high overhead and woodland insects sound their *brassy song. I know it's nearly time for our noon break, when we'll sit companionably in the shade of the trees, propped against their trunks while we eat spiced beans and salt fish and goat cheese, washed down with cold well water.*

But today things are different. Today, Vaya comes into the clearing with a sound of bells.

"You're wanted," she whispers in my ear. "They need you up the hill."

She hovers beside Dorien, who listens intently and then glances over one shoulder, as if he expects to see strangers at the clearing's edge.

"Come now," he says seriously. "Hector's back from the southern border. He has news of the Empire we're all meant to hear."

Philippa waits for us at the castle gate, and I hardly recognize the girl she was in England. We none of us look like we did there. After half a year, I'm already beginning to forget that world—the food, the clothes, the manners. And I want to forget. I throw myself willingly into learning Woodlands customs, in hopes they'll erase the memories of a home that was never home, where I was shuffled between strange houses and school like a piece of unwanted baggage. I don't ever think of our last night there anymore—I've grown a hedge around that memory.

Philippa is, as always, far tidier than Jamie and me, in a clean blue kirtle. While we've been taken in hand by Dorien and are being taught to work the Woodlands earth, she stays behind each day with Alfreya. Philippa works in the kitchen or the palace infirmary, but more often manages an ongoing correspondence with Venndarien Tarsin, and with the Emperor's numerous scribes and ambassadors.

When the three of us were asked to decide who would stay at the castle to deal with letters from the Empire, Philippa laughed.

"Give me the job where I don't have to get my hands dirty," she said.

But there's a sadness in her eyes when Jamie and I leave her behind each morning.

"Phil, aren't you happy here?" I asked her one morning as we left. "I know it's been awhile since we arrived—"

"Five months and nine days."

"—and that you worry about Mum and Dad, but Cervus promised they wouldn't even know we'd gone. Don't you think he's good for his word?"

"Of course I do." Philippa smiled so brightly she dazzled me, like sun on waves. "And I'm not unhappy, you goose. I'm far too busy for that. Now hurry along—you've got your work to do and I've got mine."

Now Philippa waits only until Jamie, Dorien, and I have reached her before turning toward the castle and catching all of us up in her wake.

We gather in the great hall, where Hector and his band of Woodlanders are tearing into the first hot meal they've had in weeks. They tell tales of the southern border—of trees felled, villages burned, and people dragged away never to be seen again. The Empire refuses to claim the raids, but we know who's behind them. We know that Tarsa is testing this country's strength.

I curl up on the floor beside Cervus, one arm around his shoulders for comfort and courage. Philippa sits alone, perched on the edge of a chair, with her face blank and her hands folded on her lap.

"Perhaps we'd better begin this war in earnest," Dorien says, running a hand across his weathered face. "With the Empire already fighting the Illyrians in the west, they'd at least be stretched thin. Are you ready, Hector?"

A muscle works in Hector's jaw. "No. We never will be, truly, but I'd hoped for more time."

"Give me a month," Philippa cuts in, looking down at her hands. "A month, and no more. If Tarsa still claws at the border after that, do what you will. But let me write to Venndarien. Time is what you hoped my brother and sister and I could get you. Let me try for it once more."

Hector looks at her, as if peering into her very soul. "And what will you attempt to win it with?"

"Flattery." Philippa smiles. "Flattery and half promises, and fables about our world. They'll go further than you think."

"Give her the month," Cervus says, and it's decided.

Later, when the hearth fires have burned low and it's well past midnight, we all go our separate ways. Jamie, Philippa, and I walk up to our bedrooms on the fourth floor, my brother and sister carrying lit lamps while I follow along in the glow they give off.

For a moment on the landing, Jamie pauses and stares out the window to the lights shining from the courtyard below. Hector's Woodlanders are camped there, the ones who've learned the sword and the bow and the determination necessary to take a life. My brother shifts restlessly. I know he's longing to join a different sort of campaign than the one Philippa runs with diplomacy and words.

When we wake in the morning, Hector and his Woodlanders are gone and Jamie's gone with them. He's left a note for Phil, which she reads with a scowl that doesn't quite hide her worry.

"Ridiculous boy," she snaps. "He'll get himself killed."

Night after night for a month, light shines out from Philippa's study, where she sits at her desk writing furiously. She never tells me what it is she says to Venndarien in her bid to hold off a war—when pressed, Philippa only smiles brilliantly and pats my hand.

"We'll be safe," she promises. "One way or another. And we'll get home when all this is done. I promise you, Ev. Leave it to me."

So the three of us each find our weapon—for Jamie the sword, for Philippa the pen, and for me the seed. Because there is power in these things—in bravery and cleverness and hope. I try to remember this as I work alongside Dorien, planning and working for the winter to come, and the spring after that. He and I fight with our belief, that there will be a Woodlands still left to plant for.

I sink every seed into the rich forest earth with a prayer for peace on my lips and under my skin.

15

WE'RE GIVEN OUR MAIL AFTER DINNER. GEORGIE CURLS up on her bed with a package of sweets and a thick letter from one of her cousins. I sit at the desk with letters from my parents and from Jamie that have been passed over in favor of a note from Tom. I try not to notice the continuing absence of anything from Philippa.

Tom's untidy scrawl rambles across a single page, eating up paper at an alarming rate.

> *Hello, Ev.*
>
> *I'd ask if you've pulled any weeds lately, but as the weather's been fine, I suppose you haven't. I'll be by again on Saturday, if it's alright with you, and I'm looking forward to the exciting groundskeeping tasks you've surely got planned for me. Here's something for you in the meantime.*
>
> *Tom Harper*

I've just opened up the little paper-wrapped box that came along with his note and found it full of toffee when Georgie speaks.

"Ev, take a moment and look at yourself, will you? Tell me what you see."

I glance back at her. I hadn't thought she was paying any attention to me.

"Go on then," Georgie coaxes. I look up at the mirror that hangs above the desk, still thinking of the note, and the gift, and that it's really terribly kind of him after so many years of sugar rationing.

And the girl staring back from the mirror's gilt frame takes me entirely by surprise. It's me, to be sure, but a me who's smiling, not just with her mouth, but with her eyes.

Georgie gets up off the bed and pads over to me in her bedroom slippers. She leans down so that her face is next to mine, and she's smiling, too. "Ev, darling, you look *happy*. Do you feel it?"

I turn inward, prod cautiously at my heart, my soul, my mind. "I think I do."

Georgie presses a quick kiss to my cheek. "Good. Then that boy is worth having around."

She retreats to her bed again, and I lean back in my chair, unable to look away from my own reflection.

I'm happy. I'm happy right here, right now. At St. Agatha's, in my cramped, familiar room with Georgie not ten feet away. The door's open, and the usual early evening sounds drift in—girls chattering and laughing, a hair dryer being run, someone practicing the violin. From where I'm sitting I can see the end of the hallway, and Max seated on a chair there. She's got it tilted back against the wall and a pile of papers that need grading rest forgotten on her lap, because a first year's regaling her with some sort of story, adoration plain on her childish face. Max nods indulgently until the girl's finished speaking, then says something with a smile and the first year skips away. The Bakelite radio next to Max's chair crackles a bit, and she leans down to turn up the sound as a new jazz standard starts up.

I snap off a bit of toffee and let it melt on my tongue, sweet and rich after the usual lumpy, tepid school dinner. I'm happy, and for once I don't wish I was elsewhere.

But I do wish it was Saturday.

I'd hate to disappoint, so when the weekend comes I get to work early, out in the large, weed-infested kitchen garden behind St. Agatha's. It's a mess of thistles and birdsfoot trefoil and dandelions with taproots as thick as my thumb. Hobb rakes up leaves that have drifted between the beds and carts them over to a sandy-soiled corner to burn. Soon the pungent smell of smoke hangs on the brisk October air.

Beyond the stone wall that borders St. Agatha's grounds, the trees are luminous, ablaze with autumn splendor. Inside the wall, the sounds of shouting and of a high-pitched whistle float over from the mown area to the side of the dormitory, where some of the girls are playing field hockey. The cook, a broad, quick-tempered woman with greying brown hair and a face the color of the tasteless mashed potatoes she serves, stumps out from the main building to inspect my handiwork. She points out a few salvageable vegetables she wants for dinner before trudging wearily back inside.

I'm on my knees pulling up turnips when Georgie appears, a copy of *Jane Eyre* and a notebook tucked under one arm. She's meant to be studying, but from the way she bounces on the balls of her feet I can tell she's full of frustrated energy and would rather be anywhere else.

"Can I help, or are you expecting your swain?" Georgie asks.

I rock back onto my heels and squint up at her in the bright morning sun. "I am expecting him, but I do need help. Did something happen?"

"I could use some fresh air," she says, picking up a spade and stabbing it into the earth fiercely. "I tried to convince Penwallis's study group to read *Annie Allen*, and got the usual lecture about sticking to good English authors for my pains. Which of course means white English authors, and before you remind me, I know, Evelyn, Cambridge, but honestly, at what cost?"

Georgie stalks off across the kitchen garden and sinks down to sit with her back against the low stone wall. We respect each other's need for distance, Georgie and I, and so I don't go after her—she always wants time after something like this, to scribble down new lines of her own verse. No one's ever allowed to read it—not me, not even Max. I suppose it's Georgie's way of wandering in the woods.

After half an hour, she sets her notebook aside and joins me. I hold the spade out wordlessly and she takes it with a sigh. So Georgie and Hobb and I all work together, putting the garden to rights. Before long there are swaths of dark, fragrant soil showing where Hobb has raked and I've weeded and Georgie has turned over the earth. When the weeding's finished I fetch another spade, and we dig without speaking as rooks call to each other from the dormitory eaves.

We're nearly finished when Tom shows up. Georgie's in better sorts, teasing Hobb about something as I straighten and brush my hands off on my dirt-stained trousers.

"Alright, Georgie?" I murmur, and she nods.

"Alright, Ev."

"You're late," I tell Tom as he stops in front of us. "There's no groundskeeping left to be done. Better turn around and walk back to St. Joe's."

"Very well," Tom says affably, and turns to go.

I hurry to catch up with him and wave goodbye to Georgie, who smiles and shakes her head.

Tucking my arm through Tom's, I steer him away from the school buildings and the front drive, and toward the back field.

"Best not go that way," I explain. "We're not allowed to leave school grounds except on special occasions, and then only with a chaperone. Must be very freeing to be a boy, and go where you will."

Tom raises an eyebrow. "I hadn't thought of it that way."

"Of course you haven't. You don't need to." We arrive at the back gate, which I open with a shove. The rusty hinges complain, but finally give. Tom stands back and watches.

"What was that about you not being able to go where you will?"

I frown. "It's just more complicated. Are you coming?"

He has to stoop very low to get through the gate. We amble down the leaf-strewn laneway, and because I have been happy for days and feel as if I'm about to shed old skin and emerge reborn, I lead us off into the woods.

Tom's as loud as an ox as he stumps through the forest, but I take off my shoes and walk in just my stockings, moving along without so much as snapping a twig. At one point, when Tom bends down to tie up his bootlace, I go on ahead and slip behind a thicket of dense undergrowth.

When he straightens, I stifle a laugh at the look of confusion that crosses his face. "Evelyn? Ev? Where've you got to?"

"Here," I call.

"Where?" Tom scans the surrounding forest, but can't place the source of my voice until I reach a hand out through the thicket and beckon to him.

He pushes through to join me, and when he's come out on my side with leaves in his hair, I point to what lies before us. "Look. I wanted to show you this."

Through the grey-brown trunks of the beeches, my birch ring gleams, the grass at its heart still jade green, even in fall.

"Now that's something I haven't seen before," Tom says, before narrowing his eyes at me suspiciously. "Ev Hapwell, are you one of the Folk? Am I being fey-led, and when we walk back out of this wood, a hundred years will have gone by?"

I make no answer, but step out onto the greensward and sink down to sit on the velvet grass.

After hanging back for a moment, Tom joins me. We lie on our backs and watch the pale blue autumn sky, and the waving tree branches, and the golden leaves, a few of which fall in a little flurry each time wind stirs the birches.

Eventually, I hear the rustle of brown paper and Tom passes me a wrinkled bag from in his coat pocket. Not toffee this time—I've eaten the last of it, I suppose—but peppermint lozenges. I put one in my mouth and suck on it as the wind travels over us and the grass ripples around us and the world turns beneath us.

By the time we sit up, it's grown a good deal colder, and shadows stretch long across the ground.

"It's like a church," Tom says, still staring at the arch of the tree branches overhead. "That's how it makes me feel. Like I shouldn't speak too loudly, and like I can't quite wrap my mind around all of it."

I reach out and take both his hands in mine. My blisters have scabbed over, and itch now rather than burn. We sit cross-legged, face-to-face in the birch ring as twilight creeps in. "Tom Harper, what if I told you I'm from another world?"

He looks at me, his grey eyes serious. "In this place, I'd believe you."

"And outside? Away from here?"

Tom turns away and smiles ruefully. "Maybe not. Would you say it to me elsewhere, though?"

I run a hand through the soft grass. No. I haven't got the courage. But I'm not sure it matters anymore.

I scramble to my feet and reach a hand down to help Tom up. "Come on. If I'm not back for dinner, the Curmudgeon will be sure to notice. And I ought to return you to St. Joe's before a hundred years have gone by."

16 ~

"YOUR SISTER WANTS A WORD WITH YOU AND YOUR
*brother, up in the study before dinner. She's had a letter from the Tar-
sin heir," Alfreya says to me one autumn afternoon, five years after our
arrival in the Woodlands. I've come up from the castle farmstead and
I'm still sweating and grimed with dirt.*

*"Is Jamie home?" I ask, delighted. He's been away with Hector and
a contingent of the army we all swear the Woodlands doesn't have.
We're still not at war with the Empire—not officially, not yet—but for
a long time now, things have been strained between us. Philippa may
have managed to stall the raids four years ago with a flurry of letters
between her and the Tarsin heir, but new outposts have gone up on the
far side of the southern border. Barracks have been built. Troops are
waiting. It can't be long now. It worries Philippa, I know—for months,
she's been quiet and withdrawn, and I catch her watching me in the
evenings with a sorrowful look in her eyes.*

*I hurry up to my room to take a bath and change, slipping into
a clean woolen kirtle belted with green. The door to the study on the
top floor of the keep is half open. I pause outside, the sound of voices*

stopping me in my tracks. I shouldn't listen—I should know better at sixteen, but curiosity gets the better of me.

Hector's inside, standing in the center of the room, which is mostly taken up by an enormous desk. She sits behind it, in the attitude I've grown so used to, her chin resting on one hand, a quill still held in the other.

"—wrote to me and said that unless his father receives oaths and an initial tithe by then, it'll mean a declaration of war," Philippa tells Hector. She sets her quill down and rubs at her forehead. "I'm sorry. I'm so sorry. I'd hoped—well, I'd hoped it wouldn't come to this. Not here, too."

Philippa turns to the long window beside her that looks down at the plangent grey sea and the little square-sailed fishing boats coming in for the evening. For a moment, she seems a world away.

"The tides of war are sometimes impossible to turn," Hector says. "But we've done everything we could to keep peace in the Woodlands. Even you've played your part."

"The tides of war," Phil says, half to the view of the sweeping sea. "What grim tides I've seen, Hector. Not battles or border skirmishes, but a war that stamped its mark on my entire world. No matter which way I turned, I couldn't escape the reminders of it. The air raids, and blackouts, and hiding in bomb shelters. The boys on street corners, missing limbs, without a bit of hope in their eyes, not knowing how they were meant to live. I don't want to see such things again. I don't want my sister to—that war hurt her even more than it hurt me."

"Philippa," Hector says. "It's not too late for you to go home."

"Isn't it, though? I—"

Booted footsteps sound on the staircase, and Jamie appears in the hall.

"Steady on, Evie," he says. "What are you doing, skulking up here?"

"Oh, shut up," I grumble, hoping Hector and Philippa haven't overheard and learned I've been eavesdropping. Jamie smells of horses, wants a shave, and still wears his faded and mud-stained travel clothes, but I throw my arms around him anyway. "I'm glad you're back."

"So am I. Did you talk to Phil yet?"

"No, I was waiting for you," I say, somewhat dishonestly. "But I don't think she has good news."

Jamie shakes his head. "No one has good news in the Woodlands right now. Things are very tense in the south. Should we go in and hear the worst of it?"

I nod, and we walk in together arm in arm, passing Hector, who's on his way out.

Philippa stands at the window now, still staring out at the mournful sea and the boats being dragged up on shore. I go to my sister and put an arm around her waist. For the briefest moment, she rests her dark head on my shoulder.

"I'm sorry, Ev," she murmurs.

"Sorry for what?"

Philippa doesn't answer. Instead, she sits down at the desk so that it stands between her and Jamie and me.

"Venndarien's coming back to the Woodlands one last time on the Emperor's behalf," she says. "A fortnight from today. I couldn't hold him off any longer, though heaven knows I've tried. He wants our allegiance and a yearly tithe or his father will declare war on the Great Wood. I've just told Hector. Alfreya already knows."

"We can't pay," I tell my sister flatly. "That's all there is to it. This is the Woodlands—we can take care of ourselves, but a wealthy country we're not."

"Don't tell me. He wants payment in timber rather than gold." Jamie's mouth turns down at the corners as he speaks, and my skin crawls. No one fells a tree in the Great Wood unless it's already standing dead.

Philippa nods. "To fuel their other war effort, against the Illyrians in the west, and which we've already contributed iron ore to behind the Empire's back."

"The Empire will have to wipe out every Woodlander in the Great Wood if he wants the forest's tinder," I say. "Surely Venndarien knows that."

"I think he does," Phil answers. She knits her hands together, an unconscious and anxious gesture. "He's pressing the point for exactly that reason. He was willing to play games for a while, and dance around the question of whether or not we'd leave the Woodlands for the Empire. But that was before fighting on the Illyrian front took up so much of the Empire's time and resources—the Illyrians are desert folk, and their land and people withstand Heraklean fire far better than the Woodlands will. The Empire needs timber to feed their flames if they're to prevail in Illyria, which means the Emperor won't wait for the Great Wood any longer."

"This is it, then," I say.

My brother nods. "I suppose so."

"No matter what preparations have been made, it will be ugly," Philippa says, her voice low. "And we'll be in the thick of things. What we lived through in London will be nothing compared to this."

I have Philippa's same memories of war. Of being desperate to escape the fear as well as the day-to-day, grinding tedium of it. Of wishing myself straight out of one world and into another. But this is the Woodlands, where I found a safe haven for a time. I love the people who live in the Great Wood, tilling its soil and singing its songs. I love the forest itself—its clearings, thick with wildflowers; its little rivers that laugh over smooth stones; its green-shadowed, tremulous depths. I love this castle by the sea, where I've lived for longer than anywhere I can remember in the world I was born to.

I was always on my way from one place to the other in England, never having time to settle and put down roots. Here, my roots go down to the very heart of the Great Wood, and plucking them up might kill me.

I know now I'd go through worse things than war if it meant keeping the Woodlands safe. And war, it seems, is finally coming.

17

THIS IS WHAT TRYING TO LIVE IN OUR WORLD LOOKS LIKE:
Saturday afternoons clearing the back field with Tom Harper.

He works as hard as three men, and it doesn't take us long to get the last of the gardens sorted. It seems natural after that to turn our attention to the field. We dig up brambles and fill in holes and patch the roof of an old cowshed near the rusty gate.

On a drizzly morning in late October I'm out back hacking away at a particularly insistent vine that's draped itself over the fence and threatens to pull sections of it down. I don't expect Tom—he'd have a terribly wet walk—but then I hear a shout and see him standing under the eaves of Hobb's hut.

"Ev! Come in out of the rain. We've got a surprise for you."

I leave the vine to live another day and hurry across the field. Hobb is just stepping out of the cottage in one of his worn grey mackintoshes, and I'm wearing its twin. He seems to have an end-less supply of them. Tom's got one on as well, and we look like a trio of overgrown gadwall ducks.

"Well, Miss Evelyn," says Hobb. "How do you fancy a drive into town?"

"Am I allowed?" I ask.

Hobb taps the side of his nose and winks broadly. "I've worked it out with the old Curmudgeon myself."

"Should I change?"

Tom shakes his head. "No. You're perfect for where we're going."

I wonder at that. I look like the muddier incarnation of a fisherman, but we pile into the front of Hobb's ancient lorry and rattle down the lane into town.

Hardwick isn't exactly a thriving metropolis. If it weren't for the nearness of both St. Agatha's and St. Joseph's, it'd just be another village in farm country. But the schools have guaranteed it a railway station with a platform and tiny depot, and there's even a sort of cinema, with folding chairs and a bedsheet for a screen. Besides that, Hardwick has a chemist and a dry goods shop, a post office and a church, and not much else.

But today is market day, and on market day Hardwick comes alive.

There are swarms of people in the streets, and Hobb has to slow his lorry. We abandon it and walk long before we reach the center of town. Temporary pens are set up for geese and sheep, there are crates of flapping ducks and chickens, and wooden stands have sprouted seemingly out of the ground, peddling hot cross buns and pasties, piping hot chestnuts and paper cups of steaming cider. Through the crowd, I catch a brief glimpse of Georgie and Max, walking arm in arm and chatting companionably with each other as they step into the post office.

"Don't mind me," Hobb says, waggling his eyebrows at Tom in a mysterious fashion. "I'm just off to make a few arrangements."

He disappears and I'm left standing with Tom on a busy, cobbled street in the cold October rain. Tom offers his arm. I take it, and we amble through the market day hubbub together, pointing out the best rams and funny-looking ducks with white topknots. All that I know comes from the Woodlands—from the time I spent with Dorien, and I miss the old stonewarden bitterly. Tom seems very knowledgeable for a St. Joseph's boy, and then I remember that he's mentioned growing up on a Yorkshire farm.

"Fancy a bite?" he asks, and I do. I'm ravenous after the morning's work in the rain.

Tom buys hot pasties and we eat them so quickly I burn my tongue. Then I buy him a sack of toasted chestnuts because I've seen him eat and I know he can't possibly be filled up after a single pasty. We share them out, sitting on a bench and watching people until Hobb reappears.

"All ready."

Tom stands and holds out a hand. I take it—my nettle burns have healed nicely, fading to faint pink—but once I'm on my feet, he doesn't let go. For a moment, I'm not sure what to do. My heart's in my throat and I'm tempted to pull away, but instead I look up at Tom. His eyes are fixed on Hobb and he's so pointedly trying not to care about our clasped hands that I know he cares a great deal. My stomach turns over at the sight of his familiar face, freckles standing out against autumn-pale skin, and I think I'd do almost anything to keep from hurting him.

Because he's only ever seen me in this world, after the Woodlands. I know myself for a sad shadow of who I used to be, a girl who wakes up each morning with barely enough strength to hold herself together. That's the only Evelyn he's known, and yet he still sees something in me that keeps him coming back.

So I hold his hand tightly as we follow Hobb through the crowd. Rain drips down my nose, and the last time I felt like this—entirely present, entirely here, without even having to try—I was on the beach below the palace, and though I didn't know it, it was our very last day in the Woodlands.

Hobb stops at a wide pen holding a half dozen placid milk cows. "Pick one out, Miss Evelyn. Cook says now the back field's cleared, we may as well put it to use and spare the kitchen help a few trips to market."

I clasp my hands together in excitement and can't stop grinning as I turn to the cattle. They're all lovely. There's a rangy Friesian and a red-and-white-spotted Guernsey with a long, mournful face. But I can't help myself when a fawn-colored Jersey comes over looking for treats, begging with her melting dark eyes. There's a sturdy calf with her, and while Hobb haggles with the farmer, Tom and I scratch the heifer's forehead.

"What're you doing over Christmas?" I ask. "Home for the holidays?"

Tom nods, resting both arms on the fence's top rail. "'Course. But I've got an uncle in London I always visit at the end of hols. That's why we ended up on the train together at start of term. I'm coming down the day after New Year's, and we could meet up at the station again if you like."

"I would. Tell me what you're looking forward to about going home."

I never really care so much about going back to London, myself. It's not that I don't love my parents, but we were sent away so often during the war that their house has just been a stopping place ever since. The Woodlands only finished a job that had already been started. London, and my parents' house, are the places I leave to journey elsewhere.

Tom stares past the cattle and the pen, past market day, seeing something that I can't. "Waking up to the rooster instead of the bell at school," he says. "Our kitchen, and the way my mum always sings when she works. The sound of my sisters laughing about something—they're terrors, but they'd take a shine to you. The way my dad keeps quiet but he's always listening and no one gives better advice if you can pry it out of him. Being back on the dales and able to go wherever I want, whenever I want."

He stops, as if surprised by all the words that have come out of him.

"Why aren't you going to farm?" I ask. "If you love your home so much, what are you doing at St. Joseph's?"

Tom grins. "Meg, my older sister, is over the moon about the farm. And my London uncle, Uncle Morris, hasn't got any children, so he's set his heart on me learning the law. He pays for my place at St. Joe's. I don't mind so much—I'm clever when I need to be, and everything works out neatly for Meg."

I squint up at him through the rain. "Will you be happy?"

Tom's grin widens. "I'd imagine once Uncle Morris passes on,

I'll make him spin in his grave and turn country solicitor rather than London barrister. I could be happy then. And I'm happy now, with you."

Across the pen, Hobb shakes hands with the farmer. Then he stumps over and hands me the Jersey's lead rope. The calf doesn't need one—she'll follow her mother anywhere. We make our way back to the lorry, and Hobb has already filled the bed with hay. Those must have been his mysterious arrangements. The cow, Buttercup, and the calf, Bluebell—named by the farmer's florally inclined daughter—settle themselves down immediately. Before either Hobb or Tom can protest (Hobb would, Tom wouldn't, but I give neither of them the opportunity), I climb up into the hay with the cows.

"Suit yourself, Miss Evelyn," Hobb grumbles, and Tom gives me a wink.

On Monday, a prefect appears in the doorway to English Lit and passes a note to Max. She takes it, reads the contents, and calls my name.

"Evelyn Hapwell, come here, please."

I walk up to her desk reluctantly. "Yes?"

"The Curmudgeon wants to see you," Max says. "I'd tell you why, but her note doesn't say. Is there something I should know?"

I shake my head in confusion. "No. I've got no idea what this is about."

"Best run along then." Max waves a hand. "Doesn't do to keep her waiting."

When I glance back over one shoulder at Georgie, she gives me a reassuring smile.

The school's rambling corridors are empty and eerie in the middle of classes. I wander through the building, going from the Old Quarter, where Max's class is housed and which is all stone hallways and narrow, grated windows, to the New Quarter at the front of the building. There, renovations have been done to impress the parents of potential students, and the hardwood of the front hall's parquet floor glows softly in the afternoon sun.

The Curmudgeon's office is just off St. Agatha's imposing entrance hall, and I knock timidly at the door. I've never been called up by her before, and can't imagine why I have been now. A quiet, careful voice tells me I'm to enter, and I slip inside.

To all intents and purposes, I might have stepped into a room in an English country house. There are ornate end tables and wingback chairs, a side table with a silver tea service, a well-mannered fire on the hearth, and even a fat pug dog I've never laid eyes on before curled up in a basket.

The Curmudgeon herself sits behind a desk of mammoth proportions and gestures to a chair across from her. "Miss Hapwell. I don't believe we've had the pleasure of a visit in my office. Do sit down."

I perch on the edge of the chair, not daring to make myself comfortable. Our headmistress is a formidable sight, figure pulled in by a corset, hair done up in last century's fashion, peering at me through a pair of pince-nez. "I suppose you know what this is about?"

"No, I'm afraid not," I answer.

The Curmudgeon looks thoroughly unimpressed by my inability to read her mind. "The *boy*, Miss Hapwell. It's about the boy."

"Oh, Tom?" I say with a smile. "What about him?"

The Curmudgeon's expression suddenly shifts to one that could freeze oil. "Not about him. About your conduct *with* him. Are you comporting yourself as a St. Agatha's girl ought to?"

I stare at her blankly. I'm not entirely sure how a St. Agatha's girl ought to behave, with boys or otherwise. It's not something I've ever troubled myself about.

"I'd hoped not to be forced into this conversation with you, Miss Hapwell. You may have your own set of difficulties, but this, at least, has not been one of your failings until now. However, I'll tell you what I had reason to remind your sister of on many occasions: any girl who disgraces the honor and good name of this school will be promptly expelled. Are we quite clear?"

I ought to nod meekly. I ought to do anything other than bristle, but I can feel myself growing prickly as a briar. Sitting up very straight, with my shoulders steady, I fix the Curmudgeon with a frigid stare even Philippa would envy. "Thank you, yes. Am I free to go?"

"Dismissed."

I'd planned to stay in tonight, and perhaps, wonder of wonders, to study for Latin. Instead I wait until the moon rises and Georgie drops off to sleep. Then I drift through the quiet dormitory and out into the night.

Gorsley's smoking behind St. Joe's, as always, and obligingly fetches Tom for me. No sooner have we made it into the cover of the woods than I turn to Tom Harper, rise up on my toes, and kiss him, mouth soft against his.

He flushes so fiercely I can see it even by moonlight.

"Now then, Ev. What's this about?"

"Honor," I tell him, knowing he won't understand.

And then, pride satisfied, I kiss him again just for the joy of it.

18

VENNDARIEN TARSIN, RIGHT HAND TO HIS FATHER
the Emperor and heir to a kingdom that covers half the world, is return-
ing to the Woodlands. The news ripples through the Great Wood, and
everywhere I go, I find Woodlanders preparing for war. Water spirits sit
on the banks of the river, naked except for their long hair, sharpening
knives made of stone. In the glens, centaurs sing war songs or spar with
one another, and the clash of their weapons is thunderous. A hundred
stonewardens have come from the western mountains, armored and
armed with pikes. They camp below the palace.

Even the tree folk are on edge. I stop at Vaya's towering beech for no
reason other than to say hello, and she dances about as a drift of leaves,
never taking shape, never speaking a word.

Philippa is at her most unreachable the day the Tarsin heir is
due to arrive. She glides about the palace with Alfreya, in constant
motion as the two of them ensure everything is ready for the coming
delegation. I know from experience that the best thing I can do is keep
out of the way.

So I put on a faded old tunic and breeches and disappear Downhill, to the rambling farmstead far below Palace Beautiful that supplies our kitchen.

Dorien blinks at the sight of me when I come upon him overseeing a line of workers with loaded handcarts preparing to make the climb to the palace. "Evie, it's an important day up the hill. Don't your brother and sister want you with them?"

I stand with my hands clasped in front of me. "I need to be busy, Dorien. Please."

At last, he nods. "Very well. There are weeds that want pulling, down by the icehouse."

The icehouse is out of sight of the palace, away from the organized chaos of preparations. Tangles of addervine and white-flowering hemephore clamber along the walls, grasping at the doorposts and tugging at the roof. I set to work tearing them away, and it's not long before I'm slick with sweat. When the walls are clear, I rip up toadfoil and pennythread from around the base of the building. I'm so distracted, trying to forget the inevitability of war, that it's ages before I notice the first notched leaves of priest's thistle.

By then the damage is done. There are dozens of wicked sprouts on the pile of pulled weeds in my wheelbarrow, and the skin on my hands is going blotchy. Frustration ties my insides up in knots, and Dorien comes around the corner just as I give the crumbling wall of the icehouse a vicious kick.

"Here now!" he blurts out, hurrying over. "What's the matter?"

I hold my hands out and blink back angry tears. "Look at this. I've pulled up a bunch of priest's thistles without gloves. I wasn't paying attention at all. Could I have done anything more stupid?"

Dorien clucks like a concerned hen, shaking his head. "Now, now. Getting upset won't heal those hands. Let me see if I can find you some salve."

He disappears around the icehouse and I tuck my hands in between my upper arms and sides, willing the pain blossoming across my skin to vanish.

Nearby, a wind rises up, whispering through the beech trees. It plays through their leaves and tugs at my hair, pulling me toward the wood. With a backward glance in the direction Dorien went, I step into the forest.

Immediately, I feel calmer, more centered. The strong, rich scent of bark and leaf mold rises up around me and I take a deep breath, holding it in. The wind continues to tease and tug, leading the way further into the trees. I let it take me where it will, pulling and prodding this way and that, over fallen logs and across little streamlets, until I come to a stand of young oaks.

The green of their leaves is shocking, and the small plants carpeting the forest floor beneath them are just as bright. All that green casts the rich red of Cervus's hide into stark relief, and I run to him, silent on my bare feet.

"Where have you been?" I ask, throwing my arms around the stag's neck as he lowers his head to rest on my shoulder. "We haven't seen you in weeks."

"The southern border."

"Oh dear. Is it dreadful?"

"Yes."

"I'm so sorry. Cervus, I'm glad you're here. Can't you do anything about all this? The Empire, and everything that's coming?"

When I step back, the stag's dark eyes are sad. "I've done all I can. I'm only the Guardian of the Great Wood, little one. I'm meant to ensure the trees stay green and growing, and to stand watch in the birch ring on the longest night of the year to see that the sun rises again. The fate of the Woodlands rests with its people."

Angry tears heat the back of my eyes. "Why does this happen? Why are there always people who want to own everything good and bright in the world, and destroy those things if they can't be bought? Isn't it enough to just know such things are there?"

"Not for some," Cervus answers.

I wipe at my eyes with the back of one hand and hiss as the salt water stings my burns. Where the priest's thistles touched me, I've blistered and swollen so I can barely move my fingers. I'll make a mess of everything tonight—I won't even be able to hold my own wineglass without fumbling.

Cervus stands for a moment, tall and proud, but not as tall as he seemed when I first came to the Great Wood.

"There's one ill I can still set right in this forest," he says, and bows his magnificent head. His velvet muzzle brushes my palms and pain blazes through me. Then, in an instant, it stops. When I pull my hands back to look at them, the skin is clear and unblemished. The pain has already receded from my mind.

"Go," Cervus says. "Stay with your brother and sister. After today there will be no stepping off the path to war."

I nod, but I'm sick with fear and rage.

Cervus shakes his head and blinks, and I think the gesture is meant to be a smile. "Gather your courage, little one. Keep it close in the days ahead."

He vanishes through the trees, leaving only the wind tugging at my sleeves and the wholeness of my hands as a reminder that he was with me at all.

19

I'M AFRAID OF WHO I'M BECOMING. I CATCH MYSELF singing when I cross the back field, early in the mornings, to visit the cows. There's something inside me—a glad, bright feeling, fragile and lovely as a dew-spangled cobweb, and I'm terrified.

When I wake, I smile at the frost patterns etched on our windowpanes. Winter is creeping in, and it's Saturday, and Tom's coming. I throw open the window and breathe the sweet, cold air, watching fog curl out of my mouth, dragon-like. Georgie's already up, so I leave the window as it is, enjoying the bite of the chilly air.

I'm halfway through plaiting my hair when a sound drifts in on the frigid breeze, coming from the forest that butts up against St. Agatha's fenced grounds. It's low and rough, mournful and utterly insistent, and sends an arrow of hope through my heart. I'd know that sound anywhere.

Somewhere in the wood, a stag is roaring.

I shut my eyes and press a hand to my mouth, waiting.

Nothing. No sudden vertigo as this world fades into the Great Wood. No tug as I'm pulled from one place to another. Familiar as the sound may be, it isn't him. It's only a red deer out in the dawning forest, calling for his hinds.

Nevertheless, that call has split me open. How long has it been since I last thought of the Woodlands? How long since I remembered?

I look into the warped mirror above the vanity and barely recognize the faithless girl who stares back at me. She's forgotten her people, forgotten her home; gladly let them go in exchange for a bit of happiness and a boy to hold her hand.

The stag roars again and I wrap my arms around myself, but it's no good. Inside, I'm shattering. Sharp cracks run through me, a spider's web of breakages, a topographical map of pain. I barely hear the knock at the door.

"Ev, are you decent?" It's Georgie, calling from the corridor, and when I don't answer, she steps inside. "What on earth have you got the window open for? Look at you, you're freezing."

She slams the casement shut and wraps a blanket around my shoulders. Though I've got my school sweater on, I can't stop shaking. "How long were you in here like that? Your hands are ice!"

I don't know. I'm not sure how long I've stood, listening to the stag and falling to pieces, but I'm cold down to my very bones.

Georgie puts an arm around me. "Ev, you've got to tell me if something's bothering you. I know I'm not Philippa, but I'm here and she isn't. You need to let me help."

I sit motionless. Dear, kindhearted Georgie. What can she do when I can't possibly explain to her the things I've seen and done? The lives I've lived?

Suddenly she brightens. "Oh! I nearly forgot—Jamie's here to see you. He must have started out awfully early, but he's waiting in the library, and I said I'd let you know. Unless you don't want to go down?"

"No. I'll go. Thank you, Georgie." I stand and push the blanket aside. I'm no warmer, and the pieces inside me prick at the soft places of my soul, but I've got to carry on.

Jamie waits at the library's far end, in one of the armchairs where Tom and I sat and watched the rain. He looks half asleep, but when he sees me, he scrambles to his feet.

"What's wrong?" I ask immediately. I know him and Philippa better than I know myself, and when he won't meet my eyes, there's something he doesn't want to tell me.

Jamie sighs and scrubs a hand across his face. "It's Phil."

"What about her?" There's not a hint of emotion in my voice, nothing to suggest I'm already carrying a heart full of splinters and that if anything's happened to my sister, I'll bleed out where I stand, killed by a thousand invisible wounds.

"She's not coming home for Christmas. She's going to stay at school, in America. I don't know why—not unless you plan to tell me what went on between the two of you—but I wanted to give you time to get used to the idea. I only just found out from Dad and Mum yesterday. I'm sorry."

I don't dare to examine what it is I'm feeling at the revelation that Philippa's staying in America. I've written so many letters, and there's never a reply. Or rather, there has been—she writes to Mum and Dad, but never to me, and rarely to Jamie. Our news comes secondhand, in the form of bright, cheerful asides. *Ev would love the artwork I'm studying. Jamie would love American politics. They'd both love the hiking in New England.*

Nothing important. Nothing of meaning.

"It's fine." I lower myself into one of the armchairs as Jamie sits down again in the other. Truthfully I'm not sure yet if it's fine, but Jamie looks so miserable to be delivering bad news that I need to make things better for him.

He leans his head against one of the armchair's wings and stares out the library window to the courtyard beyond. Everything's gold and silver with morning sun and frost.

"I can't help but blame myself, Ev. I should've done better when we came back. Should've talked about it more, should've been there for her, and for you. But I was lost in the woods. I'm still lost in the woods. We're all caught between two places now."

I straighten and fix him with an unflinching stare. Even the broken pieces scraping together inside me can do nothing to diminish its potency. "Jamie Hapwell, you belonged in the Great Wood."

"I'm glad you think so."

His smile stings, because I may know where home is, but Jamie no longer does.

I lean forward, just a bit, and speak with every bit of faith I've got left in me. "We're going back. He promised me. *A Woodlands heart always finds its way home.*"

Jamie's face crumples. "Don't, Evelyn. I can't."

He shuts his eyes. Once upon a time, I knew all the right words to say to Jamie, to my darling older brother who worked so hard to prove himself in the Great Wood, and who can't quite stop feeling like he's failing here. Now all I do is hurt him, when I want to offer words that heal.

"Hello, Ev," one of Georgie's friends says cheerfully as she walks past with a stack of books. "Saw your fellow coming up the drive."

Jamie sits up and a little of the worry fades from his face. "You're still seeing Tom, then? I'm glad of that."

I don't answer. Everything that's happened this morning has strengthened my resolve, honing it to a fine and cutting edge. The stag, Philippa's refusal to come home, my failure to reassure Jamie—it's all reminded me of something I'd nearly lost track of this term.

I'm an exile. This is not where I belong. I walk a world devoid of magic, but someday I'm leaving, and there is no point complicating my life here.

Jamie, who sees through me as easily as I see through him, shakes his head. He reaches across the space between us and takes my hands.

"Evelyn. Please don't. Tom's a good lad. He—"

I pull away and fix Jamie with an icy stare. "I am who I am, Jamie. We all know it. I'm never going to be anyone else, and I'm just biding my time. I've been a fool to let things go so far, and I'm going to stop them now before someone gets hurt."

Jamie pushes himself to his feet and looks out at the brilliant courtyard, standing with bent shoulders that were always straight when we were young in the Great Wood. "What made you change your mind?"

"A lot of things. Philippa."

Jamie's hands ball into fists at his sides. He broke two fingers once, hitting the wall at Palace Beautiful in a fit of rage over the war we couldn't avoid. He's learned circumspection, which is a thing no boy his age should know.

We're all so old in so many ways.

"We should be making a life here," Jamie argues. "We're not supposed to just wait."

"I have to choose, Jamie," I tell him. "I can't try to be here and there at the same time. And I choose the Woodlands. I'll always choose the Woodlands."

"Fine." He growls his words at me, well and truly angry, and I almost waver in my resolve. "Do what you have to, but I won't stay and watch. I'm sick of standing by while you tear yourself apart."

Jamie stalks off down the shelves and I wrap the silence of the library around myself like a cloak.

It's not long before Tom finds me. There's something so earnest about him, and he's wearing a badly knit sweater, grey and patterned with whimsical, lopsided reindeer. He stands just where Jamie did, with his hands in his pockets, and looks down at me sadly.

Grey sea. Grey sky. A stag on the beach.

Tom's not one for avoiding an issue.

"I saw your brother on my way in and he says you're going to give me the boot. He told me you can't tell me why, but that you've got a reason, which he thinks is a bad reason but you think is a good one, and he wants me to stick by you no matter what you say. To be honest, I'm a bit confused about the whole thing. I thought we were getting on well?"

Curses, Tom. I could drive you away with silence and indifference, but I can't bear lying to your face. I fold my hands in my lap and stare down at them. "We have been, yes."

"And you like me well enough?"

I swallow. Too much. I like you too much. "Yes."

"And you know I like you?"

"Yes."

"But you think we ought to stop seeing each other and won't tell me why?"

"Exactly."

Tom nods his head slowly. "I'll go, then."

Relief washes over me, tainted with regret. I'd expected a fight, though I've barely got the strength for one.

But Tom hasn't finished. "On one condition. Look me in the eyes, and tell me truthfully you don't want to see me anymore. As soon as you do, I'll leave you be."

Let my blood turn to ice. Let me be a hundred years' winter. I look up and fix my gaze on Tom, meeting his sincere grey eyes. The words form on the back of my tongue. My hands tremble. I am Evelyn of the Woodlands, walker of worlds, teller of truths.

"Tom Harper, I don't want to see you again," I lie.

Tom nods. He's red-faced and flustered with unhappiness, and though I thought I was already broken, it breaks me a little more to see him so. "Right, then. I'm going back to St. Joe's. If you change your mind, you know where to find me."

He leaves without a goodbye, and the lie burns my tongue worse than hope ever did.

I don't know who I am anymore.

I don't know who I am.

20

THE LAST TRACES OF DIRT AND THE FINAL WHIFFS OF farm smell have been scrubbed from my skin by the time I head downstairs to the great hall. There's a chill in the air, and the kirtle I wear is thick forest-green wool embroidered with rust-red threads. I can't deny it's beautiful, but it was Philippa's choice, not mine. I'd rather be in my farm clothes, if this is really the beginning of the end.

I meet Jamie on my way down the stairs. He's in the same dark green and rust colors, with Anvar, the sword Hector gave to him to carry, belted around his waist.

"Has anyone seen Venndarien yet?" I ask as we continue down to the entrance hall together. "I haven't noticed any of his retinue underfoot."

Jamie's face is grim. "Most of them are in the courtyard. He's brought a hundred soldiers at least. Hector's furious. As for Venndarien himself—" Jamie's mouth twists. "Alfreya set aside the entire east wing for him and his party. They went straight there and have been holed up ever since. We barely caught a glimpse of him or his courtiers on their way in."

The hall is half full of Woodlanders already, come to hear what the

Tarsin heir has to say. I smile and nod to those I know as we take our place at the long table. Dorien's already sitting, and a breeze shifts my hair as Vaya drops down beside me in her girl shape.

I glance this way and that, looking for Philippa.

"Where's Phil?" Jamie whispers, our minds on the same thing. "She's never been a moment late in her life."

A gentle cough draws my attention. Alfreya stands next to me, and for some reason, my stomach ties itself into knots. "Alfreya, what is it?"

"Your sister asked if I'd give this to Jamie."

When she hands Jamie a note, he unfolds the scrap of parchment and scowls as he reads. "What does she mean by this?"

But Alfreya's already gone. Jamie hands me the note and I scan it quickly.

> Jamie,
> Take off your sword.
> Philippa

"You'd better do it," I say. "You know Philippa. She doesn't draw breath without thinking about the consequences first."

Reluctantly, Jamie unbuckles Anvar, his hands lingering on the sheath. "There's a difference between not wearing my sword and not having it on hand. I'll put it under the table, if it's that important."

So Anvar is pushed unceremoniously under the table, where one of the elderly hounds that roam the castle has already taken refuge. I reach out to the dog, but a flurry of activity at the hall's entrance distracts me. The doors swing open, trumpets bray a few notes, and an Imperial crier calls out.

"Presenting His Serene Highness, Prince Venndarien Tarsin, Heir to the Great Emperor."

"He's never seemed very serene to me," I mutter to Jamie, who smiles humorlessly. "And where has Philippa got to?"

Venndarien sweeps in, surveying the room with his burning eyes. He's grown into a tall man in the past five years, his golden hair fading to a nondescript color, though his face seems ageless but for the lines at the corners of his eyes. The courtiers that follow him are all dressed in white, the color of the Empire, and the only thing that distinguishes their ranks is the sashes they wear around their waists, dyed to indicate their standing. The Tarsin heir wears no sash, and the cut of his clothes is simple.

Yet there's something about him that sends anger coursing hot through my veins. It's in the way he surveys the hall and the Woodlanders in it with a covetous air, as if all this is something to be possessed. And how he glances at my brother and me and everyone else gathered at the table, then looks away with a shrug, as if we're not worthy of notice, as if we'll pose no threat.

Venndarien Tarsin is only halfway across the room when the hall's wide doors swing open once more with a groan and a clang, revealing Philippa standing on the threshold. Venndarien turns to look at her, and there's no greed in his eyes, but satisfaction, as if it's a foregone conclusion that soon she'll belong to him.

The anger in my blood turns to fire, to match the flames behind the Tarsin heir's eyes. The words of the oath I once swore rest bitter on my tongue.

I will kill him if he touches her.

21 ⌒

Dear Philippa,
    I miss you. I'm sorry. Come back to me.

Grey sand, grey sea, grey sky.
    Salt water murmurs in my veins.
    Cervus, take me home.

22 ~

MY SISTER STANDS BEFORE THE ASSEMBLED WOOD-
landers and the Tarsin delegation in a plain spun kirtle the color of new
leaves. Yellow asters have been braided into her dark hair. I've never
seen anything lovelier, and the sight of her chokes me.

Philippa turns to Venndarien and smiles so brightly it's hard to look
straight at her. She moves to the center of the hall and kneels before
him.

"Your Highness," says my sister, bowing her head. "Welcome back to
the Woodlands. I trust you had a pleasant journey, and find the rooms
here to your liking?"

Venndarien waves a hand, as if to dismiss the question, but his eyes
fix on Philippa hungrily. "The roads in this forest are appalling and
the rooms are too small, but the view from the west wing is fine. When
I rule from Palace Beautiful as the Emperor's proxy, I shall have all the
walls in the wing torn down, to make one great chamber. That should
suit me better."

"He'll have the whole castle down on top of his head if he does that,"
Dorien mutters. "What does he think holds up all this stone?"

"As you wish, Highness" is all Philippa says with a bob of her head.

The Woodlanders whisper, and cast uncertain glances at one another. Vaya sets one weightless hand on top of mine. "Your sister's very friendly. She wouldn't—leave us, would she?"

"No!" I insist, but even as I do, ice spreads inside me.

Phil settles into a seat at Venndarien's side and finds me with her eyes. For a moment we look at one another, and I wonder if I truly know how Philippa has felt these last five years, thrown into another world by my desperate cry, then held here by her sense of duty and the need to make good on her promises.

Which promise will she hold to now? The one to look after me, or the one to serve the Woodlands? And which would I hold to in her place?

All those letters, back and forth between Philippa and the Tarsin heir, and no one to read them but her.

The banquet begins, and it's as if the Woodlanders have decided to remind themselves one last time of everything they love about this country by the sea. There are steaming tureens of fish stew; mutton roasted with phelamon spice; little cakes sweetened with honey and studded with addervine fruit; apples stuffed with nuts and goat's butter and slow cooked in a bed of coals. Musicians from the singers' school perform songs with melodies like heartbreak, and through it all, Venndarien picks at his food and broods. The laughter and tears and applause of the Woodlanders make one thing clear—this evening is not meant for him. He is nothing more than an unwanted guest.

A river girl with skin like red-brown clay is playing the harp, the sound of her music an echo of water over rocks, when Venndarien abruptly pushes his chair back and stands.

"Let's have an end to this," he says loudly enough that all those gathered will hear. "My father has humored these backwoods long enough. For the last time, will the Woodlands pay tribute to Tarsa, and will all those here gathered bend a knee before His Imperial Majesty's rightful heir?"

There's a long pause, followed by the loud scrape of chairs and benches as every Woodlander in the hall stands. No one kneels.

Until Philippa steps forward. Muttering voices nearly drown out her words.

"Don't forget your promise," she says to Venndarien, hands clasped desperately in front of her. "That if I come with you of my own accord, you'll take my brother and sister back to Tarsa, too. That we'll be safe, kept well away from the war, and when it's over you'll find a way to send us home."

Something cold and sharp blossoms inside me as she sinks to her knees in front of the Tarsin heir. Something colder and sharper presses against my throat, and when I glance wildly to one side, two Tarsin soldiers hold Jamie, a blade against his skin. We're dragged toward the door as Philippa watches in anguish. A dagger pricks my throat as I struggle against the arms holding me, and Philippa cries out as warm blood slicks my skin.

But the Woodlanders aren't content to see us go. Metal clashes on metal, and the hall is suddenly an ocean of angry shouts that I feel like I'm drowning in. Fire blazes as the Tarsin soldiers channel their power. Wind howls and water roars as the Woodlanders summon theirs. I've never seen them so before, and the wrath of the Woodlands is a fearful, wondrous thing.

A sound cuts across the uproar, deep and full-throated and achingly *familiar. When the last echoes of Cervus's call have died, he stands in the great hall's doorway, and everyone within is still.*

"Philippa Hapwell," I say, my words dropping into that profound silence like pebbles down a dark well, "what have you done?"

It's not just a question, it's an accusation, and I mean for it to burn. Sorrow and anger war within me, though the fighting in the great hall has ceased.

Cervus steps through the chaos—dishes have been knocked from the table and wine puddles on the floor. I twist my head around, though the Tarsin soldier holding me is a leech I cannot shake. Cervus stops in front of Philippa and Venndarien.

"Leave," the stag says. "Leave this place, and never return."

At his words, I'm back in the bomb shelter with Philippa's arms wrapped around me, keeping the worst of the fear away. I'm leaving home for the first time at seven years old, with Phil across from me on the train, making up games to pass the time and to help me forget how lost I feel. I'm walking into strange house after strange house, the only familiar thing in the world my sister's hand in mine.

No matter what she's done, if Cervus sends her away, it will tear me in two.

Venndarien's face is pinched and furious, his eyes burning pits.

"The Empire does not hear you," he snarls. "When I return it will be with fire and a sword, and every corner of this world will speak of how the Woodlanders burned as they died. Consider this Tarsa's declaration of war. Philippa?"

He holds out a hand to her. Tears track down Philippa's face, and she shakes her head. "I've done wrong, Venndarien. But I mean to do better, not to run from my mistakes."

Venndarien's mouth twists. "Do you know how we deal with traitors in the Empire? We flay the living flesh from their bones. You can expect no gentler treatment here if you stay. And if you survive, I will drag you back to Tarsa when I return, and make your life a misery for playing me false."

Philippa flinches, but holds her ground. The Tarsin party storms from the hall and the gathered Woodlanders wait, utterly silent. Cervus turns to my sister.

"What happened, child?" Cervus asks, and there's no judgment in his voice.

"I think—" Philippa swallows. "Oh, Cervus, I think I've lost my way."

He steps closer and she puts an arm around his ruffed shoulders as if there's no one else in the world who could hold her up.

"It's always difficult for some to find their path in the woods," the stag answers. In spite of his words, or perhaps because of them, Philippa breaks down and sobs.

By the time the sun rises again the Tarsin delegation is gone, traveling southward with the news that the Great Wood is at war.

23

GEORGIE TRIES TO MAKE CONVERSATION, BUT I SHUT
her out with short, polite answers that lead to nowhere. I sit alone
at dinner, remembering meals I've eaten, company I've kept, and
when lights are out and Georgie sleeps, I slip into the quiet night.

I've always been discreet in how I exercise my freedoms. Now
I have no interest in moderation. I stay out on the hills for hours,
soaking moonlight and cold air in through my pores. It's nearly
dawn and I'm chilled to the bone when I finally turn back toward
school. I go reluctantly—I'd rather just wander away, walking
across the hills until I can walk no more, or until I slip from one
world into the next.

But I go back. I always go back. I climb into bed with my coat
and boots still on and fall into exhausted sleep for what little is
left of each night. And when the morning gong sounds I get up
and go through the motions of breakfast, classes, study hall. The
whole time I'm dreaming, dreaming, half asleep and half alive.

When night falls, I wake. I come alive again. I go out and dance on the frozen hills. I wet my feet fording icy streams. I sing songs this world has never heard before in hopes the trees will lift their heads and join me. I raise my hands to the stars, a silent plea for one of them to come down, just for tonight.

I look for stags.

By the end of a fortnight, I've reached a comfortable place. I'm tired enough that I can't feel much, and I nap in dusty corners of the library between classes, when I should be studying. Max tries to ask me what's going on, but I brush off her questions and she stops leaving the key out for me.

No matter. I climb through the window each night, edge along the roof, and clamber down the fire ladder at the building's far end. If I can't go home, I'll be an exile in earnest, a girl with no place, no roots, no heart.

Exams are held in the refectory. I write my name on each paper, then draw leaves in the empty margins until we're let go.

> *Dear Philippa—*
> *The lights begin to twinkle from the rocks:*
> *The long day wanes: the slow moon climbs: the deep*
> *Moans round with many voices. Come, my love,*
> *'T is not too late to seek a newer world. . . .*
>
> *My purpose holds*
> *To sail beyond the sunset, and the baths*
> *Of all the western stars, until—*

I am made weak by time and fate, a grey spirit yearning in desire. I am not now that strength which in old days moved earth and heaven.

That which I am, I am.

I don't know who I am anymore.

I don't know who I am.

24

THE ONLY THING KEEPING US SAFE FROM THE
Tarsin Empire and its armies is the snow, which began to fall the
moment Venndarien Tarsin left the Great Wood. It casts us into limbo,
drifting in the forest hollows and rendering the winding track that
serves the Woodlands for a highway impassable. We're secure until
spring makes travel practical again, and I wish this winter would never
end.

The sea air buffets Palace Beautiful. I welcome the storms that come
with it, flinging sleet against the leaded glass windows. It's drafty and
cold inside. We wear furs most days, sitting snug by a fire in one of the
smaller rooms.

Philippa is quieter than ever, and more withdrawn. The Woodlanders treat her with the same unfailing courtesy, but she walks as if
she bears a weight. Most days she spends in the kitchens, sweating over
the cooking fires. She won't sit at the table in the great hall and keeps
to herself whenever she can.

When I ask her what it was Venndarien promised or threatened to
convince her to go so badly astray, all she'll tell me is this: he told her

Cervus never meant to send us home. And once he'd convinced her of that, nothing else seemed to matter. I try to be a comfort—to tell her I know what it's like to be so afraid that all you wish for is to be taken away—but she murmurs excuses, and shuts herself away in her room. There is a world between us, and I don't know how to call across the void.

On a rare day when she can bear company, Philippa and I are crossing the entrance hall arm in arm. We're careful with each other, speaking only of little, inconsequential things. Both of us look up when the castle door swings open. Hector ducks in, wearing a hooded coat, the ever-present twin swords strapped across his back. His breath still smokes from the cold, and unmelted snow dusts his black hair.

I nod in greeting and take another step, but my sister stops.

"How are the troops?" Philippa asks tentatively. "Are they in good spirits?"

Hector bows to her, gracious as only a Woodlander can be. "They are."

I hold tight to Phil's arm. Hector hesitates for a moment before speaking again. "Philippa. In the end, what you did was foolish and nothing else. No harm came of it, besides what would have come anyway. You can't punish yourself forever."

My sister winces.

"How do you manage?" she asks him. "How do you keep going, knowing you've looked into the eyes of people who will die in the days ahead?"

"We all know what we're fighting for. We're willing to lay down our lives for the Great Wood. Anyone we lose will have died defending the place they love more than any other. You know what Cervus says

about those who lose their way, either in life or death."

"Tell me again."

Hector smiles. "He says 'a Woodlands heart always finds its way home.' And we believe that, with everything in us. We know where we belong."

Philippa chews on her lower lip and shakes her head. "I don't know where I belong, Hector. Here, or in the world I came from."

Hearing her speak such words pains me. I want so badly for Philippa to feel the sense of rightness I've known in the Great Wood.

"Then stay alive when the war comes," Hector answers. "Keep searching, until your heart finds its place."

Philippa's face remains troubled as Hector walks away. Then she turns to me and smiles, so that I'm dazzled by her light.

"Evie, love, I've forgotten something upstairs. Don't wait for me."

I watch her go, gnawing at a hangnail before making up my mind. Rather than follow Philippa, I hurry after Hector.

He's in the great hall, which serves us as a makeshift armory. The hooded coat has been shed, but his swords are back in place, one over each shoulder. Hector's pushed one of the tables that litter the hall closer to the warmth of the fire. He stands before it, fletching crossbow bolts with practiced hands.

"Hector?" I say anxiously. "I need your help. I've learned everything Dorien and Vaya can teach me about trees and plants and things that grow, and Cervus says if these were brighter days, he'd let me bring in the light with him at midwinter. But I want to learn something they can't teach me."

Hector sets another bolt into his wood and iron clamp, silent and waiting for me to speak again.

"Look," I say, finally managing to get the words out. "I'm asking you to show me how to kill a man."

Hector stills. "And why would you want to learn such a thing? When all of the Woodlands and its people lie between you and the Empire? When you have your own world to return to should the Great Wood fall?"

"I'm not a soldier or a diplomat," I confess, picking at a splinter fraying from the edge of the worn wood tabletop. "I'm not brave the way my brother is, or clever like my sister. But if the Great Wood is taken, I think Venndarien Tarsin will come for Philippa. I swore on my own blood that I'd end him if he touches her and I plan to keep my word. I won't lie to you, though—the idea of killing anyone, even him, makes me sick and afraid."

For a long while, Hector does nothing, but I wait. Finally, he reaches across the table and pushes a belt and dagger toward me.

"If it's your heart that fails you, we'll teach your hands what to do. Then they will act before your heart can stop them."

25

THE DAY BEFORE HOLIDAYS, JAMIE APPEARS. I'M IN THE library, dozing in a reading nook since there's no more studying to be done. I've made a mess of my exams, but it's been years since I cared much. Jamie pops his head round the corner of a bookshelf, nods once at the sight of me, and vanishes. He returns with a chair and sets it down across from me.

Thin December light spills in through the window and pools around us, pale as snow. Jamie leans forward with his elbows resting on his knees.

"I don't want you to come home tomorrow," he says without preamble. It's so entirely not what I expect that I sit without moving, unsure if I should feel hurt or confused or relieved.

"Tom's offered to take you up to Yorkshire with him," Jamie carries on. "I know Christmas isn't ever your best time, and I thought with everything that's been going on, a change might help."

I stare at him blankly. "We're always together at Christmas."

Jamie looks down at his boots. "Don't be difficult, Ev."

"I'm coming, and that's the end of it."

Jamie sighs and pushes himself up out of the chair. "Think about it, at least. It would be better for you."

I let my eyes drift to the patch of sunlight on the library floor and unfocus them, so all the world is white and indistinct.

"I'm coming back to London. But don't call it home."

The train ride is quiet, and a little lonely. I breathe on the glass until the frost melts and I can see the winter world outside.

At the station, Jamie is waiting. He waves when I step off the train. He's so desperate in his need to make things alright for me that I want to be alright, if only just for now.

We're two-thirds of the way to whole, and I try to make the best of it. I steal looks at Jamie as we ride home, squashed together by my luggage in the back of a cab. He's the same as he was when we were older, in the Great Wood—it's like he's grown back into himself, though he hasn't realized it yet. His enthusiasm burns brighter than ever as he talks about labor reform and prison reform and goodness knows what else. Underneath that fire he's steadfast as a stone, and I know that he'll do good in this world if it gives him half a chance.

We get home and tumble out of the taxi and I paste on my most brilliant smile. There are breathless hugs with Dad and Mum, who are careful not to mention Phil, and a cold supper and hot cocoa in the kitchen and then, quite suddenly, it's dark outside and the clock is chiming midnight.

I climb up the stairs to the room that's been mine all my life.

I undress in the dark and turn my back to the empty bed that belongs to Philippa, and try not to remember the smell of the sea.

It's nearly Christmas.

And my heart pleads with my mind to stop, but I can't help recalling all the winters I have known. I remember and remember because I can't bring myself to forget.

26

ON CHRISTMAS EVE, WE CATCH A BUS TO CHURCH AND stand out under the sky that drops snow like white flowers. We light candles and sing carols.

Music rings through the great hall on Midwinter's Day. The Woodlanders gathered are fiercely happy, the more so because we know it can't last. We stay up until dawn, keeping the night vigil along with Cervus, who's miles away in the birch ring at the heart of the wood. When the first light touches the horizon, a smile brightens my sister's face.

We walk home, because it's snowing and lovely and we're all together (almost).

"Again, and stop thinking," Hector orders with a scowl when I drop my dagger for the tenth time in a row.

I try once more, letting my mind drift away, past the walls of Palace Beautiful and out among the snowy trees. Without interference, my hands move like quicksilver, doing just as they've been taught. One moment, I'm plain Evelyn Hapwell, and the next I stand armed and beneath Hector's defenses, with the end of my blade against the bare flesh of his side.

Hector shakes his head, though his scowl fades. "Better, but not good enough yet. You're still just a girl with a knife."

I push a stray lock of hair back from my eyes. "What else would I be?"

"Death," *Hector says bluntly.* "Death on soundless feet."

I shiver, and want nothing more than to walk away. But instead I sheathe my dagger and we begin again.

We go to bed after church and I lie in the dark, staring at Philippa's empty bed. Finally, I get up and tuck her Christmas gift beneath her pillow.

Icicles hang from each tree branch, and the Woodlands have become a world edged in silver. I breathe the cold, crisp air and hike out through the forest. When I stop in a clearing and turn, Cervus is waiting, finally back from his vigil at the wood's heart. He's red as autumn leaves, magnificent against the snow with that branching crown of antlers rising above his head.

We eat our Christmas breakfast and open gifts. I smile enough and speak enough to keep the others from seeing how far away I am, while I remember, remember, remember.

The snow is melting, bit by bit, dripping from the palace eaves, and none of us want it to go. Spring means war. Spring means what will likely be the beginning of the end.

I am falling into that dark place where I don't belong to one world, or two, but to none. I promised Philippa I wouldn't go back there again, but the pull is relentless as gravity.

When, on Christmas afternoon, the bell rings and I find Tom Harper standing on the doorstep looking acutely uncomfortable, it's like I've summoned him with my thoughts. He's the first real thing that's happened to me since leaving school. It's as if he's in color and the rest of the world is black and white.

"I need to go," I say before he can speak. Tom nods. I snatch my coat off its hook and shout back over one shoulder. "I'm going out!"

"Evie, who's that with you?" Dad calls, but I ignore him, poor lamb, as we always do.

Tom and I walk through the empty streets arm in arm and, being who he is, Tom doesn't say a word. Snow crunches beneath our boots and the winter sky grows soft and golden as the afternoon wears on. Light pours out of windows, revealing Christmas trees and families sitting down to dinner, and the cold air cuts away at the fog inside me. I breathe and breathe and breathe until finally I find myself, Evelyn Hapwell, walking here on a London street with a kind boy who's my brother's friend. I slip into my own body, away from the phantoms that haunt me, and with one quite ordinary step, I leave the memories of home behind.

Oh. Here I am.

"What are you doing in London?" I ask, because this is what people do—they make polite conversation. They ask about the peculiarities of one another's lives.

Tom takes off his cap and twists it in his hands. "I came down yesterday. Uncle Morris wired because he wasn't well, but by the time I got here he was on the mend. To be honest, I think he didn't want to be alone at Christmas. I rang Jamie this morning to ask after you, and he said I should come by."

I glance up at him. He's tall and ruddy-cheeked, breath puffing out in little clouds. "I'm sorry you missed being at home."

Tom shrugs and smiles when he catches me looking. "So am I.

But if I'd stayed home, I'd have missed seeing you. Evelyn—"

He stops for a moment, and swallows. I can see him gathering up his courage—I've done the same thing countless times before.

"I'm going back home tomorrow. Would you come with me?" he asks. "I know you told me to go, and you've got reasons to want to be on your own, but I'm here for you, either way. I'll take whatever you want to give."

"Yes," I say, almost before he's finished speaking. "Yes, I'll come with you."

I tighten my grip on his arm. God help this boy, but he's tethering me to the world right now and I can't let go, not after holding out for so many years. Still, I'm a Woodlander, and I have my pride.

"Tom, you don't mind at all? It's not just pity?"

He stops and steps in front of me, holding me gently in place with a hand on each of my arms. "Evelyn, sometimes things go wrong for people, and they have a hard time finding their way. I know that. I've lived that. I'm not afraid because you're still wandering."

I look past him. The streetlamps are lit, and golden motes of snow drift into the pools of light they leave.

Closer than the snow, and more solid than a stag, Tom Harper smiles and puts his hands in his pockets before speaking.

> "'She can't be unhappy,' you said,
> 'The smiles are like stars in her eyes,
> And her laughter is thistledown
> Around her low replies.'
> 'Is she unhappy?' you said—

> But who has ever known
> Another's heartbreak—
> All he can know is his own;
> And she seems hushed to me,
> As hushed as though
> Her heart were a hunter's fire
> Smothered in snow."

Tom swallows, and I can see his throat work. For a moment, there's something achingly familiar in his eyes—a grief that time has never dimmed, an unknown hurt he'll carry all his life. I recognize that look, because it haunts me from my mirror.

We stand facing each other in the light of the streetlamps, caught amid constellations of snow. There is something brighter and warmer between us than shared grief that stretches from me to Tom Harper and back again. This is the anchor holding me in place—this fearful, tenuous thing. I'll do anything to keep from damaging it, so I turn aside instead of stepping forward.

After all my years, I'm learning to be wise.

I loop my arm through Tom's. "We should go back. Mum and Dad will be wondering where I've got to."

We walk home together, and the snow smothers less than it did before.

27 ⌒

SPRING BRINGS THE MUD AND BLOOD AND FILTH OF
battle to the Woodlands, rather than green shoots and new life.

*Jamie and Philippa insist on being at the southern front—Jamie
because it's where he belongs, and Philippa because she's still doing penance. I am like every other Woodlander—ready, but still unwilling. I
don't want to go but it must be done, and I won't let my sister out of
my sight.*

*The Woodlanders fight like no army I've ever seen before—where
the Tarsin forces wear uniforms and rely on precisely planned maneu-
vers, the forest dwellers are invisible until they strike. They appear
from the trees and rain destruction on our enemies, disorienting them
entirely. By the time the Tarsin soldiers get their bearings, the Woodlanders have gone.*

*There are still losses, though. There are always losses in war. Each
evening, a party ghosts out from our hidden camp deep within the forest
to retrieve the bodies of the fallen.*

*I watch Cervus one night, picking his way between the corpses
that have been washed and dressed in green and laid out on the*

forest floor. Moonlight silvers his rust-colored flanks, and at every still form, he stops and lowers his head, brushing his muzzle against each fallen soul as a benediction. It's not until I draw closer that I hear him speaking words as well—a promise to each Woodlander we've lost.

"A Woodlands heart always finds its way home."

I pick fistfuls of snowdrops from among the last melting drifts of snow and set them between the cold, still hands of the dead. When we've finished, Cervus comes to me and lays his head on my shoulder while I stand with my arms around his neck, and the sorrow in us is so great I'm not sure who needs the other more.

So it is that here, at the end of all things, Jamie and Philippa and I find our places again. Jamie joins Hector while Philippa and Alfreya brave the blood and horror of the hospital tent. And Cervus and I tend the dead, bringing what peace and beauty we can once hope has gone. The ground is still icy, but we build stone cairns until the clearings around our secret encampment are filled with silent monuments.

The news that the Empire's forces are only a mile from our camp is brought to me late one night, along with Dorien's lifeless body. I blink back tears and rainwater as they leave him with me, and Cervus slips away. Arrows mark the stonewarden like wicked thorns.

When Cervus reappears, Jamie and Philippa are with him. They stand with their arms around each other, heartbroken just as I am. I kneel beside Dorien with his head cradled on my lap.

The noise and clamor of the frontline reach me for the first time, drifting through the trees on a gust of wind. I push myself to my feet, though I'm tired to the point of exhaustion, and join Jamie and Phil.

We stand beside our fallen friend, heads bowed, bearing the weight of worlds.

I straighten first. I will tend to the dead as I've done this past fortnight so their restless hearts will find their way home should we win the day.

I can't think of what will happen if we lose.

"Jamie," I say to my brother. "You've got to get back to the front. Draw your sword."

Jamie nods, slowly. He wipes rain from his face with one sleeve, and then a sweet steel note rings clear through the damp air as he unsheathes Anvar.

I want to call him back as he strides through the trees toward the mud and mess of the battlefield, back to his place with the fighters. But we swore. Oh, we swore.

To serve. To stand fast. And I would not break my oath for anything in all the worlds I've known.

Philippa's still motionless, staring down at Dorien's body with unseeing eyes. I reach out and put a hand on her shoulder, but she jerks back.

"Don't, Evelyn," Philippa warns, and when she finally turns her face away from Dorien, there's anguish in every line of her profile. "Don't. Not when it could be you or Jamie next."

I have no comfort to offer. The words she's spoken are true, and hard, and I can't deny them.

We go our separate ways, traveling to opposite ends of the encampment like ill-fated stars. As I go, I remember another night, long ago and a world away, and the words that stung my lips as bombs fell on

London: anywhere but here, anywhere but here, anywhere but here.

But I couldn't speak those words now if I tried. Instead, my heart-song is this: nowhere but here, nowhere but here, nowhere but here. If I'm to die, let it be as a Woodlander. Because a Woodlands heart always finds its way home.

28

I'VE NEVER ARRIVED AT A RAILWAY STATION LIKE THIS—
with my hand on someone's arm. Mum and Dad put up a bit of a
fuss at the idea of me heading off with a stranger, and a boy at that,
but Jamie silenced them with a few terse words. And it was Jamie
who drove us to the station and gave me a hug so tight it was as if
we were saying goodbye forever.

Tom is careful with me, helping me up into the train carriage.
We sit side by side in an empty compartment and share a bag of
toffee, but stay quiet for the most part. I like Tom's quietness best
about him—that he's a respecter of silence, and doesn't feel pressed
to fill it with pointless chatter.

I only realize I've fallen asleep when I wake with my head on
Tom Harper's shoulder. I keep absolutely still for a moment, eyes
shut, trying to sort out the smell of him. Burnt sugar and chocolate
from the toffee, wool and fresh air from his overcoat.

I sit up abruptly and scoot away, putting inches between us and
muttering an apology. Tom flushes, red as his hair, but there's a
smile hiding at the corners of his mouth.

The lunch trolley comes and saves us from our own awkwardness. The choices are a suspicious egg salad or the ever-present stale ham and cheese. I'm growing quite fond of those stale ham and cheese sandwiches. I'm even fonder of them after I nibble my own and watch Tom eat four in quick succession. We have more toffees after that, and tea from a thermos Tom pulls out of his bag. Outside, the dales flash by, grey and dreaming beneath a blanket of snow. The sky broods overhead and sheep gather in the valleys or huddle next to protective bluffs. I try not to see tree spirits in the wooded copses or stonewardens in the shadows of the crags, but they're always there, my own set of unbelievable ghosts.

This time, though, I see past them. I watch the sheep, the clever collie herding the flock, the shepherd working with him in a partnership without words. I look for the beauty in those things. I look for magic.

To my surprise, I find it. It's in the way the dog anticipates his master's whistle, and the way the sheep bunch and run together. It's in the starlings we frighten as we speed through the lowlands, which take wing and move of one accord in a murmuration of feathers and will. It's in the trees I've always found lifeless, that in this strange world still stretch their bare bones to the winter sky, reaching for the stars beyond.

When I turn away from the window, Tom's watching me with a curious expression.

"What did you see?" he asks.

"Everything," I say. "The world."

"And what do you think of it?"

It's a loaded question, that, seeing as I've known another. I consider my words before answering.

"I think," I tell him, "that right now I'm happy to be here, with you."

The train begins to slow and the porter comes down the aisle calling out our stop at Edgethorn Halt.

A cold trickle of nervousness works its way down my spine. This is it. The end of the line. It's time to get off the train and stand on my own two feet.

The Harper farm lies three miles from Edgethorn Halt. We haven't got much luggage—most of our belongings are still at school, and Tom told his family not to bother with coming down to the station to meet us, so we walk.

These are the things I want to remember: cold air. The grey sky clearing just enough for the sun to peer out occasionally, like a lamp switching on and off. The distant bleating of sheep carried down to us from the hills. Tom gripping both our suitcases in one of his capable hands, so the other is free to hold my own. I twine my fingers through his because I need courage—I still feel frail and rudderless, even if land is in sight. I've seen war and death and darkness, but I've never before walked home with a boy, heart in my throat, knowing that at the end of the walk will be people who love him and who will take a measure of me.

Too soon, we stop at the bottom of a hill topped by a long, two-story stone house that looks as if it grew out of the earth. We stand side by side and look up the rutted drive.

"This is it," Tom says after a moment. "Dad and Meg'll still be out in the fields, but Mum and Annie should be home. Want me to smuggle you in?"

I don't care if it will make things strange later. I snatch at the offer. "Oh, Tom, really?"

"Anything for you," he says with a crooked smile.

I don't know what to say to that. I'm off the edges of the map again (I seem to live there, only making brief forays into known country). We walk along the drive and around to the back of the house, where Tom sneaks me in through a rear entry cluttered with boots and cricket bats and barrels of potatoes. Then up a flight of narrow stairs and into a tidy guest bedroom. There's a storm-at-sea quilt on the bed and a washstand with a pitcher and basin on it. A fire crackles on the miniature hearth. Clean towels are laid out and I can smell the bar of rose soap that sits on top of them.

Tom stands in the doorway and twists his cap in his hands. "I didn't think to tell you, but we haven't got plumbing in the house yet. It's one of those things we just never get around to, and I know you're not used to that, so I feel like a fool for forgetting to mention it. If you look out the window you'll see the privy."

I push the lace curtains aside and glance out to the farmyard. There's the privy, and two long, low-lying barns, one of them with a thick-bodied heifer contentedly munching hay just outside.

"I'm sorry." The uncertainty in Tom's voice makes me turn to face him. "Do you hate it? You don't have to stay if you don't want to."

What I hate is seeing kind and quietly confident Tom Harper feel ill at ease about his house just because I'm in it.

"It's perfect." Truth suffuses the words, and Tom brightens. He sets the suitcase down on the bed.

A hesitant knock at the door draws both our attention. "Hello, Tommy."

Tom crosses the room in two steps and pulls his younger sister, Annie, into a tight hug. She peers around his shoulder at me, because she's too short to peer over it. There's an elfin quality to her clever little face, and she holds my gaze solemnly for a moment before breaking into a smile, warm and fresh as sun after rain.

Then, to my surprise, she pulls away from Tom and wraps me in a hug as sweet and unselfconscious as the one she gave him.

For a moment, I hesitate. It's been a long time since I last felt whole enough to greet a stranger with so little mistrust. But I can't help it—my arms go around Annie Harper and I feel a dart of her simple joy go into me as she whispers, "Hello, Evelyn Hapwell. I'm very happy to meet you."

"That's funny," I whisper back. "I was just about to tell you the same thing."

"You weren't here for presents," Annie says to Tom. "But I made your toffee, and I knit you another sweater. Meg didn't help at all this time—I did it all on my own."

"That's my girl," Tom says, and all I want is for someone to look at me with the raw affection I see in him for Annie.

She steps away from me and back to the door. "Are you coming down? It's not dinner yet but I'll get tea, and there are biscuits."

Tom looks to me. "It's up to Evelyn. She might want to rest before meeting everyone else."

"We'll be down right away," I tell Annie. "Tea sounds wonderful."

She smiles again, and it would take a hard person not to smile back. Once I hear her footsteps on the stairs, I give Tom a quick, fierce hug. "Thank you. Thank you for inviting me here.

Everything's perfect just the way it is."

He grins, and scuffs a boot against the braided rug.

We can hear Tom's mum before we see her. As we walk down the poky upstairs hall and the front stairway, the sounds of pots and pans and singing drift up to us, along with the smell of roasting meat and vegetables. She has a nice voice—it's not beautiful, exactly, but strong and tuneful.

When we stand at last on the threshold of the big farm kitchen, I feel recognition. I've never seen this place before, but it's homey. It's exactly where I'd imagine Tom Harper to come from, and these are exactly his sort of people. His father and Meg have just come in from the fields and stand noisily stamping their boots off in the outside doorway. It seems here in the Harper house, all doors lead to the kitchen.

Mrs. Harper is red-haired and rawboned like Tom himself, and like Meg. The three of them look very alike—lanky and bright-eyed, with smiles that would melt a snowbank. His father and Annie are the odd ones out, shorter and dark-haired, with a quieter way about them. It's not that Tom and Meg and his mother are loud, exactly, but when they're together, they fill a room with their confidence and easy laughter. Annie and Mr. Harper just stand back and watch, occasionally casting glances at each other as if they share a private joke.

I stand on the edge of this for a moment, on the fringe of their happy family chatter. It makes me glad, but there's a little ache inside me all the same. I was like this once, carefree and comfortable in my own skin, knowing exactly where I belonged.

But then my eyes light on the windowsill next to the wood-fired range. In among the oddments there, the blue glass bottles and cuttings taking root, there are two picture frames, draped with a black cloth and with fresh flowers carefully set between them. In each is a photograph of a boy in uniform, one big and straight-shouldered like Tom, the other smaller and self-possessed like his father and Annie.

The Harpers aren't carefree. They've known trouble. And they can't be as comfortable as they seem, not with the thistle of grief lodged in each of their hearts, chafing when any one of them moves the wrong way. But somehow, in spite of all this, they laugh. They love. They carry on.

I sit down on one of the benches drawn up to the long harvest table and watch, hungry to learn the trick of happiness.

Meg elbows Tom in the ribs after the first flurry of greetings and Christmas catch-up has subsided. She jerks her head in my direction and asks him something. He turns to me and smiles, a quiet, private sort of smile that's mostly in his eyes. To think I've gone through both my lives not knowing I wanted to be on the receiving end of a smile like that.

Meg says something else and crosses the kitchen, settling down on the bench beside me. She sits with her trousered legs stretched out, elbows behind her on the tabletop.

"I told him you look like a wild bird, perched there," she says, without the bother of introductions. "Just sitting and watching, not sure yet if you're going to take flight or if you trust us. And he told me that I'm quite right, but that like any wild thing, you've got to make up your own mind and we can't force you to choose us. So I suppose, given the circumstances, I should have approached rather more slowly, and with a handful of seeds."

She says that last so drily and with such a serious face that I can't help the laugh that bubbles out of me. Meg's seriousness melts away into a pleased expression, and she shoots a smug look at Tom.

I am thawing in this overheated, crowded kitchen. I can feel my winter melting into spring.

Across the kitchen, Annie retrieves her Christmas gift for Tom and he proudly pulls on the jumper, this one patterned with what might be leaves, but might also be sailboats. After a moment he tucks it back in the box and rolls up his shirtsleeves. I catch myself thinking that he's perfect, every bit of him, even his ears that stick out a little.

Annie joins us and sits down on my other side, looping her arm through mine. Tom stands before the three of us, arms crossed, wearing a ridiculous grin. There's happiness rolling off him in waves, and I don't know if it's being home or my presence or just holiday euphoria.

"Alright, Evie?" he asks, and it's the first time he's used the nickname. "You look like a rose among thorns."

Meg rolls her eyes and Annie smiles, oblivious to the joke. My face grows even hotter, but Mrs. Harper saves me, turning from the range and giving one of Tom's hands a swat with her wooden spoon. "Don't make a fool of yourself," she chides. "The girl won't like you any the better for it. Plain talk for plain folk. Evelyn, love, would you and Annie set the table together? She knows where everything is—if she fetches, you can lay it all out. Meg, wash your hands—there's half a potato field under those nails."

There is magic in the way that suddenly I've been folded into the family without pleasantries or awkward small talk. I'm just here, as if that's the way things have always been. I set the table and we eat Mrs. Harper's excellent roast dinner, Meg and Mrs. Harper and Tom chattering at each other like magpies while Mr. Harper, Annie, and I listen and laugh. I'm breathless by bedtime, with goodwill and belonging and hope.

29

MR. HARPER AND MEG ARE LONG GONE BY THE TIME I get down to the kitchen the following morning. Annie's out, too— off to visit a friend in the village. So it's just Tom and Mrs. Harper and myself, which makes for a quieter breakfast than our dinner the night before.

"Now then, Miss Evelyn," says Mrs. Harper as I take a seat and help myself to tea and a muffin. "Let me look at you."

She fixes her green eyes on me and I meet her gaze hesitantly, not sure what she'll see. I knew where I fit once, when I walked free and glad in the Great Wood. Now I'm just out-of-place Evelyn Hapwell in a skirt and cardigan, hair pulled back into a knot because I can't be bothered with a permanent. Or at least, that's the outside part of me. Even I'm not quite sure how the inside looks.

But Mrs. Harper seems to be satisfied with the inside Evelyn, because that's who she's looking at, with her stare that cuts straight to my core. After a moment, she nods and butters a slice of toast. "You be good to her, Tom. She's got a gentle heart."

That's just what Alfreya used to tell me about Philippa, on

nights when I'd creep down to the kitchen to complain about how fussy or strict my sister could be.

Oh, Phil, I miss you, nearly as much as I miss home.

I swallow a mouthful of tea to steady myself. I will stop regretting. I will stop looking back. I will look forward and be glad. I will be the gladdest thing under the sun.

"What have the two of you got planned for the day?" Mrs. Harper pushes her chair back and brushes crumbs from her ample skirt.

"I thought I'd take Ev over to Whitcomb Manor and show her the glasshouse," says Tom. "If she doesn't mind a walk."

He gives me a questioning look and I shake my head. "No, I'd love a walk."

"Then that's what we're doing." Tom gathers up his plate and silverware and takes them to the sink.

The day is fine, full of thin sunshine that glances off icicles but isn't quite strong enough to melt the hoarfrost cloaking the dales. We stump down the lane in boots and coats and mittens, cheeks red and breath puffing out in clouds, until we come to an enormous wrought-iron gate beyond which a graveled drive curves through well-kept parkland.

Tom stops in front of the gate and fumbles with the latch. The ironwork is cleverly crafted into a woodland scene, and stags hide among the metal trees. I will my heart to beat steadily, my stomach to stay calm. It's just a gate in the English countryside, made in a common enough pattern.

We pass through and the hedgerows along the road give way to manicured hills and well-tended woods. There's a small lake with a fountain at the center, shut off in winter, and I try desperately not to notice that the fountain is a stag, too, head thrown back so water will pipe out of his throat. The country house itself stands on the lakeshore, looking down at its own mellow stone reflection. It's a peaceful place, a place I might like if it wasn't for the bronze stags that guard the front door.

Tom leads me around back to the glasshouse and I keep as close as I can without crowding. I barely notice a carefully tended kitchen garden with winter crops laid in the beds and cold frames stuffed with greens. The glasshouse glitters in the sun before us and I follow Tom as he ducks inside.

Suddenly, it's as if winter's never been.

The air inside is summer-warm. A potbellied stove in one corner throws out heat, but a quantity of pans laid out on top of it bubble and steam, keeping the air moist, almost tropical. The sweet smell of lemon blossoms mingles with the sharper scents of potted herbs: tarragon, basil, rosemary. It's magic, this bit of summer in late December. I brush one finger against the velvety petals of an orchid and smile.

"Do you like it?" Tom asks. "I come round in summer when school's out and help the head gardener. The grounds all look like this then—flowers every way you turn."

"I do." The idea of walking back past all those stags is a daunting one, but I try to push the thought aside, to stay here, stay present, stay in this moment of beauty and warmth.

We linger in the glasshouse, sharing out the sour halves of a ripe lemon. When it's time to go, Tom helps me into my coat and grabs a metal pail.

"I've got one more thing to show you," he says. "Just keep a few steps back from me."

I frown but follow after him as he goes out the glasshouse's far end and trudges across the park, toward the leafless grey woods. Near the trees he shakes the bucket and calls out.

"Hey now! Come on, boys! Come on!"

For a long time, nothing happens. Tom calls again, and then they step out from the shadow of the wood—twin stags, their hides the color of autumn leaves.

He couldn't know, he couldn't, but that doesn't change the pounding of my heart, the terrible pain in my chest. I stand rooted to the spot as a hundred memories flash through my mind in an overwhelming onslaught.

Cervus in the Great Wood, the birch ring, the castle. Cervus calling me away from this world and to a place where I belonged. Cervus healing my burned hands with a touch. Cervus and me tending the dead.

One of the stags takes a mouthful of grain and rests its head on Tom's shoulder. He throws an arm around its neck.

Cervus on the beach.

Grey rain, a grey sea, a grey sky.

I turn and run, heading for the wrought-iron gate. I don't stop until I've burst through it and into the laneway, where I slip through a gap in the hedgerow and hurry on across the dales, occasionally stumbling over a stone or rabbit hole. I don't look back to see if Tom's following—I hope he isn't, because I'm drowning in memory and I'll go under soon.

When I find an outcrop of rock that offers a little protection from the brisk wind, I huddle against it and pull my knees to my chest, because

we're losing this fight.

The Empire's army tore a hole through the Great Wood, hacking and burning their way to the heart of it with ruthless Heraklean fire. There's fighting everywhere, even in the midst of our encampment now.

"Cervus!" I call out through the pandemonium. "Cervus, where are you?"

He appears suddenly, the only still spot in a world of terrible motion. I run to him, dodging a Tarsin soldier as I go.

There are so few of us already, though our enemy can't possibly know. Hector's cobbled-together army still fights like smoke in the forest, hurrying in to attack, retreating just as swiftly. They are quick and clever and desperate, but woefully outnumbered.

"Take me to my sister," I beg Cervus. We stumble across the battlefield, which is littered with bodies and abandoned weapons, the air thick with smoke from burning trees and tents.

Halfway across the clearing a great cry rises up among the Tarsin soldiers. I cast about us in confusion, and there at the edge of the trees is a chariot driven by a formidable figure in gilded armor that gleams brightly even under the halfhearted spring sun.

"Is that him?" I breathe.

"The Tarsin Emperor himself," Cervus answers. "Ruler of the Known World, should the fronts here and in Illyria fail."

But something has happened, something the Imperial troops don't seem to notice, caught up in their battle cries.

The field has emptied of Woodlanders. Though the wounded and dying still cry out, Cervus and I stand alone at the clearing's center, surrounded by the wreckage of our encampment.

"Will you surrender now, Cervus?" the Emperor calls out, his booming voice echoing back from the trees. "Bow before me and I swear I will leave a few trees standing. A handful of sad copses here and there, for a frightened remnant of Woodlanders to hide away in, telling tales of the day their country was destroyed."

Cervus stands proud beside me. Above us, a breeze sways the branches of the greening trees. I tighten my grip on Cervus, twining my fingers in his fur. The breeze overhead is a wind now, edging on toward a gale. Leaves skitter across the clearing and twist among the Empire's soldiers. Faintly, I hear a chiming laugh.

The leaves swirl and gust around the Emperor's chariot and he makes no more futile offers. He's silent, and Cervus and I exchange a look. The soldiers fix their eyes on him in confusion, and Vaya takes her girl shape as the Tarsin Emperor goes white, then blue, with her hands around his throat.

When the first soldiers make for the chariot, she vanishes, skipping away with the breeze, and the Emperor collapses to his knees, gasping for air. It's a moment of uncertainty, a moment without the threat of fire, and it's all Hector needs.

The last of the Woodlanders burst from the trees near soundlessly, barefooted or barehooved, making no hue or cry. Hector charges in at their head, and I catch sight of Jamie among their ranks. It's not until they're fighting with the very last of the Emperor's guard that the soldiers fully realize what's happening. But tree spirits move among the Tarsin army, there one instant and gone the next, reaching out to *strangle with invisible fingers and sowing terror in their wake. The Emperor's troops panic.*

And then, with a fearsome clash of his twin swords against the Tarsin Emperor's javelin, Hector reaches the chariot. There's a moment of uncertainty when I'm not sure who will win the day, but fear is already wild in the Emperor's fiery eyes.

Hector's voice rings out across the clearing. "Does the Empire hear us now?"

The Tarsin Emperor raises a hand wreathed in flame but Hector's swords flash faster. The blades bite clean, blood spurts forth and smokes, and the Ruler of the Known World falls headless onto our Woodlands soil.

"Evelyn!" Tom's voice drifts across the dales. "Ev, where've you gone? You've got to come out and tell me what happened."

The army is in a rout. They scatter and flee southward, panicked and never daring to look back. Still something nags at me, an itching worry that won't subside. Cervus pulls away and moves to where Hector and his followers have drawn back, letting the Tarsin army flee. But I turn aside and hurry to the hospital tent, with fear as tight around my throat as any tree spirit's grip.

Through all the chaos of battle, I never caught a glimpse of the Emperor's son. I never saw Venndarien Tarsin, with his hungry, covetous eyes.

"Come on, Ev." Tom's trying not to sound exasperated now, but I've heard that tone before. He's giving up on me. Tom's starting to wonder if I'm really worth the bother, and it's about time he realized the truth.

The long hospital tent is a shambles, cots overturned, crockery shattered, filthy bandages strewn about.

"Philippa?" I call out, my voice fraying at the edges. "Philippa, answer me!"

Nothing.

"Phil!"

A faint noise catches my attention from behind the curtain at the back of the tent where the dying are kept. I run for it, reaching for the dagger at my belt that I've never used, but that Hector gave me to carry.

And there behind the curtain is Venndarien Tarsin, with a knife to my sister's side and one of his dead-white hands pressed to her perfect mouth.

"I will kill her," he hisses. "I will gut her, little fawn, if you won't let me pass."

Mutely, I drop my dagger and step aside.

Venndarien pushes past me and out into the open center aisle of the hospital tent, shoving Philippa along in front of him. Her dark eyes are resigned and lifeless. Philippa might have held on to hope for me, but I don't think she ever hoped for herself.

"Evelyn . . ." Tom's voice fades away as he carries on down the lane. I'm left alone on the winter dales, with only my memories for company.

It's not as if I mind. I've spent years with these particular ghosts.

Before Venndarien can take three steps, I pull another knife from its hidden sheath in my sleeve.

"If you plan to kill a man," Hector said, long ago in winter, "always carry more than one blade."

I do what he taught me to do, which is to silence the frail and keening parts of me. In their absence, I am no longer a minister to the dead but death itself, striding forward on soundless feet. I jerk Venndarien's head back with one sure hand while the other draws my knife blade hard and clean across the Tarsin heir's throat.

Blood pours warm across my certain hands even as my uncertain heart shatters. Philippa whirls and blood spatters her, too. Venndarien Tarsin falls to his knees and then collapses, and the baleful fire behind his eyes burns out.

"Don't tell anyone," I whisper as Philippa wraps her arms around me and presses my face to her shoulder. "I kept my word, but don't tell anyone what I've done."

My vicious hands are still warm and slick, and I will never be able to wash the blood from them.

Night's fallen by the time I slip into the Harpers' warm and inviting kitchen. They're all seated around the table and turn to look when I come in. Tom's face is a confusion of relief and unhappiness.

"I'm going back to school tomorrow," I tell him.

"There's no need for that, love," Mrs. Harper says, though she looks troubled. "You can stay on with us as long as you like."

"No." Nothing will change my mind now. "I have to go."

30

I PUT ON A BRAVE FACE FOR ANNIE AND TOM. WHEN HE comes to my bedroom door the next morning, I'm calm and collected with my bags packed and my school clothes on. I smile at him with my mouth, if not my eyes, and he smiles back, though worry taints the expression. Down in the kitchen I hug Meg and Mrs. Harper, who offer invitations to come back anytime, please do, don't be a stranger, though I'm not sure if they're sincere. Mr. Harper is out in the fields already, and I hug Annie last, holding her to me as if I could freeze her in time with the pressure of my arms. She slips a paper bag of toffees into my pocket and kisses my cheek, her face open and innocent.

Stay as you are, Annie. Don't let the worlds you walk break you.

Meg drives us to the train station in the rickety farm wagon, and it's hard to be melancholy while bumping over potholes, so I'm just queasy instead. On the train I curl into a corner of the car and rest my head against the window, staring out at the passing countryside.

All I see is grey sand. Grey sea. Grey sky.

Tom doesn't try to draw me out, to press me into conversation, and he never asks what's wrong. He just sits next to me, and holds my hand in one of his. When the lunch trolley wheels past, he waves it away. I don't deserve him.

All too soon, the train chuffs to a halt in Hardwick. Tom walks me to the head of St. Agatha's road and stands, scuffing his boot against the earthen embankment where we have to part ways.

"Ev?" he says, my name a question on his lips. "Are you going to be alright?"

"I don't know," I answer truthfully. Then I pick up my bag and walk down the lane without another word, because I can't bring myself to say *goodbye*.

At school, I float across the quad and back to my room in the dormitory, which is all but empty three days before term.

I dream of the Woodlands.

Grey sand, grey sea, grey sky.

I dream of how news came to us that the Empire was falling to pieces, broken apart by infighting over the vacant throne. And each night, just as memories of that final battle and the blood on my hands seemed like they'd choke me, Philippa would come to me and stave them off with her quiet presence and gentle words. We began to be whole again together.

I dream of how, by midsummer, those of us left came fully alive once more. We would go out into the Great Wood, not to dance and sing as we used to, but to clear away bones and armor, burned branches and abandoned camp gear. And then, on the longest day, when Cervus stood watch in the birch ring until sunset to bring back the night, we began planting trees. Each sapling was a wish and a prayer. I planted a young beech in a hidden hollow and whispered the Woodlands blessing, of hearts and home, as I pressed soil down over its strong young roots, and when I stood I spoke Dorien's name as well. I planted an oak in a valley that Vaya once showed me, next to the shorn-off stump of a great tree that sang its own funeral song. I sank the sapling's roots deep into Woodlands soil, along with my grief and fear and pain, and when I left the valley I was myself again—Evelyn of the Woodlands, a girl who'd found her place.

And I dream of how on drowsy afternoons, I'd still wander in the Wood, with Cervus by my side, and together we'd just be quiet, sharing the weight of the world between us.

Away from the Great Wood, the world hangs too heavy on me, Cervus. I'm no Atlas, and I cannot bear up under it alone.

"Did you forget?" Jamie's voice asks, tearing me from one of my waking dreams. I blink, not entirely sure where I am at first, but here are the walls of the library. Here is the window out to the courtyard, showing a late winter day of fitful clouds and weak sunshine.

I scrub at my eyes with one hand. "Forget what?"

Jamie's face is a battleground, pity and anger, sadness and fear all fighting for a place. "I rang, last week. It's your birthday. I'm here to take you out—Ev, we talked about it."

It's my birthday. I'm seventeen. The same age now as I was when I left the Woodlands.

The realization makes me sway as I get to my feet and Jamie catches me by the arm. "Steady on."

If it were Philippa here, she'd be telling me right away that I've got to pull myself together, that I can't let myself fall to pieces like this, that it's unbecoming of a girl who's weathered war in not one world but two. It's Jamie, though, so he only looks at me, tense with worry. We'll be skirting around the issue all day, finally getting to his well-intentioned lecture after hours of building up to it.

I sigh, and resign myself to my fate.

"Well, what do you want to do?" Jamie asks as I lower myself onto the passenger seat of his battered old car. "Go to the cinema? Get lunch somewhere? It's your day."

I don't know. If I don't know who I am, how should I know what I want to do? I want to go home, but that's not a wish Jamie can grant.

"Just drive," I say, and lose myself in the passing countryside. We motor over hills and through valleys, past forests and streams, alongside crumbling stone walls and fields laid out like snowy quilts. Jamie stops at a pub to grab a bite, but I won't go in because I can't stand the noise and he has them pack up sandwiches. I don't eat any. I have no appetite and no words. I've lost my voice in this place as surely as the trees and animals have lost theirs.

Midafternoon it starts to rain. We keep driving, raindrops beading on the window beside me, wipers swishing at the windshield. They make a rhythmic sound, like grey waves on grey sand.

I'm waiting on the beach. Where are you?

By the time we pull back into the drive at St. Agatha's, Jamie's got the headlamps switched on. He brings the car to a slow halt and gravel crunches under the tires. I stare out through the drizzle, across the dark and rain-slick quad.

"Ev." Jamie fiddles with a loose thread on one of his driving gloves. The lecture cometh. Poor Jamie. There's defeat in the set of his mouth—he always could solve any problems but our own.

"I don't want to say this, but I think I've got to, so I'm just going to come right out with it." He stares through the windshield at the crescent of light the headlamps cast, and I freeze. This isn't the way the usual lecture starts, about being present, about living up to my role and responsibilities. This is something else.

Jamie turns to look at me, fixing me with the sort of stare that dares me to question what he's about to say. At the same time, there's a dreadful sadness behind it and I curl up inside, away from what's about to come.

"We're never going back," he says. "It's not just me, it's Philippa. It's you. None of us are ever going back. You've got to stop waiting. You've got to start living in this world. We're not Woodlanders—we never were. We're just us, and we need to make the best of it."

"Don't you remember?" The words sound strange and far away, drifting out of me in little more than a whisper. They sound like waves, like rain. *"A Woodlands heart always finds its way home. Shouldn't that mean we're going back?"*

Jamie takes his gloves off and balls them up in one hand. "You know what Cervus said to us, that last day on the beach. But you need to say it, too, Ev. I'm sorry, but you've got to."

I shake my head. "Jamie, don't make me."

He's unbending. He always has been, when there's no alternative. "Tell me what Cervus said to us on the beach, Evelyn."

Grey sand, grey sea, grey sky. My words are faint as a last breath.

"He said he won't call us again. That he can't."

"You can make a life here." There's fire in Jamie's words. "I know you can. You're strong enough for this."

"How?" I ask, desperate for hope that eludes my grip.

"Things aren't as straightforward here, I know," Jamie admits. "I think we're more like Tarsa than the Great Wood, most of the time. But you and I were born to this world, Ev, and we don't have to hack at the edges of its darkness. We can change it from the inside out. Find some good to do, something to hang on to."

But I don't know how to live in this grey country—how to find the light and shadow when they all run together so.

"I'll try," I say, and I've never spoken a greater lie. I'm done trying. I've tried for six agonizing years, held to this world by my sister and brother and the force of their wills.

Ducking out of the car without giving Jamie a chance to answer, I wait in the dormitory's entrance till he's pulled away. Once he's gone I run back out, free in the cold February air, sprinting across the gravel quad toward the back gate, past the cowshed and out into the lane, the woods, the open world that looks so achingly like home but never will be.

I sit on a hill and let the cold soak into me, because I'm cold on the inside so I may as well be cold outside. I stay until I'm shaking and can't bear the way my teeth rattle, and then I turn back and climb across the treacherously icy roof to where Georgie has left the window unlatched. Climbing into bed in my sodden clothes, I curl up around a lukewarm hot water bottle.

I have no plans to leave my bed again. I've seen this world. There's nothing in it I want anymore. Everything I've ever had, I left behind.

31 ⤴

IT'S BEEN HALF A YEAR SINCE THE WOODLANDS *went to war. Philippa and Jamie and I are on the beach, stealing a few moments together in spite of a misting grey rain that falls from the grey sky. I know they're a little at loose ends—Jamie struggling to find his place now the standing army's been disbanded, Philippa busy in the infirmary and the castle with Alfreya, but not entirely sure how to live in a world where she's been less than perfect.*

But we grew into our roles here before, and my brother and sister can do so again. The coming harvest at Palace Beautiful will be a good one. New green trees flourish throughout the Wood. The war is truly over, and the Woodlands are at peace once more. I knew all would be well with us the day Hector hired onto a fishing boat, and at long last set his swords aside.

Grey waves sigh against the shore. I am glad, and entirely alive. I know my place, know who I am. This is where I belong, in this kingdom we've all fought for. I will live and die in the service of the Great Wood. I barely remember our other life, it seems so far away.

When I look up and Cervus is coming toward us on the beach, rust-red and resplendent, my heart leaps. Then I see that his head hangs low, and his cloven hooves move heavily over the sand.

I run to him and cup his velvet muzzle with both hands, lifting his head so he can't help but look at me. "Cervus, what's wrong? What's happened?"

Jamie and Philippa come up beside me and the stag pulls away.

"Children," he says in a low voice, though we're hardly that anymore. "Your own world is waiting. I'm ready for the sending, as you asked. But be sure of your choice, for once you return, I cannot call you back."

Dread lodges in the pit of my stomach. "I'd never ask to be sent away. This is my world. I belong here. We belong here. Jamie? Philippa?"

But when I turn to my brother and sister, there's no fear in their eyes, only sorrow.

"Evie," Jamie says with a kindness that cuts. "You were only a child when we came here. It's time to go home. We never expected to stay for so long."

Philippa's arm goes around my waist, holding tight to me. "We'll be with you. Whatever world we're in, I promise. But the Great Wood is safe—you needn't worry about it anymore. This isn't where we're meant to be, Ev."

The discovery that Philippa had plotted with Tarsa was nothing compared to this—to knowing both my brother and sister have decided my fate without ever speaking a word of it to me.

"Don't ask me to go," I plead.

Jamie looks sick and Philippa's eyes fill with tears.

"Evelyn," she begs. "We have to do this. And we can't leave you behind. It would break my heart to go back on another promise, and

I swore I'd look after you. Come with us, Evie. I'm asking you to go."

I look at my sister, who I've spilled blood for. What about my heart, Philippa? What about mine? Inside, I am an ocean of grief that weeps endlessly against the shore. Outside, I stand motionless as Philippa squeezes my hand.

"We're going home at last," she says, her words heavy with relief. "Cervus, let us have done with it."

Cervus looks at me one final time and his eyes are bottomless dark pools. I want nothing more than to reach out for him, but I can't bring myself to let go of Philippa.

"I am home," I whisper.

The words don't come out clear, cutting across the sound of rain and waves. Instead, they're muffled by the earth floor and narrow metal walls of an Anderson shelter. Outside, a bomb drops so close my ears ring. The air raid sirens scream on.

Philippa and Jamie stand on either side of me, children in their nightclothes once more, and my body is not my own, my voice is not my own, this world is not my own.

32 ⌣

IN THE MORNING, GEORGIE DOESN'T TRY TO GET ME UP when the gong rings and I put my back to the room and my face to the wall. She leaves a plate of breakfast for me before walking down to the old stone church in Hardwick with the other girls. She leaves a plate of lunch. She leaves a plate of dinner. She clears them all away, untouched, at day's end.

She doesn't try to get me up the next day, either, but at some point Max appears. I know it's her because of the perfume she wears—something fresh and young, not the fussy rosewater the rest of the staff prefer. A chair scrapes across the floor and I hear her settle into it.

I expect a lecture. Instead, I hear pages turn and Max clears her throat before beginning to read. It's poetry, but I haven't heard these words before, and they pierce me to the core as she reads.

> *"The heart of a woman goes forth with the dawn,*
> *As a lone bird, soft winging, so restlessly on,*

Afar o'er life's turrets and vales does it roam
In the wake of those echoes the heart calls home.

The heart of a woman falls back with the night,
And enters some alien cage in its plight,
And tries to forget it has dreamed of the stars
While it breaks, breaks, breaks on the sheltering bars."

After that, nothing. She just sits. She has a cup of tea. She sets the book on my nightstand, and then she goes.

I know she hopes I'll read, but I can't. When the room is empty, I drink the water Georgie leaves for me. I use the lav. I get back into bed. By week's end the nurse has visited. The Curmudgeon has told me in fretful tones that my parents have been informed of my behavior, and if I keep up this shocking display much longer, they'll have to collect me.

And Mum and Dad do come. One day, the door to my bedroom opens and the shift of air brings with it the scent of lavender soap. I know without turning around that my mother is in the room. She and Philippa are the only people I know who smell so persistently of lavender, but the footsteps are quiet, and Philippa always wears heels.

There's one chair next to my bed already. I hear a scrape as the extra chair from Georgie's desk is brought over, which tells me Dad's come, too.

"Evie, what are we going to do with you?" Mum asks softly, and I keep my face resolutely to the wall. I don't know what it is she says to me—to avoid her words, I drop into memories of the Woodlands after war, of riding on the beach and casting nets over the side of a boat with Hector and racing across the meadows with Vaya.

But then a suggestion stands out, sharp and clear as broken glass, spoken in my father's voice.

"Perhaps we'd better take you home with us."

I sit up abruptly and face them, and I must look a fright because they go quite pale.

"No," I say to my parents, and the word is a command. "London would kill me."

Mum presses a handkerchief to her mouth and tears pool in her eyes. Dad looks stern, but I shake my head. "Go home. Let me be."

I set my back to them again, and can't bring myself to care that I've been cruel.

I sleep. I sleep and sleep and sleep. After so many nights spent dreaming, I think I might sleep forever.

Jamie comes. He sounds awfully low. He fumbles over his words, not knowing what to say to me. This was always Philippa's job.

He comes a second time, tries again. He says bracing things, but I can hear the hurt in his voice. I know I'm being unfair. Of course I know. But I can't see my way clear of these woods. I can't bring myself to forgive my brother and sister for what they've made me give up.

The night after one of Jamie's visits, I doze and watch the moon. Georgie's not back yet, so I've got the room to myself. I sit and pull my knees to my chest, leaning against the headboard for support. The doorknob turns and I rest my chin on my knees. I don't have the energy to climb back under the covers before Georgie steps in, and it'll give her a lift to see me sitting. Footsteps cross the room and a weight settles onto the foot of my bed, but when I look up, it's not Georgie.

It's Tom.

He catches my gaze and holds it with his own before I can look away.

"Get your coat," he says. "We're going out."

Tom stands and leaves the room before I can argue. I'm not sure I could argue—it's been more than a week since I've spoken. For a moment, I consider climbing back under the covers, making a shield of my bedspread to ward him off. But he was very decided and I haven't got the fortitude for a fight. I shrug my coat on and slide my feet into a pair of boots, then let him lead me down the hall like a lamb.

Max and Georgie hover in the front hall and nod to Tom as we pass. They're accomplices to this, though the whole thing has got Jamie's fingerprints all over it. The door shuts behind us and we're out in the night and Tom won't let go of my hand. How does he know that if he did, I'd drift, silent across the hills, and never turn back?

But he doesn't let go. He laces his fingers through mine for good measure and takes me out through the winter woods. I pay little attention to where Tom's leading, watching my feet instead. These feet have carried me so many miles, out of our world altogether, and now here they are, bound to this place forever by forces stronger than gravity.

An owl calls from somewhere in the canopy, and the moon sails across a sea of paper-thin clouds.

I let myself be led until I realize where we're going, but by then it's too late and we've already come out into the clearing. The white birches ringing it are pale and lovely in the moonlight, and tremble a bit in the breeze. I can hear them whisper—can almost make out their living voices. In any other world, their spirits would step out onto the frozen ground and dance.

But in this world, all they can do is sigh their wordless secrets. Tom lets go of my hand for the first time and I shrink between the trees.

Tom sits at the clearing's heart, but doesn't gesture to me or ask if I'll join him. Instead, he leans back on his hands and looks up at the night sky.

"Jamie came to see me," Tom says. He's almost handsome in the moonlight, sitting in the clearing like a knight in a fairy ring. "He said you lost something, and that you don't like to talk about it to other people. He told me everything reminds you of it, and that sometimes it gets to be too much. This is the second time he's hinted without actually coming right out and saying what it was."

I slide down to sit at the base of one of the birches, hidden in shadow. Tom runs a hand across his face and suddenly looks very tired. He swallows—I can see his throat work—and hunches his shoulders before speaking again.

"On April 7, 1942, my brother, Charlie, turned eighteen. He signed up for service on his birthday. He was happy to do it—Fred, the oldest of us, was nineteen and had already been in France for months. We had letters, cheerful letters, from them both, and Uncle Morris pulled some strings to get them into the same unit. After that, it's like they thought nothing could touch them, so long as they were together. I worshipped them, Ev—they were everything brave and good in my world."

I'm still as a stone, arms wrapped around myself to hold my breaking heart in. These stories always end the same way.

"On April 7, 1943, Charlie's nineteenth birthday, one year from the day he joined up, we had a visit from the army. My brothers were both killed in action in Libya. There wasn't enough left of them to bring home."

Tom turns to look at the shadows that hide me, and his sea-grey eyes are wistful. "We've all lost things we love. But it does no one any good if you lie down and quit. I think you've got the courage for living with grief, Evelyn Hapwell—in fact, I know you have. You walk like a girl out of a fairy story, and you see beauty in things that others overlook."

He scrambles to his feet and crosses the clearing to my patch of shadows. "I'll give you a hand up if you let me walk with you."

For a moment, I just look at his outstretched hand. Then I take it and let him pull me to my feet. Once I'm standing, Tom Harper wraps his arms around me, and I've never felt so safe in this world before.

"I'm sorry about your brothers," I say, and Tom holds me a little tighter.

"So am I. But we don't do the dead a service by refusing to live."

"I'm not a girl from a fairy tale, you know," I mumble against the wool of his knit jumper. "Never have been. I'm afraid I'm just Evelyn Hapwell."

Tom rests his chin on the top of my head, gently, and we might have been made to fit together. "I happen to like just Evelyn Hapwell a great deal."

I am neither a child of this world nor the Woodlands, and Cervus will never call me home. But I know, after all these years, what I need to do.

33

I PRETEND TO BE NORMAL. I SIT IN CLASS AND HALF listen. I sit in the dining hall and pretend to eat. I do the things I know will make Georgie feel better—tidy up and comb my hair and set my clothing out every evening just so. I lie in bed watching the moon scud across the winter sky, and it feels like winter inside.

Max stops at my desk one day just as Lit class ends. The other girls file out and I try not to look at her, because I haven't heard a word she's said since I walked into the room. Once we're alone, she sits at the desk opposite mine.

"You never gave me an answer about reciting in the winter concert, so I put you on the program. All the St. Joseph's boys will be coming. I expect you to be there, Evelyn, and it would be kind of you to invite your parents, like the other girls do."

The scarf wrapping her hair today is rust-red, and a waft of her perfume hits me as she walks out the door.

"Max," I call after her. "I'll recite, but I don't want my family here. When is it?"

Her voice drifts back down the hall. "The concert's tomorrow night, Evelyn, the flyers are all over school. Read something off a page if you have to, so long as you're there."

I will be. All my lives in all my worlds have led me to this place.

The refectory has been emptied of tables and lined with chairs. A makeshift stage stands at the front of the room. Bunting hangs from the ceiling in incongruous spring colors: blue, pale green, pink, and gold. I sit next to Georgie as the room fills and try to breathe through my nerves, try to keep my hands from shaking. The dull roar of voices washes over me like waves, punctuated by the scrape of chairs or outbursts of laughter.

"Alright, Ev?" Georgie asks, reaching over to squeeze my hand.

"I will be," I answer. "Whatever you hear, Georgie, I will be, I swear."

Georgie turns to me with a question in her eyes, but before she can say anything more the Curmudgeon gets up on stage and silence falls. There are the usual performances—a string quartet, recitations, and one of the girls even juggles. I'm hot and anxious and yearning for the woods by the time my name is called.

Though I'm seated near the front, the walk to the stage seems inordinately long. My footsteps sound loud, echoing off the ceiling, and my heart pounds in my chest. A white chalk line marks the place where we're meant to stand, and when I reach it, I turn.

A hundred pairs of eyes watch me. Out in the crowd, someone clears his throat expectantly.

I search the waiting faces, looking for just one. When I find Tom, he gives me a smile and waves, the movement small and contained. This is for him—the only gift I have to give. I let out a long breath and begin.

"They dropped like flakes, they dropped like stars,

Like petals from a rose,"

Beloved Dorien and a score of other Woodlanders, dead upon the forest floor.

"When suddenly across the June

A wind with fingers goes."

The Woodlands, Palace Beautiful, the girl I used to be.

"They perished in the seamless grass,—

No eye could find the place;"

Charlie and Fred Harper, brothers of my friend. Millions of people, across all of Europe, all the world.

"But God on his repealless list

Can summon every face."

Venndarien Tarsin, killed by my own hand for my sister's sake.

I miss you, Philippa. Come home to me.

I miss you, Cervus. Take me home.

The applause when I finish is muted. It's only five years since the war, and we all hide wounds that will never really heal.

Instead of taking my seat, I walk out of the refectory, and into the cold night air. Sleet mists down, and I let it bead on my hair and the wool of my school cardigan. Leaning up against the refectory wall, I wait outside the circle of light that beams from the doorway.

When the concert ends, people spill out of St. Agatha's front doors, once again happy and laughing, a transformation I've never managed to master. They vanish down the lane, and it isn't until most of them have gone that Tom appears, having dodged the chaperones from St. Joe's. He stands uncertainly in the light spilling from the building, looking this way and that. I watch him for a moment, and then call softly, unwilling to step out of the shadows.

"I'm over here."

Tom walks over and I slide my hand into his. My heart is a wild thing in my chest, anxious and crying out for home, but I bid it to be still just a moment longer.

"Thank you, Tom, for telling me about your brothers. For being here with me."

He looks at the ground and though there's not enough light to see him flush, I know he's red to the tips of his ears.

"You'd better go," I say. "It's getting awfully late."

Tom still has hold of one of my hands and he runs his thumb across the back of it. "Will I see you Saturday?"

One last time, I lie to Tom Harper. "Of course. I'll see you then."

He stands with his head bowed, then straightens. "You're right. I should get back. Are you going in?"

"Not yet."

"Alright. Good night, Ev."

"Good night, Tom."

I watch him disappear down the lane and try not to fidget. As soon as he's lost from sight, I bolt, hurrying across the field and past Hobb's cottage.

The back gate squeals softly as I slide through it and into the tame and sleeping forest. I travel the dim path to the birch ring and step out into its center, into the icy rain. There, I pull my wool sweater off and stand in my thin shirt, letting cold water wash over my skin. I kick off my shoes and peel away my wet socks so that slush oozes between my toes.

Grey sand, grey sea, grey sky. It's time for me to stand on my own.

"Cervus the Guardian, who watches over the Great Wood, call me out of this world. Honor your word. Take me back to where I belong. I swear to you, this heart beating in my chest is a Woodlands heart, and a Woodlands heart always finds its way home."

I wait in the rain until my fingers and toes are numb and the cold has leached like lead into my limbs. Drops trickle down my face, and I can't tell which have fallen from the sky and which are tears. I want to lie down and sleep, to give in to the quiet heaviness the cold has set in my bones, but I've come too far to surrender now. I'm a girl unmoored, cut free from the very last of the ties that bound me.

"Very well," I say to the dark. "If you won't call, I'll walk until I find the way."

I step forward, into the night, trusting my feet to return me home.

PHILIPPA

FEBRUARY 1950

34

WHEN A FIST HAMMERING ON MY DOOR KNOCKS ME OUT of sleep and into the cold dark of a New England night, I have a moment of perfect clarity. I know what this is about. I'm on the brink of a disaster that's been six years in the making.

Guilt lodges in my stomach, solid and unshakable and familiar as a friend. Whatever's coming, it's my fault.

The slate floors of the Women's Building are frigid in winter so I push my feet into thick slippers and pull on a dressing gown. I feel naked without powder and lipstick but there's nothing to be done about it. Smoothing my hair, I throw back my shoulders and open the door.

Professor Allard stands on the threshold. She's a tall, plain woman with a pallid complexion, and when I look at her straight on, she can't meet my eyes. She knows, like I do, that a transatlantic phone call at this hour can only be bad news. What she doesn't know are the specifics, but I can guess those without even hearing Jamie's voice on the other end of the line.

When Professor A ushers me into her sparsely furnished office and motions to the phone, I sit down and stare pointedly until she leaves. Only then do I pick up the receiver.

"Hello?" I'm counting on the long-distance crackle to erase the rough edges of sleep still clinging to my voice, and blur any traces of the shame already weighing me down.

"Philippa. It's Jamie."

"I know."

A long pause. "Oh, hang it all. What time is it there?"

I glance at the small clock on Professor Allard's desk. "Twelve minutes past three, a.m. not p.m."

"I didn't think. I'm sorry."

It's strange, listening to Jamie's disembodied voice without being able to see him in front of me. The connection gives an odd quality to his words, a static sort of tension. We're quiet for a while, listening to the snap and pop on the line. This is going to be a terribly expensive call.

That's what I'll focus on—the expense, and Professor Allard waiting outside. I won't think of anything else.

"It's Evelyn," Jamie finally says.

"Of course it is." I open one of Professor A's drawers and peer inside, but there's only stationery. I was hoping for something worth gossiping about.

"She's gone."

Oh, Evelyn. "How long has it been?"

The second drawer is pencils. There must be a hundred of them. Who on earth needs so many pencils? And sharpened already. Professor A really ought to find herself a hobby.

I won't think of Ev, even though I'm speaking of her. I won't fall to pieces in this strange woman's office. I won't, I won't.

"She's been gone two days. I'm not saying you should come home or anything like that, I just wanted you to know."

No, you wouldn't say I should come home, Jamie. You never come right out and say things, you just expect them. I think I'd be three feet taller if it wasn't for all your expectations weighing me down.

The third drawer yields a flask of whiskey. Hardly scandalous, but welcome nevertheless. I take a quick nip and pull a face. I'm not sure if it's too late or too early for alcohol, but it's definitely too something. "I'll need a day or two to make arrangements, but I can be back by week's end."

A pause again. Jamie will be paying through the nose for all these brooding silences. "You don't have to do that, Phil."

I roll my eyes, and hope he can somehow hear it through the line. "That's absurd. We both know I do, so don't be coy. I won't need a welcome or anything—I'll take a cab once the plane lands. Expect me by Friday."

He doesn't hang up. Good gracious, Jamie, are you made of money? "I'll phone again if there's any news. If we find out she just went ho—if she was called."

But if she wasn't—heat spreads across the back of my neck and I breathe, and breathe, past the guilt that's turned to nausea. When it subsides, I cling to the bitter hope my brother's offered me, that Ev is in the Great Wood after all. That in spite of Cervus telling us our days there were done, in spite of how the time slip ensured we weren't missing for more than a moment before, it may turn out she's alright.

We can't consider the alternative. *I* can't consider it. Not yet. Ev and I have put each other through all nine levels of hell, but she's my sister, and I've only ever been able to wish good things for her.

I return the flask to its place and lean my head against the back of Professor A's chair. I'm bone tired. We had a late night in town and classes start early. I already know I'll keep up my attendance until the plane leaves, just to be busy.

"Can I say good night, Jamie?"

"Yes, I'm sorry, I shouldn't have kept you so long. Good night, Philippa."

I pause, playing his game, before asking, "Can you manage until I get there?"

Jamie sighs into the phone, and if I can hear the way he's surely nodding his head, he must have heard the way I rolled my eyes before. "Yes. I can hold down the fort for now. Go get some sleep."

I hang up, and it's like he was in the room with me and just walked out the door. I'll never let anyone know how much I've missed him these last months, overbearing and self-righteous prig that he is.

A gentle tap sounds at the door. Professor A wants back into her office.

"Come in," I call out, and she crosses the threshold. I sit in her chair and watch her stand uncertainly before me, as if I'm the one who owns this space. Perhaps for the moment, I do. All I know is I've carved out a place in our worlds by learning to look as if I own the ground I stand on.

"Bad news?" Professor A twists her hands in front of her and I don't relinquish the chair—not yet.

"My younger sister's gone missing." I say the words right now, in this moment, but I've been dreading its coming for years.

Professor A's anxiety intensifies. "Is there anything I can do?"

My mouth quirks up in a humorless and involuntary smile—another trick that I learned worlds ago as a means of self-defense, to hide how very lost I felt. "No. If there was, I'd have done it myself. I'm flying home on Thursday, and I won't be back."

Professor A says something meek and contradictory, but I know now that America and college, much as I've liked them, were only ever where I came to wait for this to happen.

I'm sorry, Evelyn. I'm so very sorry.

Packing doesn't take long—I've barely got anything to my name. Goodbyes don't take long, either—I know everyone, but haven't let any of them get close enough that they deserve a face-to-face farewell. Besides, by the time I pull away from the Women's Building in a bus, word's got round that I'm leaving. I only told Professor A what's going on so I wouldn't have to bother with spreading my own news.

Fog drapes the New England woods, but melts away in the treeless streets of Queens. The plane taxis through clear air, roaring down the runway and taking off with that indescribable sensation of lift. It bears me up into a kingdom that seems strange even to me—a magic country of soft mountains and valleys, all touched by stark white light. Eventually, night descends, leaving the sky above brushed with stars.

I don't sleep on the plane. I drink coffee instead, tired but wideawake at the same time, and bluer than I like to be. The night sky is blue outside, I'm blue inside, even the upholstered seats are a faded shade of navy. It's all a bit ridiculous.

I sit and look out the tiny window, forcibly not thinking of Evelyn, of where she might be or what she might be doing or—well. I don't ponder the other what-if. That doesn't bear thinking of, not even when I'm winging my way across the Atlantic, sleepless and melancholy and suspended between worlds.

Then, below us, the eastern sky greys. We're flying over cloudless space, the sea stretching dark and restive from one horizon to the next. The grey goes crimson, goes salmon, goes gold, and a great trail of light gleams before us, sparking off the water. It's so bright it hurts to look at.

I look anyway—a family trait. A sliver of sun slides up over the sea, and quite suddenly, the night has passed. The sun leaps triumphant into the sky, flooding the waves with fire and diamonds. When I turn back to the dim cabin of the plane, transcendent light still sparks across my vision.

As we land, I'm flush with all that brilliance, aching over the reason for my homecoming, and dizzy after a missed night of sleep. But ever since the Woodlands, I've learned to love the comfortable numbness that comes with teetering on the edge of exhaustion. I'm over the edge now, into a feelingless limbo, and drag my luggage out of the airport to where a cabbie takes over for me. He has a ready smile and lined brown skin, and speaks in a Londoner's quick, offhand way. I realize, suddenly, how much I've missed this city.

The streets are a blur until I snap out of a doze to find the cab has stopped and the cabbie's holding the door open, my things sitting on the sidewalk outside the townhouse where my parents have always lived.

"Thank you." I take out the fare and a tip. The cabbie taps the peak of his cap with one hand and smiles.

"Welcome, Miss. Get a bit of a kip if you can."

I smile back, knowing it's all glitter and shine, leftover sun spilling across the ocean, because inside, the knowledge that Ev's missing has left a spreading bruise.

No one answers the door when I knock. I can't imagine where they've all gone, but I take the spare key out from under the mat and let myself in. My bags will have to wait—I dump them in the narrow front hallway and traipse up the stairs to the room I shared with Evelyn. Sliding out of my shoes and pulling the covers up is as much as I can manage before I'm half conscious.

I drift off facing my sister's bed, the empty space she's left behind, the question mark she's become.

Evelyn Hapwell, I always knew you'd break my heart. And I'd cry, but there's nothing left in me to give. I've spent every last one of my tears on you already.

35 ~

ONE MOMENT I'M LOOKING AT CERVUS AS RAIN patters onto the beach, and the next I'm in the damp, crowded confines of our bomb shelter, with Evelyn's hand in mine.

"I am home," Ev says to Cervus, but he's already gone and I've never heard such despair in so few words. I don't have time to be shocked or sick over how strange my thirteen-year-old body feels—over the suddenness of being torn from one life and thrown back into another as though no time has passed—because my sister blinks twice, like a startled fawn, and crumples to the ground.

"Jamie!" I call. His name comes out high and panicked, spoken in a child's voice. He's only two steps away, and between us we get Ev on her feet and onto the moldy cot. She curls up beside me, trembling so hard her teeth rattle. I put my arms around her as Jamie peers out the doorway, searching for our parents once again after all these years.

"Do you see them?" I ask just as another bomb goes off.

"Yes." Jamie slumps against the wall in relief. "Yes, they're coming out the door. Mum's limping—she must have had a fall, but she looks alright."

We're silent, just looking at each other, and then "Philippa, did we—"

"Yes."

"We can't tell them. We can't tell anyone. They'll think it's just that the shock of the bombing was too much for us."

I glance down at Evelyn, and brush the fair hair from her forehead. "Evie, did you hear that?"

She nods once, but won't meet my eyes.

Mum and Dad hurry into the shelter at last, Mum wincing as she sits on the edge of the cot.

"Twisted my ankle tripping over the ottoman," she says in answer to looks from Jamie and me. "Silly, really. I'm so sorry we gave you all a fright. Is Evie not feeling well?"

I tighten my hold on Ev and she burrows into me. "No, but she'll be fine."

You will be in time, Evelyn, I promise. We belong to this world and all wars pass. You'll be alright. I swear you'll be alright.

The five of us sit in the dark as the sound of planes fades away and the sirens eventually stop. But fear still eats away at my insides—fear that this is the worst thing I've done, bringing Ev home from the Woodlands. That I am born to trouble, sure as the sparks fly upward, and only harm when I want to help.

Swallowing back guilt, I hold my sister close.

36 ～

AFTERNOON LIGHT STREAMS THROUGH THE WINDOWS BY the time I make it downstairs. I may be groggy and muddleheaded, but my makeup is flawless and I haven't left a hair out of place.

Powder and pumps. Jamie once told Evelyn that's all I'm interested in since the Woodlands, but what he doesn't realize is that you can wear powder like a shield, and wield the right lipstick like a sword. I may have let the Tarsin heir's poisonous words get the better of me once, but never again. I am always on my guard now, every one of my thoughts and feelings carefully managed and accounted for, and I go nowhere unless I'm dressed for war.

Pushing open the kitchen door, I find Jamie sitting at the table, ashen-faced and nursing a cup of cold tea.

"Where are Mum and Dad?" I ask, brushing past him to freshen the kettle and set it back on the stove.

"I sent them to bed. They've been through more than enough this week." Jamie's words come out muffled and when I turn, he's got his head in his hands. That breaks me a little—I'm used to being bludgeoned by his honor, and came in ready to have it cast up to me that I left Evelyn behind.

I sit beside my brother, slide one arm through his, and rest my chin on his shoulder.

"Poor old man. Have you had a terrible time?"

He nods, but doesn't look up. "I went to St. Agatha's the morning after she disappeared. The school called Scotland Yard and they brought dogs out. The Yard traced her through the woods, found her sweater and shoes in a clearing, and the trail kept on after that for a bit. But it stopped at the—"

His voice cuts off and I pull away, pull into myself. I put my shoulders back, lengthen my neck, and set my mouth into an indomitable scarlet line. When I speak, I might be stating the time of day.

"It stopped at the river."

I can see the River Went in my mind's eye, rushing darkly along through the woods outside St. Agatha's, then over rapids and past the sheep fields outside Hardwick. My stomach turns over, but the kettle's on, so I suppose I'd better choke down some tea.

"They've been questioning everyone at St. Agatha's, and St. Joseph's, too. She was seeing a boy from St. Joe's, you know."

I glance sharply at Jamie. "Evelyn—our *sister* Evelyn—was seeing someone?"

Jamie looks up for the first time, and his face is anguished. "Don't, Philippa. Not when things are like this. I knew him and I asked him to look out for her when he could. They hit it off, and I thought—I thought it would make things better for her."

"Apparently not." The words rattle out before I can catch them, dry and wounding and not at all what I meant to say.

Jamie pushes his chair back and crosses the kitchen, standing in front of the sink and staring out the window that offers no view but a brick wall. "I couldn't handle her. I don't know how you did it all those years, but I couldn't. I tried—God knows I tried, but I think it was something I said that—"

I hate hearing Jamie lose his words because of Evelyn. I despise having to watch his hands tremble before he balls them into fists.

"Stop that. Stop it right now. Jamie Hapwell, turn around and look at me."

Jamie turns, reluctantly, and he slumps like he did in the Woodlands, when the weight of worlds rested heavy on our shoulders.

"I don't know what happened," I say. "None of us do, yet. Maybe we never will. Maybe we're going to have to live with this hanging over us. But whatever it is, it was Evelyn's choice, and it's a choice she'd been making since the moment we came home."

If only I believed my own words. As surely as I know my name, I know my sister would still be here if I hadn't left. Yet I can't bear the way Jamie is standing, like something's gone wrong on the inside. He's been the best of us for so long, the only one who managed to stay whole, and now he's finally broken. I'd tell a thousand lies and hide a lifetime of heartbreak to take away a little of his pain.

"They said there's compelling evidence," Jamie tells me. "But that without a—"

"—body—"

"—she'll have to be missing for seven years before they can declare her . . . well, anything other than just missing. Can we live in the in-between for seven years, Philippa?"

I get up and go to him. Ever since we were children, no one

has asked what we could live with. Not about the war that ripped Europe apart, not about the world that ripped Evelyn apart, not about this. I stand in front of Jamie and fix him with a battlefront look—the sort that won't give an inch, and won't allow anyone else to give, either.

"We've always been in the in-between, Jamie, and you and I live with whatever comes our way." He bows his head and when he looks at me again, I give him a smile bright as steel. "I'm here now, and I'm not leaving. We'll bear up under this together."

Something crosses his face, and it might be an answering smile or it might be the ghost of an expression he wore in the Great Wood. "You're a brick, Phil. I'm glad to have you back."

He squeezes my shoulder and leaves the kitchen. Once I'm sure he's gone, I drop into my chair.

Evelyn's empty seat across from me is a reproach.

Oh, Evelyn. Come home to us. Be alright. We've had our bedtime story with woods and magic, and now I want my happily ever after.

The kettle boils, singing shrilly from the range behind me. I make a cup of tea and I drink it, because I'm not sure what else to do.

Jamie goes out on some sort of Scotland Yard–related business. I offer to go with him, but he says not yet, not when I've only just arrived. I don't argue. I'm glad to be alone, and Mum and Dad show no sign of emerging from their room.

Drawing a bath, I sit on the edge of the tub and stare into the hot water, stirred by ripples from the dripping tap. I don't want to climb in. I don't want to let water touch me ever again, and that's why I'm doing this now, while an image of the River Went is still fresh in my mind. I learned a long time ago that the best way to overcome fear is to hold its source close.

So I sink into the bath, and the water folds around me like welcoming arms. It laps over my ears, making the sounds of the house softer and indistinct. I stay in as long as I can, trying to steady my nerves, but still scramble out, gasping, without washing my hair.

Then I get dressed, touch up my makeup, and leave, because if the bath was dreadful the silence of the house is worse. I take a bus to Trafalgar Square and hoist myself up between the paws of one of the great bronze lions guarding the base of Nelson's Column. The light is thick and syrupy, threaded through with traffic sounds, and flocks of pigeons take flight and land like anxious clouds. I pull my coat tight—having damp hair doesn't help with the cold.

The National Gallery's imposing portico rises before me. Columns soar up to the roof, higher and thicker than any tree that ever grew in the Woodlands. I remember what the Gallery was like during the war. We visited once in summer, when school was out and we were let home to London for a week as a rare treat. With its lunchtime concerts and temporary exhibitions, the Gallery was the one place where you could go to forget the bombs and the blackouts and the air raids. It was the one place where I could forget how lost Evelyn and I still were, struggling to sort out how to come home when no one knew we'd ever gone away.

I want to forget now, so I climb down from my perch and hurry up the steps. Inside, I take a guide from a bored girl at the front counter, who's as blond-haired and pink-lipped as a china doll.

"Only an hour till closing," she yawns. "Don't take your time."

It's been years since I was last at the Gallery, and some of the bomb-damaged rooms are still shut for repairs. I leaf through the guide until I find what I'm searching for, then move purposefully through the rooms, not allowing the pictures hanging on every wall to distract me from my goal.

I find her with the rest of the Rembrandts, in a room that's nearly deserted. There she is, linen hem pulled up to her thighs, about to move further into the river that already laps around her legs. Stepping up to her, I tilt my head to one side, looking for answers in her inscrutable face. Once upon a time, I thought I knew what she was thinking and feeling. She was a comfort and a guiding star, but now I mistrust that serene smile, those pale limbs exposed to the deceptively calm water.

I stand looking at her for so long, trying to divine the truth of her expression and her posture, that the room's only other visitor joins me.

My companion is an older woman, with steel-grey hair and paper-white skin that shows the veins beneath it. She has a stern air, and doesn't look at me but at the painting my attention is fixed on.

"What do you think of Rembrandt's *Woman Bathing in a Stream*?" the stranger asks.

I cross my arms. "Once I thought she was beautiful, and confident. I thought she was someone I wanted to be. But I don't trust her anymore. What if it's all just for show? Look at her face—she's smiling, but is she really happy? It's impossible to tell."

The woman next to me keeps her eyes fixed on the painting, but her thin mouth curves into a smile. "Do you know what makes a painting not just a picture, but a masterpiece?"

I could give a textbook answer, after years of studying art on my own time and a term of art history in America, but I have a feeling that's not what this woman is looking for. "Why don't you tell me?"

She steps forward and narrows her eyes, inspecting the bather critically. "It's that you don't just see what the artist painted. You look at his work, and you can't help but see a bit of yourself, as well. A bit of truth."

I'm not satisfied with that. "But I don't know what her truth is anymore."

The older woman turns her head to glance over one shoulder at me. "That's a truth in itself, realizing that there's more to others than meets the eye. At any rate, your bather's coming down for a cleaning this week. Perhaps in a month or two, once she's freshened up, she'll have more to tell you."

"Oh, please be careful with her," I blurt out before I can check myself.

The woman turns entirely, so we're facing each other for the first time. She fixes me with the same critical stare she'd given the Rembrandt. "If she unsettles you, why does it matter?"

I bite my lip and look past her, to the bather's lovely face. "Because all things should be treated with care, not just the ones I understand. I may not like her as much as I did when I thought her straightforward, but she still deserves respect. Things that mean something always do."

There's guilt in my stomach and sweat on my palms, and I can't meet this stranger's eyes. But to my surprise, the woman holds out a small card.

"I'm Presswick," she says. "I oversee the Gallery's Conservation Department, and happen to be looking for a general assistant. If you're at all interested, I think we could be of service to each other. Take my card and think it over."

"I'll need some time," I answer carefully, though the idea of spending days sorting myself out in my parents' house with all of Evelyn's empty spaces haunting me is a terrible one. "There are family matters I'm in the city attending to. How soon do you want an answer?"

Presswick smiles, her stern face softening just a little. "Take as long as you like, Miss—"

"Hapwell. Philippa Hapwell."

"Hapwell. No need to ring once you've made up your mind. Just show up in the morning, tell Kitty at the front desk that I've hired you on, and she'll take you to my office."

She walks away, and I'm struck by her confidence in me, both in offering the job and assuming I'll take it. I'm not exactly glad—my heart won't twist itself into that shape just now—but I am relieved to have something to fall back on if needed. This is, after all, my own peculiar magic—whatever circumstances I find myself in, I always land on my feet.

That thought leaves me guiltier than ever, with Evelyn's words ringing in my ears.

I want you to leave, Philippa. I need to stand on my own.

I should have known better than to listen.

37

THE SCHOOL BELL RINGS AND I HURRY AWAY FROM
Latin, hoping to catch Evelyn between classes.

I find her sitting alone on the staircase that leads to Lit, pressed up
against the wall and staring out of a window that looks toward the
nearby wood. I sit beside her and set my books down. The bell rings
again, and we ought to be in our classrooms by now, but I ignore it,
as does Ev.

"What are you thinking, darling?" I ask.

"About home." She rests her chin in her hands. "Look how the beech
leaves are starting to turn gold—they were already that color when we
left. Do you think it's snowing by now?"

"I don't know."

It's been a month since start of term, eight months since the Woodlands. It's still strange to be eleven and fourteen again, chafing under
the restrictions of school bells and lights-out and children's games. Evelyn has drawn into herself, grown still as a stone. I know that desire to
keep your troubles close, to hide your wounds until they've had a chance
to heal, and so as much as I can, I let her be. As for me, now we're back

in our own world, I've done the opposite—I feel I must keep busy or I'll founder. So I've turned this school into a project of mine, and enlisted the rest of the girls as willing troops. It's never quite enough, though.

I press a piece of paper into Evelyn's hand.

"I'm starting up a club—"

"What, another one?" she cuts in, and I roll my eyes. But I'm pleased she's even noticed my frantic activity.

"Yes. This one you'll like. I'd really love for you to join us, Ev. It would do you good."

Evelyn stares down at the hand-lettered flyer dubiously. "The St. Agatha's Aid Committee?"

"Yes. We're going to start out with sending books to soldiers in hospital. It won't be too taxing, I promise. Please, Evie?"

For the first time, Evelyn looks at me, and on the inside, I shrink away. There's no light in her eyes. It's like staring down a deep, dark well.

"Very well. If you want me to, I'll come."

"Thank you." I give her shoulders a squeeze. "I'm late for maths— I've got to get going. Don't you have somewhere you ought to be?"

Ev pulls away, and her voice goes hard. "Yes. I do."

I don't know what to say. The things I've done can't be changed, and we all made our choices on that beach. Since we got back I've lived in fear of this moment, when Evelyn finally turns on me for asking her to leave.

But she doesn't. She softens almost instantly, and offers me a smile like a gift. "Dear Philippa. What would I do without you to remind me?"

I smile back and hurry down the stairs without speaking. At the bottom, just out of view, I stop and cover my face with my hands, breathing until the prick of tears and swirl of nausea pass. I don't want to remind her. All I want is for my sister to forget.

When I've pulled myself together, I start off down the hall. There's no time to dwell, no time to wallow.

This world's war hasn't ended, and I have work to do.

38

AN UNFAMILIAR CAR SITS OUT FRONT OF THE HOUSE, IN A puddle of light that drips from the streetlamp. I step past it and push open the front door.

"Hello?" Shedding my coat and scarf, I peer into the empty sitting room. No Mum and Dad. No Jamie.

"Philippa." My brother's voice drifts from the kitchen. "We're back here."

There are two men seated at the table along with Jamie and Dad. Mum stands at the sink, mechanically washing a pair of teacups. My parents are quiet and colorless enough they might be ghosts. It's Jamie who's taken charge, who leans forward, speaking earnestly to the unfamiliar men, and little pieces of pain hide in the way he holds his mouth.

"These are Inspectors Dawes and Singh." Jamie gestures to the men, who look up and nod. The younger of them, Inspector Singh, smiles reassuringly. He has kind brown eyes and wears a neat mustache, black against his terra-cotta-brown skin. The older man, Dawes, a hard-bitten-looking fellow with a weathered and ruddy white face, stands and holds out a hand that I shake before taking a seat. I'm keenly conscious of which chair was left over, of whose place I'm sitting in, though the inspectors can't know.

But we know, all of us Hapwells, and there's a breathless moment, a charge in the air, as I lower myself onto it. Dawes leafs through his notebook, unaware of what I've had to do, of the little deaths I die.

"Miss Hapwell, I'd like to ask you a few questions about your sister, Evelyn."

I nod. "Of course. I've been away in America for some time, though, so I don't have much recent information."

Mum wordlessly sets a cup of tea down before me, her slippered feet silent on the flagstone floor.

"What was your relationship like with your sister?" Dawes taps his pencil against his chin.

"Complicated." I take a sip of tea, wanting the warmth to fortify me. It's hot and bitter, just the way I like it. Though the war's left us behind, it cured me permanently of my taste for sweet things. "We could both be difficult to live with, but I loved her, of course."

"And did she write to you, while you were away?"

"Yes."

"Did she mention anything in her letters? Anything that was bothering her, any worries about someone from the village, or a boy from St. Joseph's, perhaps?"

"I don't know." I look down into my teacup as I own up to this. "I never read the letters."

Inspector Singh cuts into the conversation for the first time, watching me thoughtfully. "Why is that, Miss Hapwell? Did you have a falling out?"

I sigh, and the steam rising from my tea twists and writhes. "Yes, before I left. I'm just—I couldn't bear to hear from her, not when I was so far away."

I'm sorry, Ev. I'm sorry. But we're all drowning and I'd held you up for so long. I couldn't take the weight anymore, not if I wanted to keep my own head above water.

Inspector Dawes stirs in his chair. "Mr. and Mrs. Hapwell," he says in a gruff voice, "if you could step out, I'd like a moment to question your daughter in private."

Mum and Dad vanish, leaving Jamie and me alone with the inspectors. As soon as Dad goes, I move to his chair, so Evelyn's spot is empty once more. Dawes frowns, but I offer no explanation.

"Miss Hapwell." Inspector Singh pauses after saying my name, seeming reluctant to put his next question to me. "Do you have any reason to believe your sister might harm herself?"

I keep quiet and fix my eyes on Evelyn's empty place.

"Did she ever do herself harm in the past?"

Jamie's stare is so intent I can feel it burning my skin. There are so many secrets between Evelyn and me that have never come to light, that ought to stay in the dark, but here we are dredging them up, and Evelyn, my love, where *are* you?

"Yes."

The word is small, just a little thing like a round marble that nevertheless sounds profoundly loud as it drops from my lips.

"Oh, Philippa," Jamie says.

Silence falls over us, heavy as a shroud.

With a scrape, Inspector Dawes pushes his chair back and gets to his feet. "I think that'll be all for now. If we've got any further questions, we'll be in touch. I'll trouble you for those letters, though, Miss Hapwell."

There's a flurry of activity as he and Inspector Singh prepare to leave and I trudge upstairs to dig Evelyn's letters out of the bottom of my valise, careful not to look at her familiar handwriting. I'd worry that they're full of memories of the Great Wood, were it not for the promise we made after coming back—never to write any of that story down, and never to speak of it, except to each other.

The inspectors take the letters and nod their goodbyes. Then Jamie and I are alone in the kitchen, with only cold mugs of tea scattered around the room to show the interview ever happened. I don't know where Mum and Dad have gone—their bedroom, or the sitting room.

"You never told me," Jamie says.

I stand and pace the kitchen floor, restless and wanting to be out of the house. No, what I really want is to be on horseback. I want Palace Beautiful's tall plow horse, Gensa, and the beach below the cliffs. Were I there now, I'd set my heels to his sides and gallop until the sand gave way to horizon.

Instead, I wrap my arms around my waist and stare out the kitchen window at the brick wall beyond. "I never would have told you, if this hadn't happened."

"Do you want to—talk about it?" Jamie's offer is hesitant. He's not sure he wants to make it, and not sure if I'll accept.

"No. Absolutely not. I need some fresh air."

I gather up my coat and plunge back into the lamplit London streets. My mind is made up. First thing on Monday I'll stop at the Gallery, and tell Presswick I want the job she offered. I need to be busy, or I'll fall to pieces.

And I refuse to end up like my sister.

The Gallery looms above me as I climb the front steps Monday morning, clutching a thermos of coffee. I'm always tired, but sleep is hard to come by, across the room from Evelyn's empty bed.

The doors have only just opened and I make my way to the front counter, where the same bored young woman I saw on Saturday is surreptitiously finishing a cup of tea.

"I'm looking for Presswick," I say. "She offered me a job, as general assistant."

The clerk's blank expression vanishes. She shifts forward, eyes sparking with interest. "*Presswick? Presswick hired you?* That's impossible—she'd have to like you to give you a job, and she doesn't like anyone. Are you *sure* it was Presswick? What did she look like?"

"Grey. Prickly as a Scotch thistle."

The clerk's mouth forms a little O. "That's Presswick, alright. What did you say to her?"

I lift one shoulder, by just an inch, an elegant gesture that implies *whatever Philippa wants, Philippa gets*, and that it isn't odd for jobs to fall into my lap. "We talked about art, that's all. Perhaps I make a good first impression."

Jamie would throw his head back and laugh if he heard me speak those words so guilelessly. I make exactly the sort of first impression I mean to, and have done for years. The truth is, though, with

Presswick I was honest. I was my unguarded self, as I so seldom am, and it's as much of a surprise to me as it is to the girl behind the counter that anything good came of that honesty.

"I should say you do." There's a look of admiration on the girl's face, and I can't help but smile.

"I'm Philippa Hapwell," I say, holding out a gloved hand. "You can call me Phil, if you like."

"Kitty Foster." The girl shakes my hand and calls to a guard crossing the far end of the room. "Albright! This is Philippa—*Presswick* hired her. Can you take her back to the old battle-ax's office for me? I can't leave the desk."

Albright's still in uniform, but carrying a bag and undoubtedly just coming off his shift.

"Oh, come on, Kitty," he says tiredly. "I'm headed home. Can't you have Billings do it?"

But he makes the mistake of glancing over at me. Poor Albright's a good fifteen years my senior, pasty from working indoors and going a little to seed, but I'm dressed for battle in a navy suit and matching pumps. I favor him with a slow and secret smile, and he's lost. Behold, the powers of lipstick and a good permanent.

Powder and pumps, indeed. You forget I was thrown over by nothing more than words once, Jamie, and now my life is a constant offensive of charm and smiles, lest it happen again.

"S'alright." Albright's gruff and awkward, trying to hide the white flag that might as well be waving over his head. "I could use the walk anyway. Come on, Miss—"

"Hapwell." I speak my name like a note of music and he stumps off, expecting me to follow. I do, pumps making a satisfying sound on the tile of the hall floor, but I take enough time to look over one shoulder at Kitty. She's watching, and I raise my eyebrows and quirk my mouth, as if Albright's sudden surrender is a private joke between us. She smiles and shakes her head, but anyone can see she's pleased.

We walk through what seems like miles of galleries—some open and lit and hung with pictures, others still bomb-damaged, half full of tarps and rubble. I fall suddenly and fiercely in love with this place, which presents a serene and beautiful front to the public, but hides rooms that have been gutted and are only now undergoing the long, slow process of being put back together.

Albright leaves me outside the shut door of an office after grunting something about Presswick. He hasn't surrendered with very good grace and I'll have to work on him. If everything goes well, we'll be seeing each other again.

I don't watch him go. Instead, I knock at the office door.

"Come in," Presswick's acerbic voice says from inside. I step in and shut the door behind me.

The woman I met while looking at Rembrandts sits behind a desk in an austerely furnished office. She's thin-faced, hair pulled severely back, and wears a tweed jacket and trousers. I take a seat and wait when she doesn't bother looking up from whatever it is she's writing on a thick sheet of paper.

Finally, she finishes and sets her pen aside. She leans back in her chair and takes a measure of me. "Well, what do you want, girl? Out with it."

I refuse to let myself be cowed. "You hired me the day before yesterday. I'm your new general assistant."

"Oh. Yes. I'd forgot about you. *Woman Bathing in a Stream.* Here—you can fair copy these letters for now."

I glance down at the stack of untidy pages she pushes toward me. "Have you got a typewriter?"

Presswick looks up abruptly. "Is there something wrong with your handwriting?"

"No," I assure her. "It's just that a typewriter would be much faster."

Presswick scoffs. "Nasty machines, all those buttons and noises, and the typeface is an affront to one's artistic sensibilities. Copying the letters out neatly by hand will be fine, thank you."

"What exactly does this job entail?" I ask before she can turn back to her work.

"I have no idea." Presswick waves a dismissive hand in the air. "But Director Hendy's been telling me I need an assistant since the war ended—ever since the Conservation Department first came into being—and all the candidates he's sent for me to interview were absolutely unsuitable."

I watch her closely, trying to sort out what it was about our conversation that convinced this odd woman to hire me. "What makes me suitable when they weren't?"

Presswick peers at me over her reading glasses. "I suspect you're a careful person—not the sort who rushes into decisions or does things heedlessly. That's the impression I got on Saturday, at any rate. If it turns out I'm wrong, which I seldom am, I'll just sack you."

"That seems fair enough," I say, and begin copying the first of Presswick's letters. It's not long before I'm lost in a new sort of politics, learning the intricacies of the Gallery's world as I write.

My head is still full of solvents and inpainting and Old Masters when I arrive home and find Jamie's bags sitting by the door.

39 ⌒

*I HAD HOPED, VAINLY, THAT IT WAS THE WAR GIVING
Evelyn such a hard time, and that once it ended things would be better.
But now, standing all together in the National Gallery a month after V-E
Day and a year and a half after the Woodlands, I realize I was wrong.*

*The Gallery is mobbed. Everyone wants a glimpse of the Old Mas-
ters, brought back from their wartime sojourn in a Welsh cave. I turn
away from the front counter and see Ev standing alone, in a bubble of
solitude she seems to take with her wherever she goes. Mum and Dad
are a few feet away, talking in low tones and occasionally glancing at
Ev. They're talking about her, of course, and when I bring our tickets
over, Mum pulls me aside.*

*"Philippa, what went on at school this year? Your sister doesn't seem
herself."*

*I bite my lip and swallow. If I had a sixpence for every time I've
been asked what happened to Evelyn—first it was Max. Then several more teachers, and finally the Curmudgeon herself. After that it
was our school nurse, and a doctor from Hardwick who never could
find anything wrong.*

And here's Mum asking me the same question I can never answer. But really, what would we say if we wanted to speak up? No one would believe our story. They already whisper things about Evelyn, about her health. If Jamie and I were to come forward with tales of a mysterious country where we spent years as only a moment passed by in a bomb shelter, the same shadows of madness folk cast upon Ev would fall on us, too.

"I expect it's just difficult for her to be back in London." I pat Mum on the shoulder. "It's not you or Dad, of course, it's just with all the rubble the city's not a very cheerful place."

I slip away and take Ev by the arm, steering her through the Gallery until we find what I'm looking for. Evelyn's docile and uninterested beside me until we step up to the painting.

It's a Rembrandt. I've seen it in art books before, but never in person. The simple background, the single female figure stepping further into the stream—it's an elegant image, understated and intimate. There's a confidence to the woman in the painting, and she immediately gives an impression that she knows more than she'll ever say.

Beside me, Ev leans forward and her lips part.

"Look at her," she whispers, and I can barely hear her over the murmur of the holiday crowds. "She's so still, on the inside. She knows exactly who she is, and where she belongs."

We stay and look at the bather for as long as we can before carrying on. When we walk away, I see an unguarded smile on Evelyn's face.

Though it's midsummer, I've been frozen inside. But I can feel myself thaw in the afterglow of that smile. Things will get better now. They will. They must.

40

I STAND IN THE FRONT HALL WITH MY HANDS IN MY sweater pockets and try not to feel lost because my brother's leaving.

"I've got to get back to school," Jamie says, an apology in his tone. "If you need anything, Philippa, just ring. Or come up on a weekend. Oxford's not far. And I don't think you'll be bothered much by the Yard, so you needn't worry on that count."

"Don't fuss." I smile, though I'm wretched over Jamie going. "I've already got a job, actually, and Mum and Dad . . ."

My voice trails off. The truth is, Jamie and I haven't been very good children, so wrapped up in our worries about the Woodlands and Ev and each other, so intent on never letting our shared secret slip, that we didn't realize until it was too late how our complete autonomy cut our parents out. We lead parallel lives now, and I'm not sure how to bridge the gap between us. I'm not even sure anyone wants that. The thread that binds us together is Evelyn's absence, and it's a foundation that I, for one, have no interest in building on.

I hug Jamie tightly. He's the only one left now who knows the things I know, the only one who understands the real reason for Evelyn's disappearance. When he walks out the door, I have to lean against the wall for support. If anything were to happen to my brother, too, I'm not sure I could go on.

Mum smiles when I step into the kitchen, but it's a halfhearted expression that fails to touch her eyes. She hands me a cup of tea and we sit in silence. When I can't take the unspoken things between us any longer, I push my chair back and mumble an excuse. I wish I was braver, not just in this moment, but in all my moments. I wish I could go back and undo the things I've done.

Alone in our—my—upstairs bedroom, I get into my pajamas in the dark and lay staring at Evelyn's empty bed. Light from the streetlamp cuts through the gap in the curtains and divides the bed neatly in half, two swaths of darkness shot through by a single bright patch.

I hope there's truth in the picture I'm looking at. I hope that even if Jamie and I are left wandering in the dark, that somewhere, Evelyn's found happiness and light.

After a long time, I get up and cross the room. Gingerly, I lie down on my side in the space my sister's left behind and hug her pillow to me, breathing in the last faint trace of her scent. I stay and ache and wait until I'm incandescent with longing for a perfect world the like of which I've never known.

Where have you gone, Ev?

What have you done?

Kitty's behind the ticket counter on my second day, looking peaked, but she perks up a bit as I walk in.

"Well, hello again. And how was your first day in the Conversation Department?"

I wrinkle my nose. "Conversation Department?"

"Mm." Kitty pulls out her hidden mug and sneaks a mouthful of tea. "All the rest of us call it that on account of how much endless talking goes on down there. They must generate a thousand pages of paperwork for every painting they actually clean. And the *meetings*, my goodness! Of course, they're all running scared after what happened to Director Clark."

I frown. "Sorry, I ought to know, but I've been a bit preoccupied the last few years."

Kitty leans closer with a surreptitious look and lowers her voice. "There was *such* a scandal, Philippa. You know they hauled all the paintings off during the war? Stuck them in some cave in Wales, but while they were there, the keepers cleaned a good lot of them. You can't blame them for that, what else is there to do in Wales? But when they were brought back, some people thought they'd been damaged by the restoration work—that the folks in Wales had got a bit carried away. There was a committee investigation and everything, and Director Clark was quietly packed off to Oxford. That's how Director Hendy came to be here, and *that's* why the Conversation Department was started."

"Gracious," I say mildly, but it's all coming together now—why Presswick wants a careful assistant, and why there's so much bloody paperwork to be done.

"Presswick rules the Conversation Department with an iron fist," Kitty goes on. "If you're cozy with her, put in a good word for me. She's got the director's ear, and I want out from behind this desk. I'm *dying* to help with acquisitions."

"It might take some time," I say. "And I can't make any promises. But if I ever get a chance to mention you, I will."

Kitty blows a kiss. "You're a love. I'm going out dancing with some girls Friday night. Care to join us?"

I should say yes, and I would have done before Evelyn's disappearance. I'd have set myself the task of adding London to my list of conquests and managed it by September.

But I'm not who I was. I haven't got the heart for games of wills and words. I just want to be here, to fit in as a little cog in the complex workings of the Gallery. For once, someone else can be the key that turns the gears.

"I'll let you know," I tell Kitty. "You're sweet to offer."

41

THINGS DO GET BETTER SOMETIMES, USUALLY IN
the spring. By our third spring away from the Woodlands, I realize this
is how it will be—worse in winter, better at its end. The days lengthen,
the world goes green, and my sister comes out of her shell. Every moment
she can, she spends lingering in the back field or wandering the woods
outside St. Agatha's. When she's able to be in the forest, she comes back
brighter, more present, almost as she was before. I talk with Max about
her, and we come to an agreement. Max will leave a key out for Evelyn,
if I'll watch over her when she's off school grounds.

So, though I've come back to this world, I finally learn to walk the
Woodlands way. I learn to be silent in the forest, so that Evelyn will
not know I follow along as faithfully as her shadow. When she walks,
I walk. When she sits, I sit. When she speaks whispered and wistful
remembrances to the trees, I am the one who hears them.

One night, I trail along behind Evelyn to her favorite haunt—a
birch ring at the heart of the forest. A sickle moon hangs above us, and
the air is soft and sweet. I hang back as Evelyn steps forward, into a
pool of moonlight and bluebells. Slowly, with a smile on her silver-lit

face, she unbraids her hair and shakes out the golden length of it.

She's bewitching in the woodland night, a creature from another world. When she turns her face to the sky and begins to sing, even the sleeping trees of the English countryside bend closer to listen.

She sings a song we learned once upon a time in a palace by the sea. The birches sway and tremble, as if Evelyn's clear, high voice pierces them to the quick. It pierces me, and I stand adrift, lost on a spit of grey sand beneath a grey sky, along the shores of a grey sea.

42

SCOTLAND YARD REQUESTS MY PRESENCE, DESPITE
Jamie's assurance to the contrary. Accordingly, I squeeze into a little
office early one morning with Inspectors Singh and Dawes, trying
not to cough in the overpowering haze of cigarette smoke. Part of
me wants to be cowed by them—they seem much larger in the tiny
windowless cubicle than they did in my parents' kitchen. Instead I
sit straight-backed and calm, hands folded in my lap, acting like I
don't know what questions are coming and like my stomach's not
ruined by nerves.

"Miss Hapwell," Dawes says briskly. "I know you were reluctant
to speak about it in front of family, but I need to ask you more
about your sister's history. You gave the impression that she was a
troubled girl."

Oh, Evelyn.

"Are there any untroubled girls?" I ask without flinching. "But
yes. Ev had a hard time dealing with things that came up in life.
Sometimes she couldn't cope."

Dawes taps his fingers on the arm of his chair. "And what did that look like? Not coping?"

I don't want to think about it. I don't want to remember Evelyn's darker times. "Sometimes she shut down. Stayed in bed. Didn't eat, didn't speak. Other times she went out at night—wandered until daybreak."

Inspector Singh cuts in. "You mentioned she'd harmed herself before?"

I don't like that *before*, which implies that we know what's happened to Ev, that this investigation is merely a formality.

"Yes. She cut herself, once. Had to have stitches put in. But there were other, smaller things. Leaving her coat off on the coldest days of the year. Going barefoot through a patch of briars. I'm not even sure I noticed everything."

Inspector Dawes sits back in his chair and regards me for a moment. "Would you say you're the person who knew your sister best?"

I think of the connections between Ev and me, the unseen years of shared history and upheaval. We're bound together through time and across worlds, and nothing will change that. "Yes, I would."

"But you left the country, even though you were aware she was unstable?"

I'm not sure if this is a question or a reproach, and Inspector Singh's eyes flash to Dawes.

"Why is that, Miss Hapwell?" Dawes presses when I don't answer.

"Excuse me for a moment," I say. I make it past the typing pool and the front desk and into the bathroom, where I'm quietly and efficiently sick into the toilet. Goodness knows I've had practice, after all the weeks and months in which my nerves were frayed to a ragged edge, not knowing if Ev would still be down the hallway or across the room from me each morning. When the shaking stops, I sit on the floor, not caring a bit about the state of my clothes, and let the wall take my weight.

I couldn't stay. I couldn't hold up anymore, couldn't watch Ev fall to pieces again, wondering if this would be it, if this time there'd be no putting her back together. Trying to keep us both whole was tearing me apart, and the bitter words that passed between us were just the excuse I needed to finally leave.

But I'm not sure I can live with this, either. With not knowing what's happened to my sister. With the constant, draining guilt brought about by always wondering *what if*.

What if I'd stayed.

The answer's simple. Evelyn would still be here. I talked her back from the edge often enough to know that this is true.

Whatever's happened, I might have worked a dark magic and banished her myself. These are my unforgivable sins—that I brought Evelyn home from the Woodlands and left her, and in my absence, she couldn't cope.

I get up off the bathroom floor, rinse my mouth at the sink, tuck a peppermint under my tongue, and carefully reapply a layer of lipstick.

"Sorry," I tell Dawes, settling back into the chair across from his. "Where were we?"

"Your reasons for leaving."

"I had a scholarship," I say, and I know my face is serene and unreadable. "A very good one. You can check the college records. I'd given up years of my time watching over Evelyn—I wasn't about to give this up, too."

It's true I had a scholarship. I've got a decent enough brain. But I'd been offered one by Christ Church at Oxford as well, and that would have meant being minutes away from Jamie and only a short train ride from Ev.

The thought of the train ride, the phone calls I'd get, the dozens of panicked trips I'd have to take, is what made me cross an ocean in search of freedom.

Now here I sit, chained more tightly by guilt than I ever was by obligation.

"That'll be all for now," Inspector Dawes says. "We may have more questions down the road, though, and ask for your cooperation."

"Have I not been cooperative already?" I lean forward in my chair, but it's not the Philippa Hapwell I've become who leans—the one weighed down by her failures. It's the Philippa who's walked between worlds, and seen more than anyone can possibly know. When she leans, the motion is wide with meaning. "I would give anything—*anything*—to see my sister step through that door behind us, whole and well. I hope that, at least, is abundantly clear."

"We'd never doubt it," Inspector Singh reassures me. I gather up my handbag and gloves and hurry out before they can see how my hands shake, or divine that my stomach still roils inside me.

43 ~

IT'S OCTOBER. I'M SEVENTEEN, AND ABOUT TO HAVE
the worst night of my life. Evelyn is fourteen, and it's been more than
three years since the Woodlands, since Cervus told us we'd never be
called back.

I wake at one in the morning to a knock on my door. Not a gentle
knock, mind you, a frantic pounding and a voice calling for me in a
piercing whisper.

"Philippa! Philippa, it's Georgie. Wake up."

I roll out of bed, pull on a dressing gown, and am out the door
before my roommate, Millie, can ask what the matter is. Georgie stands
in the shadowy hallway, wringing her hands.

"Ev got up in the night and you know she hasn't been herself lately.
I thought she might be ill, so when she didn't come back I went to check
on her, but she won't let me into the bathroom and I think there's
something wrong."

Inside, my blood freezes and my stomach fills with frightened
wings. "Georgie, it'll be alright. I'm sure she's just had a stomach
upset or something of the sort. You're so kind, looking out for her, but

I'll take care of it now."

Despite the way my pulse is racing, the words come out measured and reasonable. Slowly, the panicked light leaves Georgie's eyes. She nods and returns to the bedroom she and Ev share, shutting the door behind her. Only then do I turn and fly down the hall to the bathroom at the end.

"Evelyn." Her name comes out soft as a moth's wing. "Evelyn, are you alright?"

I reach for the doorknob and find it locked. Pulling a hairpin from my dressing gown pocket, I fiddle with the lock, poking at its inner workings in the half-light and hardly breathing until I hear a telltale click. By then, my hands shake so badly the doorknob rattles as I push into the bathroom and shut the door behind me.

White moonlight pours through the single window, washing over Evelyn and silvering the blood on her hands, her legs, her underclothes, the nightgown hitched up around her waist. Beside her, abandoned on the tile floor, metal gleams wickedly.

"Evie." I take her face in my hands and she stares at me with blank eyes. "Evie, darling, where's the blood coming from? Evie, what did you do?"

"I don't know who I am anymore, Philippa." Evelyn's voice is thin as a thread, hardly loud enough for me to hear. "I don't look the way I'm supposed to. I don't feel the way I should. I had a scar—"

Evelyn's hand goes to her side, to the place where she'd caught herself on a long nail in the cowshed outside Palace Beautiful, years and worlds ago. I see it then, beneath her blood-slick fingers—a ragged gash that stretches from the curve of her waist to her navel, the twin of the wound she bore in the Woodlands.

I pull her hand away because fresh blood still seeps from the cut. Then I drape my dressing gown around her and pull her close.

"Evelyn," I whisper, hating myself even as I speak. "We've got to get into the castle so I can patch you up. It's just across the courtyard. Can you walk?"

Her eyes shine. "If you help me, Philippa."

We flit through the dark, down the stairs and to the main floor of the dormitory, where I find the nurse's stuffy office blessedly unlocked. I haven't the patience for hairpins again.

Inside, I switch on the electric light and blink in the sudden glare. Evelyn lays herself obediently down on the bare mattress that serves the nurse for an examining table. I rummage through drawers and cupboards, acutely aware that each moment means more of my sister's blood lost. Though I don't think she's hurt herself seriously, an endless litany runs through my head—I hate I hate I hate this, I just want the night to end.

Finally I come up with catgut and a needle.

"Ev," I mumble as I bite off the thread. "I'm going to stitch you up. It'll hurt, just like it did at home. But I'm here, same as I was then."

"Of course you are." Ev's face is beatific. "And when we go back, we'll be together, too."

Dampening a cloth, I sponge the blood from Evelyn's wound. Nothing can be done about her nightgown and underthings—they'll have to be hidden and then burned, some night when I'm able to get away unnoticed. Threading the needle, I take a shallow breath and fight against the heat that spreads across the back of my neck. I can't be sick, not now, there isn't time.

Ev winces at the first prick of the needle, her smile strained but still firmly in place. Twenty-four stitches I put in, hands rock-steady and fighting nausea all the while, but my sister should heal cleanly, and have only a fine scar.

I've lost count of the number of people I've sewn back together, on the battlefield or in the infirmary at Palace Beautiful. This is by far the most dreadful the work has ever been.

When I've finished, I bandage the injury. I make Ev swear not to show it to anyone, to hide it as best she can. I'm not sure how much of what I say gets through to her, but I have to try. If anyone were to find out—well. I'd die before I let my sister be sent to one of the places they claim are hospitals for girls with troubles like hers.

I tuck Evelyn back into bed, wearing my nightgown. Hers still waits in the nurse's office, and under my dressing gown I'm naked as the day I was born. But I haven't time to fetch new nightclothes.

I hurry back downstairs and scrub every trace of Ev's blood from the nurse's office. I flip the mattress so the rust-red patch she left on it won't show. I bundle the cloths I used to wash her in the nightgown, and steal fresh ones for the bathroom upstairs.

By the time I've cleaned the tiles and hidden the evidence of Evelyn's lapse, the moon has set and birds sing sleepily in the trees. Morning is well on its way, and there's no point taking out fresh nightclothes. I pull on my school things and fall wearily into bed for a few moments' sleep.

I see Ev at breakfast, where she sits talking and laughing with a few girls from her year. There's a spark in her eyes that hasn't been there for months, and I wish I was glad to see it.

Instead, I'm raw and heart-sore, but one of my own friends slides into the empty space beside me. "Long night, Philippa? Out with a St. Joseph's boy, or was it a townie this time?"

I flash her a smile so bright it dazzles, a trick of the light that's never failed to hide any darkness in me. "You know I never kiss and tell."

Evelyn leaves the refectory, light-footed and alone, walking with a Woodlander's silent steps.

44

I DRINK COFFEE, BLACK, ALL MORNING, TRYING TO forget the interview with Scotland Yard and to lose myself in the fair copying Presswick has set out. The coffee eats at my empty stomach and I don't even realize the rapid-fire tapping sound in the room is my own foot until Presswick snaps at me.

"Hapwell! What's gotten into you today, girl? Take these files to the restoration room and go the long way—walk off some of those nerves."

I gather up the files and bolt. There are stairs up to the restoration room not far from Presswick's office, but I don't take them. Instead I wander aimlessly past and through the rooms of the Ground Floor—the Scientific Department, where X-rays and photographs are made of pictures prior to cleaning, and the Reference Section, where paintings are kept in limbo, awaiting restoration or rehanging. Some of them have been waiting for years, ever since the war.

At the Ground Floor's far end, I duck through one of the open rooms and up the stairs to the Main Floor. Kitty's at the front counter, as always, hiding a mug of tea, as always, and I wave, but don't go over. I haven't the patience for a conversation just now. I'm buzzing with anxiety, guilt, regret, exhaustion—an entire toxic cocktail of emotions, shaken and stirred with an unconscionable amount of caffeine.

Not even the quiet of the Main Floor can calm me—the beautiful damask-hung walls, the hum of low voices, the meditative pace at which the visitors walk. And I refuse to glance up at the paintings on the walls. Whatever their truths are, I don't want to know them. The only truth I'm interested in now is what's happened to my sister, and for all their secrets and symbols, the Old Masters can't tell me that.

I've taken a terribly roundabout way through the Gallery, and at the end of my walk I've got five rooms of construction to pick my way through. The Ministry of Works laborers are on the job, sanding and plastering and doing goodness knows what else. It's dusty and messy and loud, not at all like the carefully planned exhibitions in the open wings.

Finally, I come to the restoration room. Presswick's walked me past it, but I haven't yet been inside. I step across the threshold and freeze.

Inside, the restoration room is a long, cavernous space with a glass-paned ceiling that lets in a flood of daylight. The floor is a jumble of easels and tables and stands, but the walls to my right and left are empty, drawing my attention forward to where three paintings hang in a row on the far wall.

Each one is a reproach in oil and brushstrokes.

The first is simple, a green landscape on a day of fitful rain, bathed with grey storm light that cuts through a rent in the clouds. A river runs through the fields, and a stand of trees masks the distant highlands. It must be from those trees that the stag has leapt, for he occupies the foreground, frozen in midstride. The whites of his eyes show and he's caught forever, twisting toward the frothing hound that's launched itself at his throat.

The second painting is more complicated, a lush Grecian landscape with purple vistas and a crumbling, columned ruin. Men armed with bows and trailed by dogs stand alongside a river, and a stag on the opposite bank regards them mildly, seeming not to care about the tight-strung bow trained upon him, the arrow nocked to the string, its shaft gleaming with promises of death.

The last picture is a confusion of figures, done mostly in sepia, as if all the color has bled out of the world. Men and dogs riot across the panel, and the chaos and clamor break over an unlikely pair in the foreground like waves on sand. A woman crouches before an arrow-pierced stag. She cradles the great creature's head in her arms, and they regard each other, faces bare inches apart. Caught in the center of that frantic scene, they're an island of calm, neither of their expressions strained or grieved. Instead, they're wistful, weighted by memory, bound together in a moment of recognition and resignation that seems as if it will never end.

In the span of a heartbeat I take this all in, and swallow against the sourness in the back of my throat.

"You can't be serious," I mutter. The words come out bitter, and it's only then I notice I'm not alone. I'd thought the room was empty when I first walked in.

A young man straightens from where he's been bent over a table, the painting spread on it depicting a stag standing proud in a land-scape of mist and heather. I catch a glimpse of his profile before he turns to me—brown hair, brown eyes, regular features, his white complexion a bit pale from too much time spent indoors. He's an ordinary sort of handsome, pleasant and serious-looking.

But then he turns and I read his whole history in an instant, in the burns that pucker one side of his face and pull his mouth into an odd shape, that thin his hair and mottle the skin of his left hand—a hand from which three fingers are missing. I read it in the way he favors his injured side, the pained hitch in his step, and the mismatch of his shoes that means it's not just fingers he's lost, but a limb.

There are boys like this all over England. There were Wood-landers like this, too, following the war. Their sacrifice never sat easy with me then and it still doesn't now.

The young man before me is flushed and miserable though he's gallantly trying to get past it. One side of his mouth pulls up into a rueful smile but his eyes skitter away from mine and embarrass-ment creeps hot from under his collar.

"They should have warned you. I know it's a bit of a wrench."

My stomach drops out from inside me and I can feel the heat of tears I've held back since that disastrous interview at Scotland Yard.

"No, please," I beg. "That's not at all what I meant. I've had a ghastly morning, and look at the paintings—they're all stags, and that means something to me, something I can't get away from. I'm sorry. I'm so sorry, I didn't know, and I couldn't even see."

I don't know how to make things right, and I can't bear the idea of causing pain, not when I've spent a lifetime at war, not when all my worlds have been filled with young people that time and circumstances tore to pieces.

I can't take back what I've said, and can't think of new words to mend the damage I've done. There is grief caught inside me, disastrously close to the surface, and I won't burden this young man with my tears—won't let them spill out like small knives to force his sympathy. I hurry out of the restoration studio and manage to keep myself whole until I find one blessedly empty room. It's strewn with tarps I have to step around and I stumble twice, finally giving up in defeat and sitting down on a pile of rubble to cry.

Fitting, that I should end up here, when all my words bring such ruin. Words that, in the end, were not quite enough to keep the Woodlands from war. Words that led me to strike a bargain with a tyrant. Words I spoke to Evelyn on the beach, the day we came home. Words said in anger, before I left. And now this. I've become the girl from the old story. No matter what I say, no matter the intent, it's toads and snakes that drop from my lips.

If I could only speak roses and gemstones instead, I'd happily cut my tongue on their thorns and edges.

Uneven footsteps echo in the room beyond. I hide my face in my hands because I can't bear to be seen.

"Look, I believe you," a kind voice says after a time. "And I'm sorry, too. I'm used to thinking the worst of people. It's easier than being let down."

When I look up, the young man from the restoration room crouches before me. He stands, a little unsteadily, then finds his balance and holds out a hand. I take it and allow myself to be pulled to my feet.

There's a brief moment where we might let go. But I don't, because I'm desperate to hold on to someone, and I'm hungry for the sympathy in this stranger's brown eyes. He doesn't let go either, for reasons of his own. Instead we stand, close as lovers, with my hand held fast in his.

He looks at me with an expression I can't quite parse the meaning of, and I place the files Presswick gave me into his free hand. The embarrassment's left his face and heats my own now, because this is not how I behave. For two lifetimes I've been cool and aloof, untouchable on a pedestal of my own making, but Ev's absence has toppled me, has turned me into a muddled girl who weeps in back rooms because everything's suddenly become too much.

"Hapwell!" Presswick's voice rings out over the construction noises in the next room. "Where have you got to? I said take a walk, not climb a mountain."

"Thank you for believing me," I whisper, and press a kiss to the young man's scarred cheek. "I have to go."

Presswick says nothing about my flushed and tearstained face, just shakes her head and mutters something about young people as she shepherds me back downstairs.

When I lie down at night, across from Evelyn's empty bed, my insides are still tied up in knots. Sleep is a long time coming, but when it does, I dream a perfect dream. It's as though somewhere, beyond the borders of this world, Cervus is trying to apologize for all the dreadful things I've had to remember.

In it, I find myself in my favorite Woodlands haunt. Returned to a place I can never reach while waking, I sit on the trunk of a half-fallen tree that overhangs a sleepy river. The water is clear as glass, reflecting the sky. Turtles sun themselves on the bank, and the only noise is an occasional buzz of flies or the ripple of a fish as it breaks the surface. It might be any lazy summer afternoon on which I decided to escape my duties and hide out for an hour or so, except for one thing.

In this dream, I'm light as a feather. Completely free.

There's no awareness of things I ought to be doing. No memory of how close I came to playing the Woodlands false. No nagging reminders that I'm worlds away from home.

No worry about my brother and sister. No wondering how the time is passing in England, and if my parents still cry for us at night. We have always, *always*, since the moment Cervus called us, been torn in two. In this dream, there's not even a scar where the wound has healed. It's simply never been.

I am whole. I am well. And the awareness that the people I love are whole and well too fills me like light.

I sit and sing and dip my toes in the river, until finally I wake at dawn with that dream clinging to me like shreds of hope, and what is it Evelyn used to say about hope? *She would sing while I was weeping; If I listened, she would cease.*

Perched on the edge of my bed, I pretend that this hope will last once I walk through the door rather than burst like a soap bubble. I stare down at the rug and try to hold on to that brief moment of freedom, but it's already slipping away. I'm already forgetting how it felt.

When I've put on my lipstick and powder, combed my hair and slipped into a pair of pumps, I brave the kitchen. Mum's seated at the table. I pull strength from the memory of my light-filled dream, enough to sit down across from her and smile as she pours me a cup of tea.

"How are you, Mum?" I ask, and though the question terrifies me, the words ring true.

To my surprise, she reaches out a hand and squeezes mine. "Philippa, your father and I will be fine, do you know that? You don't need to hold us all up on those competent shoulders of yours."

I take a swallow of too-hot tea that burns as it goes down, I'm so shocked by her answer.

"If we haven't been very present lately, it's because we don't want to burden you," Mum goes on. "You take on weight you were never meant to carry. No one expected you to stay with Evelyn forever. Not even Ev. It was only a matter of time before she had to try coping on her own."

I can't breathe. I've tried to hide the guilt that dogs my steps. No one, let alone Mum, was supposed to see it. I'll have to do better.

Mum reaches across the table and sets something beside my cup. It's a little box, covered in Christmas wrapping paper, and the note stuck to it bears my name in a familiar, looping scrawl.

"I wasn't sure if I should give this to you or not," Mum says. "I found it in your bedroom, before the Yard went through every-thing. It just felt private, so I hid it away, and here it is. Whatever we might want or not want now, *she* wanted you to have it, so go on. Open it."

My hands sit in my lap like dead things.

"Will you do it for me?" I whisper.

Mum takes the gift back and unwraps it carefully, folding the foil paper and setting it aside. The box beneath is plain, with a gilt emblem on top I don't recognize. Mum pushes back the lid and a small sigh escapes her. "Now isn't that lovely?"

She lifts out a thin silver chain from which a pendant dangles, cleverly worked into the shape of a leaping stag. Once I've seen what it is, I can't bring myself to look straight at it again. Coming around the table, Mum clasps the chain around my neck, handling it as reverently as if it's a relic. The pendant rests against my skin, cool and unfamiliar. Only three people in this world know the depth of meaning behind such a gift, and how heavily it will hang upon me.

I've been a fool to think anyone else could uncover the truth of what's happened to Evelyn. Scotland Yard might as well be bumbling about in the dark. As always, the care and keeping of my broken sister falls to me.

It's time to go looking for Ev. And I listen for the hope I felt on first waking, but I can no longer hear it sing.

45

"I NEED TO TAKE A HALF DAY ON FRIDAY," I TELL Presswick. I've spent nearly a fortnight working up the nerve to ask her. The pendant from Ev lies hidden beneath my blouse, next to my heart. "I'm sorry to ask when you've only just hired me, but I've got family matters that need seeing to."

Presswick sets her pen down and gives me a shrewd look. "Family matters?"

"*Private* family matters."

But she reaches into her desk drawer and pulls out a newspaper. My stomach clenches, already sour with black coffee and not much else.

Search for Missing Girl Continues, the headline reads, and one of Ev's school pictures stares out at me, serious and solemn-eyed, her golden hair haloed with the light of another world.

"Your sister," Presswick says simply. I set my bag down and sit before my legs give way.

"How long have you known?"

Presswick shrugs. "I guessed, when you first told me your name.

You had that look about you, of a person who's living with unanswered questions."

I narrow my eyes at the older woman across from me, plain and severe in her tweed suit. "And how do you know that look?"

Presswick returns the newspaper to its drawer and removes a framed photograph from the same place. She hands it to me and I look down at the face of a young man in uniform.

"His name was Arthur Merritt," Presswick says, and the edge to her voice melts away. "We were engaged, before the Great War, when I was just a girl. He flew fighter planes until he was shot down over France. They found the wreckage, but never a body."

Carefully, Presswick takes the picture back and hides it away again. She picks up her pen and speaks over the sound of it scratching away on paper.

"Take the time you need, Hapwell, and find whatever answers you can. I will, of course, expect you to catch up on Monday."

Bowing my head over my own work, I let out a slow breath.

I'll find you, Evelyn. I'm coming for you. I'll make right the wrong I've done.

Presswick's gone out on lunch break when a faint knock sounds at the door.

"Come in," I call without looking up. The door groans a little on its hinges and there's the squeak of wheels as someone pushes a cart inside. I ignore the sounds of movement, the whisper of a panel sliding into place against the wall.

But then there's a polite cough, so I push the papers in front of me aside and glance at the doorway.

It's not the doorway I notice, though, or the person standing in it. I'm riveted by the painted panel on the wall. It's blue-green, the color of the sea below Palace Beautiful, the color of grief, the color of my heart. The background is stark in its simplicity, the female figures deceptive in their primitive rendering. Dressed in folds of plain blue cloth, they stand, heads bowed together, taking comfort from each other's presence. I feel, for the second time in as many days, as if something's being said to me in a language without words, and a chill runs down my spine.

"Oh, come *on*," I mutter. "The stags were bad enough, but what's that doing here? It's supposed to be in Leningrad."

"Do you know," the figure in the doorway says, a hint of amusement in his voice, "I've never met anyone who reacts to things quite the same way you do."

My hands fly involuntarily to my face, cool against my burning cheeks, because of course it's him—the young man from the restoration room, with whom I made such a fool of myself.

"I'm Jack Summerfield." He moves forward, a hitch in his step, leaning a little on an unornamented cane and holding out his free hand. "I don't think before counted as an introduction, so here we are. Charmed, and all that."

"Philippa Hapwell." I shake his offered hand, careful not to hold on for too long. "Look, I'm so sorry about—well, everything. Do you think we could start over? If you'd rather not, I understand and I can try to keep out of your way—"

"We are starting over. That's why I came down in the first place." He smiles, one side of his mouth tilting up, humor in his dark eyes.

I look away, a little horrified at the spectacle I keep making of myself. Pull yourself together, Philippa, you've handled foreign kings and declarations of war with better grace than this.

Jack ignores my lack of composure and turns instead so that he's standing next to me and we both face the painting on the wall.

"What is it you have against Picasso?" he asks.

I shake my head and stare at the pair of sad figures. "It's not Picasso, just this picture."

"*The Two Sisters*?"

"Exactly."

"Should I inquire further?"

"I'd prefer you didn't. But you could tell me why it's here in the first place."

Jack smiles again. "I'm good at my job, I have a friend at the Hermitage, and they've got no conservation department to speak of. It's not a very exciting story."

Absently, I slip the silver pendant out of my blouse and rub the little stag figure between two fingers, as if it can bring me luck. "You must be more than good at your job to have someone send a picture all the way from Leningrad."

"It's not that." Jack shakes his head. "I'm just—"

"Wait," I cut in. "Did Presswick hire you?"

"Yes, a little over two years ago."

"Then let me guess," I say. "You're careful?"

Jack's smile turns to a grin. "Exactly. I'd assume that's why she hired you as well?"

"Yes. She seems to value that particular trait quite highly."

Stepping forward, Jack straightens *The Two Sisters*, a tiny adjustment I hadn't even noticed was needed. "No one who doesn't have the patience of a saint would last long in this department—all the work is slow, and the lead up to it is even slower. I suppose that's why she looks for cautious people to employ. Though I can't say you came off as cautious at our first meeting."

I raise my eyebrows. "Oh, come on, that's not fair. I've already apologized for the scene I made."

"I know," he says. "And I shouldn't tease. It's forgotten. If Presswick's not around, do you mind if I sit for a minute before tackling the stairs again? Don't let me interrupt you, though, just go on with what you were doing."

"Please." I gesture to her chair and take my own seat. But it's hard to focus with him sitting across from me. I can still remember the warmth of his hand in mine, and I'm certainly not about to go on eating my sandwich and peppering myself with crumbs.

"You know," Jack says after a moment. "I don't usually ask complete strangers to dinner. But what would you think if I did?"

I glance up quickly. He's not looking at me, just toying with a pencil, and there's a bemused expression on his face.

I lower my head and keep on doggedly writing away. "That depends. Am I the stranger?"

Jack echoes my words about *The Two Sisters*. "I'd prefer you didn't inquire further."

"In that case, I think it's very easy to find yourself living a life full of regret," I tell him. "And that you should always make the courageous decision, even when doing so seems hard."

When I look up again, Jack's not exactly smiling but he still manages to seem pleased. "That's a very good answer, Philippa

Hapwell. I've got a feeling you're frightfully clever. Now I really should be getting back."

He sets his cane on top of the cart he brought *The Two Sisters* in on and wheels it out the door. I stand in the hallway and watch him go, back through the Gallery's labyrinth toward the restoration room.

"Hang on," I call after him. "Have you asked me to dinner or not?"

"Not," Jack says.

"Are you going to?"

He raises a hand to wave but doesn't turn back, just keeps pushing the cart on down the hall. "I'm not sure yet. We aren't all as brave as you, Philippa."

I don't want to let anything sour the moment, but, oh, if only he knew.

46

MAX AND I ARE IN LIT CLASS, SORTING THROUGH books to be mailed to a hospital in Leeds. The rest of the Aid Committee will be along shortly, including Ev, and I glance out the window impatiently.

We've made it four years since the Woodlands. It's January, the middle of Evelyn's bad season, which starts in October when the stags fill the woods with their insistent, mournful calls. Looking up, I freeze at the sight of my sister crossing the quad. Despite the blowing snow and the ice that glazes the windowpanes, she's coatless, not even wearing a school sweater. Something's gone wrong with her feet, too, because each step she takes is slow and pained.

"I'll just run out and use the lav before everyone gets here," I say to Max, and hurry down the stairs and through the nearest outside door.

It's bitterly cold—the sort of cold that rips your breath out of your chest. I meet Evelyn halfway across the quad and wrap my arms around her, chivvying her indoors. When we stand inside, in the poky back hall beneath the Lit staircase, I shake my head.

"Evie, you've got to wear your coat. You're going to catch your death out there like that. If I see you without it again, I'll come to your room and put it on you myself."

"Yes, Philippa," Ev answers meekly. She's trembling from the cold, but when she glances up at me, her eyes are clear.

"And what happened to your feet?" I sigh. "Did you walk through a snowbank barefoot? Or—don't tell me. You left the window open all night because Georgie's away."

Evelyn gives me a sarcastic look. "Really, Phil. The things you think of. My shoes are too small."

I'm so relieved to be met with such a mundane answer, I laugh out loud, and then stop abruptly as the laughter turns to nausea.

"Are you alright?" Ev asks.

I let out a slow breath and smile. "Of course I am. Now come on, we've got books to send out."

But later, after lights-out, I creep across the hall to Evelyn's room and silently open the door, just a crack.

She sits on the edge of the bed. Untouched on the desk is a parcel from my parents, shaped suspiciously like a shoe box. I watch as Evelyn pulls off her shoes and socks, a sharp hiss escaping her as she does so.

The backs of her feet aren't blistered. They might have been, once, but they're beyond that now. Instead, round suppurating patches mark her heels, an angry and raw red against her pale skin. I slump against the wall and swallow. I'll have to bully Ev into the nurse's office tomorrow, though I hate to do it. Any time I'm forced to allow others into my sister's secret world, it's a danger to her. Who knows when someone might take it into their head that she'd be better off in an institution? And that, I know, would kill us both.

I lean my head back, praying this winter will be short, and soon melt into the relief of spring.

47

I HAVEN'T GOT THE COURAGE TO TELL MUM AND DAD
what I'm planning, so I leave them a note on Friday morning before
heading to the Gallery. Once there, I'm so distracted that Presswick
casts murderous glances in my direction and sends me off an hour
early.

At Charing Cross, which is impersonal and crowded and unfamiliar, I buy a ticket for a train that's just leaving and have to run
to catch it. I slide into a carriage that's empty except for a traveling
businessman, and rebuff his attempts at conversation with frigid,
one-word answers. After that I'm left to my own thoughts, and the
passing late-winter countryside.

The leafless beeches wave to me, and at noon an attendant
brings a cart round with stale ham and cheese sandwiches. My
companion has two, but I couldn't eat a bite if I tried. Instead, I
drink coffee, and try to think of what I'll say to Max, to Georgie,
to the Curmudgeon, if my nerve doesn't fail and I don't go straight
home on the next London-bound train.

All too soon they call out the stop at Hardwick.

The little open-air platform seems to have shrunk since the last time I stood on it, and Hardwick itself seems smaller and faded, too. No one's expecting me, so I walk the two miles out to St. Agatha's, passing by St. Joseph's on my way. The wind is icy, so I tuck my chin into the collar of my coat and keep my head down. I climb a rise in the road and St. Agatha's appears below like magic, set against the grey and dreaming wood and warmed by the last long rays of the setting sun. It looks as if it's grown out of the forest itself, like the sort of place where fairy stories might begin, rather than end, and I can't decide if I love or hate it.

But there's no turning back now, and the necklace that is Evelyn's last gift to me rests cold against my skin. I clutch my overnight bag and hurry down the slope.

Classes have let out for the day, and the girls are going to clubs. Groups of them race across the quad, not wanting to stay out in the cold longer than they must. A smell of tough, boiled beef wafts out from the kitchen, mingling with the scent of wood smoke and melting snow. I glance across the quad to the dorm, but I'm not ready for that yet. Instead, I duck into the refectory where I once held court.

The girls inside look so frightfully young. I see faces I know, but they're bright and open and untouched by trouble. Not wanting to dim that brightness, I keep to the edges of the vast dining room and slip down a hallway unrecognized. At every turn I'm met with memories of Ev, but I pass through them like mist until I reach a back stairwell.

The door at the top is shut. I knock and let myself in before an answer comes.

Max stands with her back to me, staring out a window at the nearby forest, arms crossed in front of her.

"What happened to my sister, Max?" I can't keep the desperation from my voice.

She turns, and at the sight of me is across the room in a moment.

"Oh, Philippa," Max murmurs with her arms around me. "I'm so sorry. So very sorry."

"Please. I need to know."

Max seems to shrink, to retreat inside herself. "It was nothing you hadn't seen before. I stopped leaving her the key, for fear she'd wander off and not come back, but she found ways out. Then the evening of the winter concert she recited, and did it brilliantly, and I thought perhaps she'd take a turn for the better. But in the crowd afterward, she vanished."

"I want to see her room."

Max nods. "The Yard took all her things away, you know. In case she'd left something behind, to indicate her state of mind."

"And Jamie says there was a boy," I add. "I need to speak with him."

"You can't." Max's mouth tucks in at the edges. "He's gone home to Yorkshire, for at least the rest of term."

I narrow my eyes. "Why? Was there some sort of suspicion?"

"Of course not." Suddenly Max looks very tired. "If you met him, you'd know he could never. But he was the last to see her, and he took it very hard."

"They're not giving you any trouble, are they?" I ask.

"No. But then, we all saw this coming."

"Yes, we did. And yet I still left."

"Philippa, it's not your—" Max begins, but I raise a hand to stop her.

"Could I see Ev's room, please?"

The dormitory's worse than the refectory. Girls loiter about the halls or linger in their bedrooms with the doors open. Several times I hear my name called, but hurry along without answering.

Max turns a key in the lock of the door to Evelyn's room.

"We've moved Georgie in with me," she explains. "She's more cut up over all this than she lets on, and the only other options were leaving her in here across from an empty bed or having another girl take Ev's place. Neither seemed quite fair, so the room's been sitting unused."

When the door swings open, a blast of cold night air hits us. Max switches on the electric light and hurries to shut the window, which has been left ajar.

"Faulty spring," she says. "It never quite latches."

The room is bare. No sheets on the beds, no personal belongings strewn about, and the wardrobe gapes open, showing its hollow insides. I'm not sure what I'm hoping to find.

"May I have a moment?"

Max stops in the doorway. "I've got to be in the refectory shortly. Are you alright on your own for a bit? If you need anything, my rooms are open. Help yourself to tea, or the telephone."

"Yes." I sit gingerly on the edge of Evelyn's bed. "I'm fine. Thank you, Max, truly. For everything. I don't know what either of us would have done without you."

The door shuts behind her, and I'm left alone in this too-cold, empty room, which feels more like a cell than any sort of home. The bare light bulb casts harsh shadows against the walls, and flickers when a gust of wind rattles the window. With a little pop, the faulty spring gives way again, and the window slides open an inch.

I walk over to it, and the sight of the woods ensnares me, restless and sighing in the wind. Shutting the window, I set my jaw. No one here can tell me anything about Evelyn I didn't already know.

But the river where Ev's trail ran cold might.

Outside, the wind's grown icier, and I'm in entirely the wrong sort of shoes for a trek through the forest. I traipse across the back field with my shoulders bent to keep in as much warmth as I can, and pound on the door to Hobb's cottage.

There's a clatter, the sound of shuffling feet, and the door swings open. Light and heat and the smell of something cooking pour out around me. Hobb stands blinking on the threshold.

"Miss Hapwell? Is that you?"

"It is. May I come in, Hobb?"

"Oh, aye."

He steps aside, and I enter, setting my overnight bag next to the door. It's a little place, the gardener's cottage, just a single long room with a bed off to one side and space for a wood-burning stove, a table, and two chairs. But there's a pot of stew bubbling on the stovetop and music crackling from the wireless, which Hobb shuffles over to and turns down, so we can hear ourselves think. Silently, he pulls out a chair and I sit.

Still without speaking, Hobb ladles out two bowls of stew and sets one in front of me, then takes the remaining chair. I eat a mouthful to be polite, and it's far better than school fare—savory, and thick with meat and winter vegetables. I've only got through half of mine by the time Hobb pushes his empty bowl aside and leans back with an expectant look.

"I need to borrow a pair of boots and a torch," I tell him, setting my spoon down. "I'm going out to the river."

Hobb nods. "Very well, Miss. But I'll be going with you."

I nearly argue, but he fixes his eyes on mine and I read regret there, of the same sort I've been feeling since I woke in the New England dark.

"Alright." I bow my head in assent. "If you insist, Hobb."

"I do."

It's not long before we're both fitted out in tall boots and Hobb produces a lantern from a high shelf. Not an electric torch, but a genuine kerosene lantern, which he carefully fills and trims before we set out. Bracing ourselves, we plunge into the wild night.

The gale in the treetops murmurs and moans. At the rusted back gate, Hobb squeezes through first, then reaches back with a gnarled hand to help me. The entire evening seems strange, two steps removed from my London life, as if there's magic in these English woods, and in the wizened, lamplit face of my guide. I follow after Hobb and the bobbing circle cast by his lantern. Last autumn's dried leaves skitter across the trail and cold, brackish puddles lie in the hollows. Once, an owl swoops soundlessly overhead. It's a fey night, a quicksilver night, a night for passing between the worlds.

But I've gone through the veil before—had my return trip and paid for it in blood and pain and tears. No matter how sly and half awake the woods may seem at night, I know this: the trees are only trees, and the beckoning shadows no more than trickery.

We walk by the birch ring, a white gleam away to my right, but don't stop to enter. The river's roaring with meltwater, already calling out with its full-throated song. Hobb and I press on.

"Tell me a story, Miss Hapwell," Hobb calls over one shoulder. "It's a night for remembering home and hearth, to keep our feet from wandering."

Caught up in the witchery of the woods, I begin speaking words I ought not to.

"Once upon a time, there were three children—a brother and two sisters—who loved each other very much. They lived ordinary lives in an ordinary place, until one day—"

Pebbles shift on the trail beneath me, and I nearly lose my footing. Hobb grabs my elbow to steady me. The river lies ahead.

Another step and the trees are behind us. There is only the stony riverbank, and the song of the water, and the spark of moonlight on frothing rapids.

And though I'm standing on the bank with Hobb's hand still on my arm, I can feel the cold river close around my knees, my waist, my ribs, my shoulders, then lap hungrily at my hair, my neck, my lips—

With a gasp, I turn to Hobb. He's more inscrutable than ever, here in this halfway place.

"You know what they say about her," he rasps. "They say she—"

"Please," I cut in, and there's water still purring around my throat, making the rest of me weightless. "Please don't you say it, too. Not here, not now. I couldn't bear it."

Hobb pulls a pipe from the pocket of his greatcoat, fills it, and lights it with a guttering match. Only after the first draw has coiled back out of his mouth like dragon smoke does he speak again. "I never believed it, Miss Hapwell. Not of our Miss Evelyn. Gone off on some adventure, she has, or been taken by the Folk. But not that, and not her. Maybe I'm a fool for hoping, and maybe you are, too, but we'll go on doing so, won't we? Until the very end."

I have always been a fool to hope. I see that now. Reaching up, I unclasp the chain that hangs around my neck. Moving forward, I make my way to where the river tugs at the toes of my borrowed boots. There, holding the stag pendant so tight in one hand that the miniature antlers dig into my palm, I whisper a last confession.

"I'm sorry, Ev."

My sister's final gift drops into the dark water and is carried away.

On the damp, bone-chilling walk back to St. Agatha's, I try to feel some measure of peace. But when I've collected my things from Hobb's cottage and am bypassing the dormitory, intent on catching a train home and never returning to this place, a voice stops me.

"Miss!"

A first-year student in a winter coat and scarf runs across the gravel. It's nearly lights-out, and I can't imagine why she's outdoors.

"Miss." The girl stops in front of me, breathless and red-cheeked. "You dropped this in the quad, Miss. Here you are."

On her gloved hand rests a silver chain and a silver pendant, worked in the shape of a leaping stag, with a bit of river weed still clinging to it.

I take it from her and watch as she hurries into the dormitory. When she's gone, I clasp the chain around my neck once more. It's yet another whisper in that language without words, but I don't know who's speaking. I don't know what any of this means.

I do know I was a fool to hope even for this—that any offering of mine might be acceptable. There are bonds that join Evelyn and me, across time and across the worlds. Nothing but the truth will set me free, and I have no idea where to find it.

48

THE PICASSO IS STILL IN PRESSWICK'S OFFICE ON MONDAY, waiting to make its journey home to Leningrad. I'm glad my back is to it over the course of the morning, and when Presswick takes her lunch break, I eat in the office as usual but don't change seats. I can't bring myself to sit with those two sad figures in my peripheral vision.

As always, I'm so absorbed by my fair copying that I startle when Presswick sweeps in with a lean man in a suit. She seems surprised to see me, though I've been sitting across the desk from her every day.

"Oh. Hapwell," she says. "I forgot about you again. This is Director Hendy, and we've got business to discuss. Go make yourself useful elsewhere, will you? Have someone in the restoration room show you what they're about, or something of the sort."

With that, I'm unceremoniously escorted into the hallway, where the door is shut behind me with a decisive click. I haven't been dismissed in such a perfunctory way in, oh, lifetimes. Not since before the Woodlands. I can't help but smile, and there's no dazzle in it, just dry amusement.

I take the stairs up to the restoration room and pointedly ignore the stags still hanging on the wall. There's a fan set up in the far doorway, in a vain attempt to keep plaster dust from the construction out of the room, and three restorers are at work. A middle-aged woman with black hair pulled back into a tidy knot bends over a table, using a heated spatula to repair damaged bits of canvas. An older man in spectacles stands nearby, mixing colors on a palette and inpainting damaged areas of another picture.

Jack Summerfield sits in front of an easel, closest to the far door. I cross the room as if I'm meant to be there, as if I haven't just been turned out by Presswick and left to my own devices.

Jack's intent on his work, cleaning the painting before him with a cotton swab and some sort of fluid that smells sharp and astringent. It's my old nemesis, *A Woman Bathing in a Stream*, who Presswick did promise would be getting a cleaning. I watch for a moment, lips parted, mesmerized by the slow, assured motion of Jack's hand, working in small circles, revealing details that were previously obscured by dirt and discoloration. The rich colors of the tapestry mounded behind the bather show brighter, glowing orange-red and gold. The deft folds of her linen shirt stand out in clear relief, and the shadows on her upper thighs have deepened, grown more alluring.

"Hello, you," Jack says when I clear my throat softly so as not to startle him. He sounds so pleased to see me I could melt. "This is a nice surprise."

"Presswick's kicked me out of the office for a while," I answer. "She and Director Hendy are having an impromptu meeting so I thought I'd come see what you do."

Jack nods. "Pull up a stool. You can stay as long as you like."

I do as I'm told and by the time I'm back Jack's picked up his swab and is working again, smoothing the bather's hair, moving slowly toward her face.

"What do you want to know?" he asks, and I shrug.

"Whatever you can tell me. I don't know a thing about restoration, to be honest. I was at school for art history, in America, until—well, until I had to come home."

The bather's hair isn't the dark brown I thought it was. There's more red to it, and an undertone of gold. Jack's swab moves steadily down, brushing against her forehead. "Is your coming home something I shouldn't ask about?"

"Yes," I say tartly. "And this isn't a lesson in Philippa Hapwell, anyhow, it's a lesson in restoration work."

"Duly noted. In that case, it's not a particularly difficult thing to understand. Do you see how clouded the uncleaned bits look?"

I nod. There's a muddied, yellow appearance to the untouched parts of the canvas, a sort of golden haze that darkens the shadows and obscures details. It still sits like a veil across the bather's face, and I chew on my lower lip as Jack's swab touches her eyes.

"That's varnish. It's applied to protect the paint layer, but it discolors over time—goes yellow. It darkens warm colors, and changes cool ones entirely. Blue looks green, that sort of thing. Layers of varnish have built up over the years, so now I'm cleaning them off, but I've got to take care not to touch the paint layer."

"And how do you know when to stop?" I ask. "How do you

know when you can't go any further, or you'll damage her?"

Jack smiles, though he keeps cleaning, keeps his eyes on the bather. "A great deal of practice, and a bit of intuition."

"What are those?" I point to a trio of spots marring the smooth curve of the bather's legs.

Jack glances down. "We call them losses. They're places where the paint has cracked a bit, and someone's patched the damage. But it's likely the original loss isn't anywhere near that large—the patches discolor, and have to be patched themselves, and so on and so forth, until you end up with an ugly mark that's much larger than the loss that started it all."

I let out a small breath. Damage breeds damage. That's a familiar story. "Can you fix a problem like that?"

"Yes." The bather's eyes are unveiled now, and there's a wistfulness to her expression, as if her thoughts are very far away. "But you've got to get back to the original loss. I'll scrape away all the added paint, *very carefully*—if only Presswick was around to hear me say that—until just the original paint layer and the original loss are left. Then I'll fill the crack with something we call gesso, and paint it over again, but the repair will be much smaller and unnoticeable, and hopefully won't discolor as the paints we've got now are a far sight more advanced than those they had around the last time this piece was cleaned."

The whole of the bather's face has appeared. I'd hoped she'd tell me something true, something about my sister or myself or the unbreakable bond between us, but she only stares into the water with that bittersweet smile, her thoughts an eternal mystery.

"What's this?" I point to a faint gold line along the bather's shoulder, like an aura, or the imprint of a ghost.

Jack squints. "It's original. It may have been intentional, or it might be pentimenti—sometimes it's impossible to know."

"*Pentimenti*?"

Setting down his swab, Jack wipes his hands on a rag and presses two fingers to the bridge of his nose, as though his head's started aching. "Something the artist changed. It means 'repentances.' Sometimes you can see the ghost of what it was they meant to do, underneath what they've painted over."

The ghost of what I meant to do faces me every night in the form of Ev's empty bed, and it sometimes seems my whole life is a series of repentances. Repentances for all the promises I've broken, both here and in the Woodlands. Repentances for bringing my sister home, repentances for leaving her behind. Repentances for not being strong enough to bear either her absence or her presence.

"Fancy a walk?" Jack asks, taking his cane from where it's hooked over one of the easel's supports. "I need some air."

"Yes. Thank you."

I stare at the bather as Jack clears things away, putting lids on solvent bottles, disposing of cotton swabs. She won't meet my eyes, won't tell me her secrets, no matter how badly I want her to. She just stands, poised in the river, about to take another step.

"Ready?" Jack asks. "Mrs. Zhang, Mr. Haas, we're stepping out for a minute."

We navigate through the mess of the Ministry of Works'

construction, and out past the quiet, contemplative galleries, into bright sunshine on the portico. The early spring air is still chilly, but the Gallery's a drafty old place and I had a sweater on anyhow. Still, we've only just made it down the steps when Jack hands me his overcoat.

"Take it if you like," he says. "I've got my jacket and scarf. I'm quite comfortable."

I shrug into his coat and it smells of the restoration room—of cleaners and solvents and paint. We amble across Trafalgar Square, past Nelson's Column and the lions that guard its base, past the fountains and the winter grass, and out onto the Mall. Jack's limping badly, but it gets better as we carry on, and I wonder if it's sitting for too long that bothers him.

"Do they hurt?" I ask. "Your burns, I mean."

"Sometimes," he says. "But I broke bones that didn't set right, and that's worse, depending on the weather. I suppose I'm used to it, though. Does whatever's brought you home from America hurt you?" I glance at him sharply and he gives me a look. "You don't talk about it, so I assume you came back because of something difficult, is all."

I slip the stag pendant out and rub at the cool metal, a reminder of all my failings. "My sister's gone missing. It's been nearly"—the words threaten to choke me—"a month. She disappeared from school, but she'd been having a hard time coping with a lot of things. So I think Scotland Yard has made up their minds about it, and about her, but I'm still not certain. And honestly at this point I'd rather know one way or the other, because not knowing is worse. I *hate* not being sure what to do with myself—whether I should hurt or hope, because I can't manage both at once, and I'm caught between the two."

We step through the entrance to St. James's Park and the city streets give way to grass and trees, which are faintly green with the promise of spring. It feels like a betrayal, that spring will come whether Ev is here or not, that the trees would dare to bud and the flowers to bloom in her absence.

Jack hasn't said anything, as if he knows there's more, and so I go on, because he may as well hear it all.

"We fought, and I left her. I went to America because I thought I couldn't bear being with Evelyn anymore. And I'm never going to stop regretting that, because if I'd stayed, she'd still be here. I'd pulled her through hard times before, and I could have done it again. But I left instead. Now I have to live with that, and it's eating me up inside."

I can't see straight, and selfish creature that I am, I'm not sure if the tears blurring my vision are for myself or Evelyn.

Jack's damaged left hand slides into my own and I cling to it.

"Handkerchief's in the coat pocket," he says simply.

I take it out and wipe at my face. "I'm so sorry. That's probably more of an answer than you bargained for, and now I've gone and made a mess of myself again."

"Philippa," Jack says. "Please stop apologizing to me. If you keep that up, I'm going to want to kiss you, just to prove everything's alright, and—"

"I'm sorry, Jack," I repeat, blinking away the last rebellious tears. "I'm sorry, I'm sorry."

I don't have time to be breathless before he kisses me, and I'm lost in the mingling smell of paint and my own lavender scent. Around us the trees sway and whisper, promising a spring that will come without Evelyn, and I've never been so happy or so terribly low, everything in me aching with loss and longing until I think I'll fall apart.

49 ~

LONDON'S CAUGHT IN FOG, AND SO AM I. I CAN'T SEE MY
way clear of it, and I'm beginning to forget the sound of my sister's
voice, so I decide to beard the lion in its den.

Whitehall's sidewalks are emptier than they were during the
war, when queues for the Army Recruiting Office stretched from
one street to the next. But the New Scotland Yard building is as
imposing now as it was then—tall and severe, with a blank-faced
brick exterior. I pace the walkway for a few minutes, trying to
ignore the gnawing pain in my stomach, before sucking in a breath
of damp air and pushing my way inside.

Everyone here is busy and impersonal, from the secretaries to
the line of telephone operators to the inspectors, who walk about
with their heads down as if their busyness is somehow superior
to that of ordinary mortals. After inquiring at several desks, I'm
directed up a flight of stairs and to a small waiting room that
smells of cheap perfume and cigarette smoke. I settle into a chair
and leaf absently through a magazine, trying to appear untroubled and uncaring.

I've only just managed to snap a facade of serenity into place when Inspector Dawes blusters into the room. Bother. I'd been hoping for Inspector Singh, who seems the more understanding of the pair.

But I get to my feet, and even Dawes is caught for a moment by my glamour, uncertain whether he should shake the hand I offer or bow over it with a kiss. I smile as he shakes it, a slow, enigmatic expression, and the inspector scowls.

"What is it you want, Miss Hapwell?"

"I've come for my sister's letters," I tell him. "You've had them quite long enough to read through. I should like to look at them myself."

Inspector Dawes's formidable eyebrows grow even closer together. "You're taking an interest now, when you couldn't be troubled to read them before? That seems like too little too late, doesn't it, Miss?"

I want nothing more than to crumble at his words. Instead, I barely blink.

"I beg your pardon, sir," I say to the inspector, "but you know nothing about me. I'd ask you not to judge what you have no knowledge of."

"That's the trouble with girls like you," Dawes grouses. "No one knows you, not even yourselves. You're too caught up in mysteries of your own making."

He stumps out of the room, presumably to fetch Evelyn's letters. I drop into a chair and bury my face in my hands till the sound of his footsteps in the corridor brings me once more to my feet.

Ev's letters have all been torn open, and the envelopes smudged, but I take them from Dawes as if each one of them is worth a pound of gold.

"Thank you," I say, meaning it with every bit of me. "For reading my sister's words when I couldn't. And I'm sorry, whether you believe it or not, for being who I am, and for not being here when I ought to have been. You may not know me, but you should know this—I will spend the rest of my life doing penance for the mistakes I've made."

Dawes has no answer for that. He just stands watching as I leave the waiting room, clutching my sister's last words.

Across from Evelyn's empty bed, her letters sit on my lap, and they're heavy as consequence, burdensome as guilt.

Before I can falter, I slide the first from its envelope and smooth creases from the paper.

It's poetry.

I'd expected something else. Entreaties for me to come home, or feigned cheerfulness. Instead I find verse.

> *Beautiful Evelyn, Hope is dead!*
> *Sit and watch by her side an hour.*
> *That is her book-shelf, this her bed;*
> *She plucked that piece of geranium-flower,*
> *Beginning to die too, in the glass;*
> *Little has yet been changed, I think:*
> *The shutters are shut, no light may pass*
> *Save two long rays thro' the hinge's chink.*

There are pages upon pages of poetry—every letter a window made of words.

> *The lights begin to twinkle from the rocks:*
> *The long day wanes: the slow moon climbs: the deep*
> *Moans round with many voices. Come, my friends,*
> *'T is not too late to seek a newer world.*
> *Push off, and sitting well in order smite*
> *The sounding furrows; for my purpose holds*
> *To sail beyond the sunset, and the baths*
> *Of all the western stars.*
> *It may be that the gulfs will wash us down:*
> *It may be we shall touch the Happy Isles,*
> *And see the great Achilles, whom we knew.*
> *Tho' much is taken, much abides; and tho'*
> *We are not now that strength which in old days*
> *Moved earth and heaven, that which we are, we are;*
> *One equal temper of heroic hearts,*
> *Made weak by time and fate, but strong in will*
> *To strive, to seek, to find, and not to yield.*

And at the very last,

> *When I go back to earth*
> *And all my joyous body*
> *Puts off the red and white*
> *That once had been so proud,*

If men should pass above
With false and feeble pity,
My dust will find a voice
To answer them aloud:

"Be still, I am content,
Take back your poor compassion,
Joy was a flame in me
Too steady to destroy;
Lithe as a bending reed
Loving the storm that sways her—
I found more joy in sorrow
Than you could find in joy."

I read feverishly, looking for Evelyn, searching for a single word of her own. It's as if she erased herself and her voice long before finally vanishing, and all I want is one leftover glimmer, a small lingering spark of who she was.

And then, in her final letter, I find it.

Dear Philippa,
I love you. I miss you. I'm going home.

It's something. There are no answers to be read there, but if I've failed to find truth elsewhere, I can't expect it to appear in Evelyn's own familiar writing. Still, I run one finger across the loops and swirls of dried ink, wishing to read in the shape of them whether she was happy, whether her resolve brought her peace.

Evelyn of the Woodlands, walker of worlds, heart of my very heart, what have you done?

50

"—YOU SHOULD THINK ABOUT IT, PHILIPPA. MY parents would love to have you, and I've got three older brothers you could civilize."

Millie Green is speaking, though I'm hardly listening to her. We're all at our usual table, under the window in the refectory, but Ev isn't with us. She's sat at the fringes for so long, always where I can keep an eye on her, but this year, things have changed. I scan the long, table-filled room, desperate to catch a glimpse of my sister.

And there she is, alone, at the back of the room, a book (of poetry, if I know Ev) propped up against the saltcellar. I remember how she looked, our first winter after the Woodlands—set apart, as if nothing and no one could touch her. She looks like that now.

Which is why, when Millie repeats her invitation to visit her family in Boston after graduation in spring, I all but snap.

"No, thank you," I tell Millie coolly. "I've got too much to do here in England. I can't think of gadding about overseas."

I feel guilty enough that I went so far as to send an application to an American college. I knew, even as I was doing it, that it would

*never be more than a lovely idea. There is too much holding me back.
And that idea became just another disappointment when an acceptance
letter arrived. I did what I had to, crumpling it up and tossing it into
the bin.*

*One of the girls jokes that I've become quite a snob since the war,
but Millie only gives me a worried look.*

*After dinner, she corners me in the dormitory stairwell, her red-
brown hair put up in rollers and a stack of bath towels in her hands.*

*"I meant what I said," she tells me, purposely pitching her voice
not to carry. "About you being welcome at my family's place in Boston
anytime."*

*I cross my arms and lean back against the wall, turning myself into
a picture of indifference. "Of course, darling. And I meant what I said,
about having too much to keep me here."*

*Millie sets her bath towels down on the steps. When she looks at me
again, it's with a seriousness I've never seen her show before. "Phil. I
know why you don't want to leave. All the girls do. Do you think we
can't see? We know what Evelyn's like, and we've watched you break
your back over her for five years. I talked to everyone, and we all think
you need to get away. You're wearing yourself out, and it's just not fair."*

*I straighten and fix Millie with a stare meant to make grown men
cower. I should be better, should be kinder, but when it comes to Ev, my
heart is an open wound. "Walk. Away. Do not speak to me again. You
know nothing about my sister and me, and you never will."*

American to the core, Millie doesn't falter. "Phil—"

*"Go." The word's a command, and reluctantly, she starts back up
the steps with her towels in hand.*

"If you change your m—"

"Are you really still speaking to me?"

She vanishes at the top of the stairwell. A moment later, Evelyn appears in her place, as if summoned by my unhappiness. I sit down on the steps, and Ev sits beside me. She says nothing, but rests her golden head on my shoulder. I put one arm around her and we sit until lights-out, just the two of us together against all our worlds.

51

I LIVE IN A REALM OF LIGHT AND SHADOW. BY DAY, there's the brightness of the Gallery—of learning the workings of the Conservation Department, and willing myself not to flush each time Jack favors me with his quiet smile. That's all I get from him, though—smiles and courtesy and kindness. No more kisses in the park. No invitations to dinner. But I don't push. I'm afraid of my own capacity for damaging things.

By night, there's the darkness of Evelyn's empty bed, which serves as a constant reproach from the other side of the room. I stay as late as I can at work, and ride the bus for hours after I have to leave. Even when I get home, I slide under the covers and lie awake, unable to avoid thoughts of what might have been.

But spring cannot be stopped and the weather grows warm. Soon I no longer have to wear a long coat on the ride to work, and settle for soft cardigans instead. One afternoon I'm drooping over my fair copying in the chair across from Presswick when she glances up.

"Hapwell. Stop yawning and take a break. Go out to the square for once to have your lunch—I'm tired of you leaving bread crumbs on my desk."

If there's one thing I've learned, it's that there's no gainsaying Presswick, so I grab my sweater and lunch and go.

Gathering my courage, I head down the dimly lit and tumble-down hallway that ends in the staircase up to the restoration studio. There are a few other restorers there, bent over worktables, and I notice with a tightening of my throat that every painting on the wall depicts a forest. Bruegel's *Ambush in the Woods*. Monet's *Olive Tree Wood in the Moreno Garden*. Van Gogh's *Trees and Undergrowth*. Worst of all is Klimt's *Lakeside with Birch Trees*. Serene as the meadow and the white trees and the still water appear to be, all they remind me of is the birch ring outside St. Agatha's, and Evelyn's trail gone cold on the riverbank.

I stop next to Jack's table, where he's doing what looks like an incredibly fiddly bit of inpainting, not on the *Woman Bathing in a Stream*, but on Gainsborough's *View of Dedham*. A forest again. More whispers without words.

"Do you always restore paintings according to subject matter?" I ask, pitching my voice low so it won't carry across the quiet room. "It's just, that seems a very strange way to work."

Jack takes a moment to finish what he's doing and sets his brush aside. Then he peers at me like a puzzled owl. "Sorry, what?"

I gesture to the paintings on the walls. "Look. They're all of woods. Isn't that odd?"

He looks at the walls as if seeing the paintings there for the first time. "You're right. It is. I don't think it's been done on purpose, though?"

"And when I came in the first time, don't you remember—every picture in here was of a stag."

"Oh. Yes, I did find that funny at the time."

I can feel a frown creasing my forehead. "Do you believe in coincidence?"

Jack wipes his hands on a damp cloth and puts it away. "Coincidence, no. Providence, yes. Are you going to lunch?"

I'd nearly forgotten the paper bag I'm holding, and the reason I came up here in the first place. "I am. Presswick's tired of me, so I walked up to tell you I'll be out in the square for the next half hour."

"I could use a break myself—I've been hunched over that canvas all morning."

We stop at the door, where Jack hangs up his apron and takes his cane from the umbrella stand.

There are school tours wandering through the open rooms, and the galleries are louder than usual, full of stage whispers and children's laughter. Kitty waves lazily from behind the front counter as we head out into the square and the spring sunshine, where water chatters in the fountains and Lord Nelson keeps a perpetual watch atop his column.

I set my lunch down and sit with my back to one of the portico's pillars, watching light play on the fountain water and pigeons flutter about the square. Jack's eating an apple with his shirtsleeves rolled up to the elbows, and the skin on his injured arm is a patchwork of burns, pulled tight or puckered in places.

"Penny," Jack says after a minute, and I sigh.

"My sister, Evelyn, loved spring. She was always better once things started getting warmer, brighter. I can't help but expect that one day, I'll turn around and she'll be here. Maybe she'll look a little different, and have a story to tell, but it'll be *her*, and all this will be over, and I'll finally be able to sleep at night."

Oh, Ev. You wore me to a raveling and I'd give anything to have you back.

Jack's voice is kind, and a little sad. "I don't know what's happened to your sister. Maybe someday she'll turn up. Maybe she won't. But even if she does come home, things aren't going to be the same. I hope—I hope you're prepared for that. One way or another, your life's different now than it was before. And perhaps it's just going to be the difference of not knowing, of learning to live without looking back."

I cross my arms stubbornly. "Jack Summerfield, I will never stop waiting for my sister. Not until her bones or mine go into the ground."

"Don't be cross," he says. "And wait if you must, but while you're doing it you've got to build a life for yourself, where you are and with what you've been given. Trust me—I know a few things about living with regret. About wondering what might have been. If that's all you do, it'll leave you hollow and bitter, Philippa."

I don't say what I'm thinking because I've no interest in a fight. But the fact of the matter is, I've *chosen* to put myself in limbo. I managed life in the Woodlands and after, and I could manage now if I chose to. There's fire and steel at my core, and no world will break me unless I let it.

But I don't deserve to be happy. I don't deserve to move on, not after all the promises I've broken. Not after bringing my sister back here and abandoning her to her demons. I can't build a life if Evelyn's no longer living.

I don't even deserve this moment, of sitting in the sun on a spring day in London, so I scramble to my feet and start back toward the front doors.

"Philippa," Jack calls after me. "You haven't had your lunch."

"Feed it to the pigeons," I tell him. "I'll get a coffee at the canteen."

Then one night I stumble upstairs after work and Evelyn's bed is gone. My own bed's been pulled to the center of the room and the rug moved. It's as if she never was. As if she's never coming back.

This is infinitely worse than having to sleep next to a constant reminder of her absence. I march down the stairs and into the kitchen, slamming the door behind me. Mum's sitting at the table with a cup of tea, though it's late, and looks up with a start.

"Oh, Philippa! You gave me a fright."

Even Evelyn's chair is missing. I can hardly speak, I'm so angry. Instead I shove the chairs back to the way they were, moving mine to where hers ought to be and leaving a gaping hole at my place.

"Oh dear." Mum sighs. "I see. Philippa, will you sit?"

"No. I'm going out, and I won't be back." I storm out of the kitchen and Mum follows as I hurry up the stairs and into the bedroom, where I pull clothes and cosmetics from drawers and stuff them into my valise.

"Philippa, darling, let me explain. We watched your sister hold on to something for years. What it was, I don't know. The three of you have always been a closed book to your father and me. But we have eyes. We know that's what broke your sister in the end."

She steps forward and puts a hand on my arm, but I pull away.

"I refuse to see the same thing happen to you," Mum says.

Anger and regret threaten to strangle me, and I'm not ready to count Evelyn out yet. Maybe that will be my undoing—maybe I'll fall apart holding on to her the way she fell apart holding on to the Woodlands, but I don't know what else to do, or who else to be.

I'm not letting go, Ev. I won't forget you. Let everyone else erase your memory, and I'll still be here, standing fast until the very end.

I leave the house without another word.

It's raining, and I get on a bus just to stay dry. The raindrops against the window make phantom images of the streetlamps— an endless series of pentimenti, repentances in light and water. We drive and drive until I fall asleep and wake with a start, completely disoriented, fear pouring ice through my veins.

I can't stay on a bus all night, so I get off at the only sanctuary I know.

The Gallery looms tall after dark and its pillars cast long shadows. I drift up the steps and hammer on the door until Albright appears in his night guard's uniform. He shakes his head at the sight of me, bedraggled and damp, toting a bag of clothes and shoes, but opens the door and lets me in.

We stand in the silent lobby and I'm not sure what he'll do. Then he heaves a sigh and beckons to me to follow him. "The workmen dragged a few old couches into the shut-off rooms, for when they're on break. I can't say as they're very clean, but if you're out of the way before morning shift starts, we'll keep this between you and me."

I look up at him, and there's no pride left in my posture, or in the puddle of rainwater I've left on the lobby floor. "It might be for a while, Albright. Do you mind?"

He shrugs. "The higher-ups might, but I don't, and what they don't know won't hurt them."

Relief washes over me. "Thank you. I couldn't think where else to go."

"S'alright, Miss. Don't say anything else about it."

Albright leads me to a back room where rubble lies in heaps in the corners and the walls are seamed with cracks. An overstuffed couch sits off to one side, cotton batting bursting through its worn upholstery. There's only one window with glass in it, the rest being covered over with tarps. That single window stares out at the wreckage that is all that's left of Room 10.

Drop cloths serve me for a pillow and a blanket. No sooner has Albright gone than I sink into sleep.

And I dream.

Grey rain. Grey sea. Grey sky.

Evelyn beside me and Cervus before us, as I break my sister's heart because I can't let her go.

When I wake in the small hours before dawn, rain still drums against the makeshift tin roof. I put myself together in one of the Gallery's tiny staff lavatories, and a haunted face peers out from the mirror. I look like Ev.

So I put on powder and lipstick with even more care than usual. I spray myself with scent to hide the smell of plaster dust. I brush my hair till it shines, and slip on red pumps with silver buckles. When I look again, my face is a perfect mask that blocks off any glimpse of the lost girl within.

52

IN THE END, IT'S MY BEASTLY STOMACH THAT GIVES out. *By spring of our last year together, Ev's wandering the woods ceaselessly and I can't keep anything down.*

The nurse and Hardwick's fusty doctor are brought in. They tell me I have an ulcer, and confine me to the school infirmary for a week. They say it's to minimize stress and that I've got to stop pushing myself so hard. My courtiers divide up the various committees and clubs I oversee between them, and I'm left with nothing to do but read and think.

I don't recover as quickly as the doctor would like. Of course not—cooped up in the infirmary, I'm wild with worry over Evelyn. At least until an unlikely delegation comes to visit.

Max, Georgie, and Millie Green appear in the door one afternoon. I'm only glad I fixed my hair and put on lipstick, though there's nothing that can be done about the fact that I'm in pajamas at three p.m.

"We're here about Ev," Max says simply as they pull up chairs, hemming me in like a captive. "Whether you've asked for it or not, it's time you had help, Philippa. You need to get away, and to trust that in your absence, what will be is just what will be. Millie told us you made it into an American college. You ought to go."

To my everlasting shame, I bury my face in my hands and cry.

"I can't," I sob. "I can't. I promised to look out for her, and I won't break a promise again."

As a last resort, they send in Evelyn. She steps into the infirmary barefooted one afternoon, smelling of the woods and the clean spring wind, with daisies still braided in her hair. Ev sits on the side of my bed and takes my hand.

"Philippa, you should go," she says, the light of hope shining in her eyes. "I'll be alright. I know I'm not always at my best, but I can muddle through on my own until it's time to go home."

She looks so much like the girl she was. Like Evelyn of the Woodlands, who was strong of heart and will, and loved the Great Wood with every bone in her body. Like the girl who wanted nothing more than to grow things in the good earth, but who nevertheless found the courage to kill for me.

But I know how deep her darkness can become. And I know, too, that when winter returns, she'll remember the truth—that she's never going home. So, God help me, I remind her, because she needs to remember and because I can't bear to be sent away.

"Evie." I can't look at her when I say the words. "You're not going back. None of us are. Cervus said so himself."

Ev's eyes well with tears.

"Why would you say that?" she asks. "A Woodlands heart always finds its way home. Do I not have a Woodlands heart?"

I swallow, and swallow again, fighting back frustration. "You were born here, just like Jamie and me. This is where we belong, together."

In all our years since the Woodlands, Evelyn has only once come close to reproaching me for my greatest failing—not my near-betrayal of the Woodlanders, but that I couldn't leave without her. I couldn't live in her world so I brought her back, and now she can't live in mine.

Ev whispers something and pulls her hand away.

"I can't hear you, love." I push myself up further in bed and lean forward to catch her words.

"You should have left me," she says. "You shouldn't have brought me with you. It was wrong to take me away."

At first, all I can do is sit and breathe. I will never forgive myself for the things I've done, and I've always marveled at the greatness of Evelyn's heart, that she could so completely overlook my part in her distress. But she hasn't forgiven me, just buried the hurt as deep as the taproot of an ancient oak. We've both been consumed on the inside by that moment on the beach.

"Evelyn, I'm so sorry." I twist the covers desperately between two hands. "I never thought things would be like this. When we were in the Woodlands I missed home terribly, but I still got by. I only meant to keep my word, and to keep you safe."

"I want you to go," she says, sitting straight-backed and lovely with those flowers in her hair. "I don't just think it would be for the best. I want you to leave, Philippa. Stop deciding for me. Stop propping me up. I need to stand on my own again, and if I fall, I fall. But I don't need you and I don't want you. It would be better for both of us if you left."

I've known many bleak moments in my life. I've known desperation and shame and sorrow and fear. But in this moment my battered heart finally breaks and it pains me so, I think I might die of it.

The very last thing I have is my pride. I gather the tattered vestiges of it around me like a cloak and fix my sister with an icy stare. "I'll go then. I see no reason to stay where I'm not wanted. Millie's asked me to visit her family in America, and there's a school there holding a place for me."

"Good." Evelyn smiles softly, even as she deals me one final blow. "All I've ever wanted is to remember, Philippa, and you're determined to make me forget."

She stands and pads away, soundless on her bare feet. I watch her go, and refuse the softer part of me that wants to call out after her.

53

"I'M SORRY."

The words startle me out of my thoughts as Jack Summerfield limps into Presswick's office and takes a seat in her empty chair. "I shouldn't have lectured you. That's not what you need right now. What *do* you need, Philippa? I want to help."

I press one hand to my chest, where the little silver stag rests against my collarbone. "Are you asking in earnest? Don't offer unless you mean it."

Jack leans forward and nods, his brown eyes sincere. "I am. Tell me what I can do."

I should give him some small errand, to make him feel as if he's done his bit. Have him fill my thermos with coffee, or take me for a walk. I shouldn't be truthful, but I am.

"I need to go to Yorkshire. Ev was there over Christmas, visiting a friend. I'd ask my brother to come, but he's started studying for exams, and I hate to take him away. And I'd go alone, but—I'm afraid to."

It brings me very low to admit that. I stare down at the stack of papers before me until Jack reaches across the desk and takes my hand in his.

"I've got a car, and some time off coming to me," he says simply. "Will Presswick give you a day if you ask for it? We could leave early Saturday morning, get rooms at an inn, and drive back Monday. You'd have Sunday to make your inquiries about Evelyn. What do you say?"

"Why are you so kind to me?" I ask, looking at him in bewilderment. "I am sharp-tongued and faithless and I live my life shutting out other people when I'm not using them for my own ends. I know these things about myself. So why are you doing this?"

Jack gets up and comes around the desk. He sets his cane aside, and slowly, carefully, mindful of his prosthetic, lowers himself to his knees in front of me.

I nearly choke. In the Woodlands, no one knelt except to swear their lives to the Great Wood's cause in time of war. I heard so many oaths like this, and watched so many of those oathtakers die. I swore the same oath myself only to break it in spirit, if not, in the end, in deed.

"Do you know what I see when I look at you, Philippa Hapwell?" This time, Jack takes both my hands in his own. "In the short time that I've known you, I've seen loyalty, and courage, and a determination to find the good in those around you. You show mercy to others, and save none for yourself."

I look away and press my lips together for fear I'll cry in front of him again. I thought I'd spent all my tears, but Jack Summerfield seems to have found an inexhaustible well of them.

"Let me help you," he says. "You don't have to do this on your own."

I turn back to him and nod. "Alright. But will you do something else for me first?"

Jack smiles. "Anything. Name it."

"I've only been waiting for you to kiss me again."

He rises up on his knees and I lower my mouth to his, and it's true I don't deserve this, don't deserve the small and fierce joy of knowing him, but now I've been given it, I don't plan to let it go.

On Saturday before dawn, I meet Jack outside the tall brick house where he rents rooms. He pushes up the door to the garage and reveals a well-kept Morris Minor.

I'm holding my thermos of coffee like a lifeline and still only half awake in the dim grey light as Jack switches on the headlamps and we make our way out of London. The streets are relatively empty so early in the morning on a weekend, and before long we're free of the city, and out into the open countryside.

"There's a blanket in the back seat," Jack says after I hide a yawn for the third time. I tuck it in around my shoulders, then rest my head on one arm propped up against the passenger window ledge, but I can't sleep. I'm too anxious about what's to come in Yorkshire, and too nervous about being in this quiet, sensible car next to this equally quiet, sensible young man.

Instead I watch the market towns roll past, with their sleepy houses and shops and leftover air raid sirens. I build castles in the air, imagining impossible things—that I'll find Evelyn at the end of this drive, that she's somewhere in Yorkshire, that this last connection will be the one that matters, that brings me peace.

I'm so lost in thought that it takes me ages to realize Jack is humming, so softly as to be almost under his breath. I sit up with a sigh and he turns to me with a smile. "Hello, you."

"How far have we come?" I ask. It's only now I notice that Jack's got a road map on one knee, and that I've been a completely useless passenger when I might have helped.

"Not halfway yet." Jack glances down at the map. "We're almost to Kettering, if you want to stop. I wouldn't mind a bite to eat, and I'm sure you're hungry, too."

"No, but I'd have another coffee."

Jack frowns but says nothing besides, "It's settled then. We'll take a bit of a break."

I bite my lip, not sure I'm in a place to be making suggestions, but he notices. "Go on; if you've got something to say, out with it."

"Can we just stop a moment? Pick up some sandwiches and find somewhere quieter to eat them? I don't think I could manage sitting in a pub for long, is all."

Jack nods. "Of course. England's not lacking for fields. I'm sure we can find one to oblige us."

In Kettering we stop at a pub and walk in to order sandwiches and coffee. Though it's not terribly busy, I was right—the noise and the people would be more than I can bear just now. I stand next to Jack while we wait, and can't keep from tapping one foot compulsively until he shifts a bit closer so his shoulder brushes mine. I'm not sure why he did it, to get weight off his bad leg, or to steady me, but having him so close makes me feel less adrift.

I keep still until our sandwiches are ready, nicely wrapped up in brown paper.

We carry on for a while until Jack brings the car to a stop alongside an empty, flat stretch of road. There's nothing to see in any direction except fields and hedgerows and grazing sheep.

"Will this do?" he asks.

I smile in answer and get out of the car. Together, we spread the blanket on the green grass between the hedgerow and the road, and make a picnic of our lunch. I take a sandwich to please Jack and nibble at it unconvincingly, but he's had my thermos refilled with coffee at the pub. We pass it back and forth between us and watch the new lambs gamboling about beside their mothers. The wind still has an edge to it, but I'm warm enough in my sweater and scarf and wool stockings.

"Philippa," Jack says eventually. "What is it you're hoping to find in Yorkshire? Only I'd hate to see you disappointed, is all."

I set the thermos down. "To be honest, I don't know. And I understand that it's foolish for me to expect to find anything, but I can't stop looking. I owe it to my sister, to ask all the questions, to turn over all the stones."

Jack smiles. "I hope someday I've got someone who believes in me half as much as you believe in your Evelyn."

Pulling up a handful of grass, I let it be carried away by the wind, one blade at a time. "I left her when I shouldn't have. I'm more at fault in this than anyone else cares to admit. It's not just painters who have to make repentances."

Jack leans back on his hands and squints at me in the afternoon sun. "If I thought you'd listen, I'd tell you that you can't be responsible for another person's choices. But I know there's no changing your mind."

"No." I squint back at him. "I'm afraid you can add stubbornness to my list of terrible qualities."

We sit a little longer, watching the sheep and soaking in the sunshine, and I wish I could stay in this moment forever—that I could capture this fragile, transient happiness and keep it for my own. But eventually clouds pile up away eastward, and the wind gets colder, and we're forced back into the car as it begins to rain.

The wipers are working double time and I've got my knees pulled up to my chest, and the blanket, still smelling vaguely of grass, wrapped around my shoulders when a derelict barracks with boarded-up windows looms alongside the road. A tall fence topped with barbed wire surrounds it, and the whole thing looks closed off and menacing.

Jack's knuckles go white for a moment on the wheel.

"I'm sorry," I say, though I'm not sure what for. For everything, really—for how life is so often just a long, slow way of dying. "The war's impossible to forget, isn't it? Just when you think you have, something crops up. A place like that, or an old leaflet, or you're silly and use up your sugar ration too soon."

"I don't need any of that." Jack raises his left hand. "I carry my reminders a good bit closer."

For a while the only sound is the rain and the wipers, hurrying back and forth.

"You can ask what happened," Jack says finally. "People always want to know."

I shake my head. "*I* don't have to know. Not if you don't like to talk about it."

Jack shrugs. "I'd rather you did, though I'll warn you, it's a very short story, and a stunningly unheroic one."

Pulling the blanket tighter, I watch him driving, his scars still visible in the low light. "Tell me, then."

"Very well." Jack stares straight ahead, into the driving rain. "I enlisted the day after I turned eighteen, spent a few months in training, then shipped out to Italy. I was there for two weeks before I ended up trapped in a building during a bombing. Not much of the house was left, but what was caught fire, and so I am as you see me now. Spent the rest of the war in a convalescent ward."

"And of course it was entirely natural to go straight from hospital to the National Gallery," I point out drily.

Jack gives me a sidelong look. "Before the war, I thought I'd paint. Afterward, for obvious reasons, I decided I'd rather give damaged things a new lease on life. So I studied in hospital—there was precious little else to do—finished up my degree in record time, and then Presswick hired me on. I shouldn't have got the job, not without any experience, but you know how Presswick is."

"Of course." I hug my knees tight and rest my chin on them, still watching his face in profile, his hands on the wheel. "And I think you're right, you weren't a hero, but you *were* brave."

Jack tilts his head to one side, trying to sort that out. "Oh? What's the difference?"

"Heroes do something extraordinary, when they might have chosen to do otherwise. Brave people just bear up under their circumstances and do their best. There's a whole world full of brave people out there, all trying to muddle through. And honestly, I don't think heroes are worth more at the end of the day. Sometimes it takes greater courage to learn to live again when you think your life's over, than it does to risk it in the first place."

Jack pulls the car over to the side of a windswept, rainy road, and turns in his seat. "Which one are you, then? Heroic or brave?"

I shake my head. "Neither. I've already told you. I'm only a girl trying to fix her mistakes."

"Then you'd better not think of me as brave," Jack warns. "It's just pigheadedness. I don't give up on things easily. Never have. Don't mistake me for something I'm not."

I've made a great many mistakes in life, but I know this isn't one of them.

"As you wish," I concede. "Call it stubbornness, then, but from where I'm sitting, your stubbornness and courage look very much alike."

"Will you ever let me win an argument?" He smiles his crooked smile and I can't help but smile back.

"Unlikely. But it's your own fault—no one asked you to add me to the lists of damaged things you're trying to restore."

We're quiet for a minute, listening to the hiss of the wipers and the murmur of the rain.

"Phil," Jack says finally, "whatever courage I have or haven't got, people aren't paintings. I can't erase your troubles, no matter how much I'd like to. But I can be with you while you sort them out yourself, as long as you'll allow it."

He looks down at his hands on the wheel, one marred by war,

the other lean and whole. "The truth is, I like you a great deal— more than anyone else I've ever known. God help me, but I've always liked complicated things, and I don't believe I could ever get to the end of you, not if I spent my whole life trying. So if you think I'm here because you're in pieces, you're wrong—I'm here because those pieces make up something I can't look away from."

I lean across the little distance between us and brush a kiss against the burned side of his face. "Jack Summerfield, swear you're not going to leave me. I know you think you won't, but I've had things change before, things I was as certain of as gravity, and I'm not sure I can do without you any longer."

"You'd be fine without me. You'll manage no matter what." Jack reaches for my hand, and twines his fingers through my own. "But I promise you, I'm not going anywhere. I'm right here."

We drive on, and inside me, fear blossoms alongside the guilt I carry. I trust Jack to be steadfast as the sunrise. What I don't trust is my own self, who's been torn out of this world and sent back from another, and who couldn't stand by her sister in the end. Who let a few thoughtless words drive her away.

Jack I'm certain of. But I've never been anything other than faithless—a girl who breaks her promises. A girl who leaves.

54

THE INN AT EDGETHORN HALT IS A THATCH-ROOFED building with a low-ceilinged great room and a wide fireplace at one end. The booths are cramped, the lighting dim, the back staircase precipitous, and the rooms Spartan in their comforts. In short, it's everything an out-of-the-way country stopping place ought to be.

I sleep better than usual, without the worry of being caught camping out in the Gallery, and in the morning I go down buzzing with nerves.

This is it. There's no other place I can think of that might lead me to a last truth from Evelyn. If I don't find anything here, I'm back at the riverbank, with her trail gone cold.

We have breakfast—for Jack, buttered toast, for me, black coffee *and* buttered toast, which he orders and hawkishly watches me eat. When we've finished, we hurry through the misting rain to the car. I'm quiet on the drive out of Edgethorn and into the countryside, worrying at a hangnail with my teeth until Jack takes my hand in his own.

All too soon, we slow at the base of the hill where the Harpers' farmhouse stands. I peer up between sheets of rain and can see it's the sort of place Ev would like—stone, unassuming, looking of a piece with the surrounding dales.

"Are you ready?" Jack asks. I nod.

His Morris Minor purrs steadily up the drive and then we're parked in the farmyard, taking umbrellas from the back seat and dodging puddles to get to the door. On the front step, I pause a moment to steady myself, then raise a hand to knock. There's a sound of voices from inside, calling back and forth. I give Jack a nervous look.

The door opens at last to reveal a wiry young woman with a riot of red hair spilling out from under a Sunday hat. She frowns at the sight of us.

"Hello. I'm so sorry, I'd ask you in but we're on the way to church and probably don't want whatever it is you're selling, anyhow. Better luck next time."

She moves to shut the door and I freeze, heart pounding in my ears, stomach a knot of pain. It's Jack who holds up a hand to stop her.

"This is Philippa Hapwell," he explains. "Evelyn's sister. She was hoping for a word with your family."

"Oh." The girl manages to infuse the single syllable with eighteen different meanings, then turns and shouts over her shoulder. "Mum, put the kettle on! Dad, take your coat off, and Annie fetch Tom—Ev's sister's come by, so we're staying in."

"Oh no, please don't trouble yourselves," I beg. "We can come back later. It's really alright."

"Nonsense." The girl reaches out and pulls Jack and me inside before I can protest again.

We find ourselves in an enormous farmhouse kitchen, with flagstone floors and a long harvest table off to one side. Mrs. Harper, who's got a bit of grey threaded through her red hair, is setting a kettle on the wood-fired range. There are *things* everywhere—cast-iron pots and pans and dried onions and garlic hanging from the ceiling beams, bottles and potted plants and picture frames on the windowsills, coats on hooks along the wall, but somehow it doesn't seem crowded, just homey and comfortable.

"Tea?" Mrs. Harper calls over to us, and I press closer to Jack, because I can just see Evelyn here, sitting at one of the benches drawn up to the table. She'd have her elbows on her knees and her chin in her hands, and take in the easy way this family has, letting it wash over her like waves.

"Yes, please," I murmur.

"I'm Meg," the young woman tells us. "I'm sure Tom's who you really want to see, and he'll be in shortly—Annie's gone to get him from the barn. We're so terribly sorry for everything, by the way."

"Thank you."

Mrs. Harper turns to us as the kettle begins to steam. "Please don't be shy. Take a seat and make yourselves comfortable. Meg, don't just chatter at them—fetch a plate of biscuits."

Meg disappears into what I'd imagine is a pantry, and with a sudden rush of damp air, a small girl and a gangly, ginger-haired boy step in from the outdoors. The child, Annie, clings to her brother's hand and looks up at him uncertainly, as if she's not sure how he'll take our sudden intrusion into the Harper household.

And it's true Tom Harper looks acutely unhappy to find us in his kitchen. He pulls away from Annie and stuffs his hands into his pockets.

"Well," he mumbles, "what is it you want?"

Mrs. Harper sets a tray down with a clatter. "Thomas Albert Harper, you'll mind your manners, or so help me—"

"Sorry, Mum." Tom hunches his shoulders. "I already spoke to the Yard, is all, so I don't know why they've come."

He lowers himself onto a bench and I follow suit, only dimly aware of Jack crossing the kitchen and saying something civil to Mrs. Harper before making himself useful setting out tea things on the tray.

"How was she?" I ask Tom quietly. "That's all I want to know—what happened when she came here over Christmas, if she was happy. I'd give anything to hear she was happy."

Tom goes pale beneath his freckles and runs a hand through his hair. "And I wish I could tell you so, but she was a disaster. She kept falling apart, and I kept trying to put her back together, but I couldn't manage it."

I shake my head, and the constant guilt I carry is an iron band inside me. "You should never have had to try."

Tom glances up at his mother and sisters, and at Jack. "Can I say something to you? In private? If you've come all this way, I think you ought to hear it."

"Of course."

"Mum, we're stepping out to the barn," he says, and Mrs. Harper nods. Jack gives me a questioning look, and I shrug in response.

The cobbled farmyard is slick with rain and I take careful steps, though I've worn my most sensible pair of shoes. Inside the barn the air is sweet and dusty with the smell of hay. A row of placid dairy cows chew their cud in the gloom. Tom and I stop just inside the barn door, but leave it open for the light.

"There's no gentle way of saying this," Tom tells me, and there's agony written across his features. "But it's my fault your sister's gone. I suppose you know I was the last to see her. If I'd paid closer attention, or said something differently, she might still be here."

He sits down on a row of hay bales pushed up against the wall, but I stay on my feet, rooted to the spot. I know this boy's pain. I've held it close and nursed it through many a long night. It is a bitter thorn to carry through life, lodged in the secret places of your soul. And I cannot watch someone else do penance for sins that were mine alone. I won't.

I must be who I was in the Woodlands now, before I went astray. I summon every bit of confidence and pride I've ever had in myself, and hold them tight enough that they sink into my very skin and bones. Then I hold out a hand to Tom, which he takes before looking up at me, his plain face guileless and anguished.

"Tom Harper, this was never your fault." The words come out clearly, ringing bell-like in the quiet of the barn. If there was ever any power in my words and wit, I draw upon it now, to infuse the pardon I'm offering with immutable truth. "Her fate wasn't your burden, I promise you that. *I* should have been here—I was meant to look after her, and the only failing is mine. Do you understand? Look at me—do you really think you could have taken my place?"

He blinks. I may be wearing a wrinkled traveling suit, with my hair pulled back and not a bit of makeup to shield me from the world, but memories of magic sing from my heart through my veins.

"I don't know." Tom stumbles over the words. "But I ought to have done something. Ought to have seen what she meant to do."

"Six years," I tell him. "That's how long Evelyn's been battling her ghosts, and that's how long I've stood beside her. Even I couldn't always guess the right words to say, or keep her from the choices she made, though most of the time I managed. But you were sent into a trench with nothing more than goodwill for a weapon, and left to carry on a war that I'd abandoned. Foot soldiers aren't held responsible for a rout, at least not where I come from—it's their general who carries the blame."

Tom's not happy with my answer. "So you're saying the fault isn't mine, because it's yours? That hardly seems fair."

"Life isn't fair," I answer grimly. Mine certainly hasn't been, not since long before the moment Ev reached for another world in the darkness and Cervus called to us from across the void. I slip the silver stag pendant from the neck of my blouse and press it between two fingers. "Tom, I'm begging you. Please don't let this hurt more than it has to. The only person blaming you is yourself."

"I'll think on it, I promise you that." Tom turns toward the house, but I stop him with a word.

"Wait. Did Evelyn—did she say anything, about me? Leave a note, perhaps?"

He looks back and there's pity in his honest face. "No. I'm sorry."

"Oh well. It was worth asking."

"Coming in?"

"Shortly."

He steps out into the rain and I drop onto one of the hay bales, tired in body and soul. I came north looking for absolution, but here I've gone and given it away.

55

I SHOULD HAVE TOLD JAMIE AND OUR PARENTS THAT I was leaving sooner. I would have, if I'd had the courage. But I didn't, and now here we all sit at the breakfast table with an invisible wall between Evelyn and me as she asks me what day I'm leaving.

Ev doesn't even notice the shock wave reverberating around the table. She just takes a bite of toast, still waiting for an answer to her question about my flight to New York.

"I leave two weeks from today," I tell her. "But I can take a cab— no one needs to bother with driving me."

"Does term start sooner in America than here?" Evelyn asks, her voice colorless and flat. "Only that seems a little early for school."

She stirs her tea methodically, the spoon going round and round and round as I answer. "They let overseas students settle in during the week before term begins, but I'm staying with Millie's family for a while, first."

Evelyn stares down at her untouched plate, and at Old Nick, who's resting his grizzled muzzle on her lap.

"Ev, would you take a walk with me after we've cleared up breakfast?" I ask, feeling desperate. "We could go down to the park, feed the ducks. Spend the morning together, just the two of us."

"I don't think so," Evelyn says. "I'm awfully busy. I owe Georgie a letter, and I'm still trying to catch up on everything I missed last term, when I was—ill."

"Alright. If you change your mind—"

"Yes. Of course."

It's not until Ev gets up and leaves the room that Jamie and our parents turn to me wide-eyed, and I'm forced to confess that I'm really going. They're lovely, of course—they smile and congratulate and fuss about how I should have told them sooner. But I might never have told them if Evelyn hadn't forced my hand. Secretly, I've been hoping all my plans would come to naught.

That she'd ask me to stay.

Over the next fortnight I learn how easy it is for two people to live in the same house and sleep in the same room while barely speaking to one another. Hardly a word passes between Evelyn and me until the morning I'm to leave, when I stand at the doorway with my bags ready, hugging Mum and Dad and Jamie goodbye.

"Where's Evie?" I ask, when there's no more time and I really have to be off.

Jamie frowns. "Wasn't she in your room? She's not down here."

"No." My pulse begins to race, and a familiar nervous pain springs to life in my belly. "I haven't seen—"

The door opens with a soft click, and when I turn, Evelyn is standing in the doorway, framed by the morning sun. It glints on her golden hair, and when she steps inside, I can see that her arms are full of daisies.

"It's selfish to buy you flowers as a going-away gift, I know," she says. "They're really for me, since you can't take them on the plane."

I put my arms around her and hug her tight, never minding what happens to the flowers.

"I'm sorry," I whisper, but Ev shakes her head.

"Don't be. I'm not a shackle for you to wear."

When I step back and hold her at arm's length, hands still on her shoulders, my eyes burn and my throat tightens. Because my sister, with whom I've walked through worlds and wars, is smiling—a smile bright as the sun, so bright it dazzles.

I know that smile because I've worn it myself so many times before, and looking at her now, it's as if she's snatched the expression from my face.

Jamie and Mum and Dad exclaim over the flowers, and their relief to see her looking so well is palpable. We go through our goodbyes yet again, though I'm nearly late as it is, and then I'm out the door and into a cab.

Evelyn stands on the doorstep as the cabbie loads my bags into the boot of the car, and the last thing I see of home is her waving, still smiling brilliantly. When we've turned the corner, I press a hand to my mouth to keep from sobbing.

I've never worn that look of intolerable brightness unless it's to hide a hurt so deep I refuse to speak or think of it. Unless I hope to blind everyone else to my heartbreak, and in doing so, blunt the edges of the pain.

"Chin up, love," the cabbie says, shifting in his seat to nod at me. "It's always a wrench leaving family behind. But you'll get through it, I've no doubt about that."

"Thank you," I tell him, and smile through my tears.

A smile like the sun, a smile that dazzles, a smile that's both a refuge and a cage.

56

WE TRAVEL SLOWLY ON THE WAY HOME, AND STOP overnight again. It's all very proper—separate rooms and meeting in the inn's dining room for dinner. We make the last short leg of the journey Monday morning, arriving back in London with time to leave Jack's car at his building and walk the short distance to the Gallery from there.

"There's someone here for Philippa," Kitty says from the front counter as we step into the Gallery. "A young man. *Quite* handsome, and he's been waiting. Are we allowed to entertain gentleman callers during working hours now?"

I give her a killing look.

"Does this young man have a name?" Jack asks blandly. I can't imagine who it would be—I knew enough people before leaving for America, but haven't seen any of them since coming back.

"Jamie."

My heartbeat goes wild. I'm not expecting Jamie. If he's here, there must be news.

"That's my brother." I fight to keep calm. "If he's come down from Oxford there may be an emergency. Jack, can you tell Presswick?"

"Of course. And if you need anything, Phil, you know where I am."

I find Jamie in front of my old nemesis, *A Woman Bathing in a Stream*. One glance at the way he's standing and my stomach drops clear through the floor to the reference rooms below. Whatever he has to say, it's not good news, and I don't want to hear it.

But this isn't the first time I've walked straight toward heartache, with my footsteps unfaltering and my head held high. I put my hands on Jamie's shoulders and kiss him lightly on either cheek.

"Darling. What a nice surprise. Walk with me?"

Before any of the guards or Kitty have a chance to overhear a word of my troubles, I lead Jamie back through the Gallery and out the front door.

"What is it?" I ask breathlessly as soon as we're out. "What's happened? Don't keep me waiting."

Jamie's face is a ruin. "There's—they found a body, Phil."

I stand still as a stone, as if doing so could turn back the clock, to the moment before I heard those words. "Do Mum and Dad know?"

Jamie shakes his head. "No. I asked the Yard to contact me first if there were any developments. They want someone to go down and take a look—to say yes, it's her, or no, it isn't—and I thought it would be better not to say anything unless we're certain."

"Of course." Even when he's wretched, my brother's always done what's best.

Stuffing his hands in his pockets, Jamie stares down at the

ground miserably. "I don't think I can do this on my own. That's why I'm here. I'm sorry."

"Oh, stop," I tell him, though on the inside, I'm slowly dying. "You were right to come. We'll manage together, the way we've always done."

But there were three of us to manage before, and now there's only two.

I try not to think, try not to feel, as we get into a cab and drive through the London streets, then step out and down into a dim waiting area that smells of unpleasant chemicals—not at all like the solvent and cleaners and paint of the Gallery.

Inspector Singh is there, and I'm weak with relief that it's him and not Dawes. He leads us along a narrow corridor to another room, where there's a steel table holding something underneath a sheet.

Jamie's white as death beside me.

"I can't—" He chokes. "Where's the toilet?"

Inspector Singh points down a hall and my brother hurries away.

I'm left alone, in this room full of flat fluorescent light, with the inspector and the shape of a body that might be Ev. Letting out a quavering breath, I step forward.

"Show her to me."

"Don't you want to wait for your brother, Miss?" Inspector Singh's eyes are sympathetic.

"No. Show her to me."

We used to sit in the back garden and make daisy chains, before the war. Then when war came and we were sent away from home, the two of us started the journey hand in hand. Evelyn was still holding tight to me on that dark and deadly night, when Cervus called us away to the Woodlands. There she was love and light and laughter, everything beautiful and wild, and I did whatever I could to shield her from hardship.

Then at home, when her light flickered and dimmed, when sometimes it seemed like the last spark would go out, I could always find ways to rekindle her fire.

Oh, Evelyn, my heart.

Inspector Singh pulls back the sheet.

When Jamie comes out of the toilet, looking peaked, I'm waiting by the door.

"Let's go," I say flatly. "It wasn't her."

I start down the hall but he doesn't follow. "Philippa, wait. Are you sure?"

"Yes," I snap, and round on him. "Yes, I'm sure. It looked a bit like her, as much as it could, but it was someone else."

Jamie's not giving in. "Do you think I should look, just to be certain? I know you don't want it to be her—"

"It's not her!" I'm shouting now, because if I don't shout, I'll sob. "She had a scar, a long one, from cutting herself open one night at school because she wanted to look the way she did when we were *there*. I stitched it together myself, Jamie, because if the staff had found out, they'd have sent her away, to one of those terrible places for people who can't cope. So don't suggest, don't suggest for an *instant*, that I'm not certain the poor dead girl in there wasn't Ev."

I turn and sweep out of the door and there's a bus just stopping. I don't care where it goes so I climb onboard, torn to pieces now I've seen how a drowned girl looks, and endlessly repenting for every mistake I've ever made.

I'm sorry, Evelyn.

I'm sorry.

I'm sorry.

I'm sorry.

57

THE GALLERY'S SHUT BY THE TIME I GET BACK, BUT Albright opens up after some persistent knocking. I go straight to Presswick's office, shed my sweater, and begin feverishly fair copying the day's stack of paperwork. Thinking now would be a disaster.

It's ages before I notice the incongruous, crackling sound of a gramophone playing jazz. The only thing I'm used to hearing in the Gallery after hours is Albright's tuneless whistling. Drawn to the music like metal to a magnet, I leave my work to slip down the hallway and up the stairs. The door to the restoration studio is open, letting light spill out, and I peer in.

Among the cupboards and lockers that hold the restorers' supplies, Jack's seated with his back to the wall, a book in one hand and a bottle of lager in the other. His legs are stretched out in front of him, though on one side his trousers are flat and empty below the knee—sure of privacy, he's set both his cane and his prosthetic off to one side.

I knock, gently, not wanting to startle him. "May I come in?"

Jack's head jerks up but before he can say anything I cross the room and pull off my pumps, dropping them carelessly to the floor next to his prosthetic. I slide down and sit at his side.

Jack fishes a thermos out of his bag and hands it to me. "You're here for so long after hours most nights, I thought I'd stay, too, and see if you came back before going home. Bad news?"

"Yes and no." I unscrew the thermos cap and grimace at the smell of chamomile and honey. Piano and trumpet filter out from the gramophone as Ella Fitzgerald picks up the refrain of "I Hadn't Anyone Till You." "The Yard had my brother come down from Oxford. They found a body."

Silence. Then, "Phil, I'm so sorry."

"It wasn't her." I lean my head back against the wall and shut my eyes, though even with them closed I can see the dead girl's face. "But I read on the file next to her that she'd drowned. And it was *awful*, Jack. Whoever it was, she'd been in the water too long and she didn't even look human anymore. If Ev—"

I stop a moment before going on. "What are you reading? Tell me what you're reading, please, I'd like to think about anything but this and I haven't been able to get it out of my head."

Jack's voice is calm, an anchor in the storm. "The latest Poirot."

"Do you like mysteries?" Ella's voice pours over me like moonlight, and I'm waiting for it to wash away the horror of the day.

"I do. I like how tidily everything wraps up at the end. And I was given a box of mysteries in hospital, which helped keep me from dwelling on my troubles."

"That's just what I need," I say from in the dark of my own making. "Do you mind reading aloud?"

Jack's voice and Ella's twine together in a counterpoint of jazz and murder, and I doze, dreamlessly, finally worn to a last thread, until he murmurs to me, "Philippa. It's late. We should be getting home."

I'm still half asleep and at some point while I was dozing he must have put his prosthetic back on. Once I've slid into my shoes, Jack helps me to my feet and we walk through the quiet emptiness of the Gallery together. I ought to say I've forgotten something and need to go back to get it, because the door will lock behind us and I'll have to knock until Albright lets me in, but I don't want to say good night just yet. I don't want to face being alone. Instead I go out into the cool night air with Jack and when I shiver, he puts an arm around me.

"Well," he says at the top of the museum steps, "I'm just a few streets over that way. Do you want me to walk you to the bus?"

"No. I'll be fine. Good night."

"Good night, then."

I hurry down the steps and to the bus stop. When I look back and see that Jack's vanished and the square is empty, I turn and trudge wearily up to the portico.

But Jack hasn't gone. He's leaning against the doorway, with his hands in his pockets and a bemused look on his face. "I never see you go home. Don't you have a place to stay?"

I wrap my arms around my waist, trying to keep myself in one piece. "Of course I do. I'm staying here."

Jack steps forward. "Look, you can come with me if you like, just for tonight, until we can find a better arrangement. I'll take the sofa. But we've got to keep quiet—my landlady would have a fit if she saw me bring someone home."

So we walk the short distance to his flat, through the shadows of St. James's Park and along the dreaming London streets. His rooms are cramped—there are only two of them, one with space enough for a couch, a sink, and a hot plate, the other with a bed and a nightstand. I've left my few things behind at the Gallery, and he hands me a pair of striped pajamas without a word before shutting himself in the bedroom.

After a moment, I knock.

"Come in," Jack calls, and I do. He's half changed already, his back to me and his head bowed as he buttons his pajama shirt.

"Let me see you," I say softly. Slowly, he turns.

The whole left side of his body is spackled with burns, the skin slick in some places and puckered in others. I've never wanted anyone so badly, to have and to hold, perhaps forever, but when he raises his head his eyes are sad.

"Sorry. Not much to look at, I know. If you ever change your mind about me, Philippa, I'm not going to hold it against you, I hope that's clear."

I take three steps across the tiny bedroom and put my hands on his bare skin. He draws in a breath and then I kiss him and he kisses me until I slide the shirt from his shoulders and it falls to the floor.

But when I stop to fumble with the neck of my blouse, there's a shift of air and the click of the door shutting between us.

I drop my hands in frustration and stare at the closed door as Jack's voice drifts, muffled, from the other side. "I can't, Phil. Not now. I'm not exactly modern, and—well, I've got this foolish idea that I'll ask you to marry me someday. Sooner rather than later, I hope."

I press my forehead to the door and sigh. "Oh, come on, Jack. You haven't even managed to ask me to dinner yet."

"I've been waiting for the right moment," he says. "Besides, I don't think you're in any shape to be making decisions tonight."

I stretch my hands and shake tension from my arms. The drowned girl's eyeless sockets are staring blankly at me in the tortured mess of my own mind, and I can't dodge the image, no matter how hard I try. "You're right. I promise to behave. Can I at least bring you your shirt and fix a cup of tea?"

The door opens, and I hand Jack's shirt over demurely.

"I'm sor—" I begin, but he presses a finger to my lips.

"Don't be. Let's have that tea you mentioned."

We have our tea, and suddenly I'm dead tired, hardly able to keep awake. I fall asleep alone in Jack Summerfield's bed, and it's not a grey beach that haunts my dreams, or the way a drowned girl looks, but the smell of paint and canvas.

58

"IT'S NOT MUCH, BUT IT'S YOURS IF YOU WANT IT," SAYS Mrs. Hammond, Jack's blowsy and accommodating landlady, a round and apple-cheeked woman with greying blond hair. First thing in the morning he smuggled me out of the house to ring the doorbell and introduce myself as his friend, who's looking for a place to stay.

There's very little to this room under the eaves. Just a bed, a wardrobe, and an old-fashioned washstand with a pitcher and basin on it that Mrs. Hammond says she'll fill for me during the days. The bathroom and the lav are shared, off the hall outside Jack's own rooms. This is what I've come to, in my waiting and my endless repentances—a girl who pays rent, but who's really living on charity, stuffed into the corners of other people's lives, because they pity me, because they see I'm falling apart.

"It's exactly what I need," I say with a smile as bright as the sun. "Could I have a moment?"

I can hear them speaking in low voices as they retreat down the hallway, Mrs. Hammond sounding anxious, Jack quiet and self-assured.

"How long will she stay, do you think?"

"I don't know. As long as she needs to."

"Is she good for the rent?"

"Of course, Mrs. Hammond. We work together, you know. I'd vouch for her anywhere."

Once they've gone, I walk over to the wardrobe and glance inside. When I open the door, mothballs roll out, accompanied by a scent of cedar. It's empty, with more than enough room for the few things I have to my name.

For the first time, I wonder if Evelyn felt this way—as if she was existing on crumbs of compassion, on fading goodwill, always on the edges, in the shadowland between worlds.

"Evie, my love," I whisper, into the silence of the attic room. "How I miss you."

When I walk down the hall to the restoration studio the following day to meet Jack for lunch, he's already waiting outside the door. The hello I was about to offer dies on my lips. "What is it? What's wrong?"

Jack runs a hand across his face and shakes his head. "Nothing. Just promise me you'll keep out of the studio for a few days."

My breath catches in my throat. "Why?"

"Please. Just promise."

But I push past him and stop on the threshold, pressing a hand to my mouth to hold in the frightened sound that wants to escape.

Three paintings hang on the far wall. Each of them depicts a single female figure. The first sits in a little boat, about to set off downstream, her face a study in heartbreak—Waterhouse's *Lady of Shalott*, sailing to her death. The second lies on her back in the water itself, being borne away by the current, unseeing eyes turned skyward—Millais's *Ophelia*, who walked willingly into the river.

And between the two, stark and simpler in its rendering, is Watts's *Found Drowned*. Its lonely, lifeless figure lies cast up on the shore of the Thames, with water still lapping at her while London broods in the distance.

Jack takes me by the arm and steers me away, through the quieter galleries and out the front doors into the sun. I can hear him speaking distantly, saying meaningless, comforting things. But I'm waking in the New England dark again, and hearing Jamie's voice across the Atlantic. I'm standing on the bank of the River Went with Hobb, feeling the cold water close over my head. I'm sitting in the Harpers' barn, offering hope to Tom that I can't keep for myself. I'm knocking on the bathroom door, and jimmying the lock only to find Evelyn seated in a pool of her own blood, holding a blade sharper than truth.

There's a commotion building in the square below us, and it filters through my remembering. I look down in confusion as people push away from the square's far end. Shocked exclamations ring through the spring air.

Impossibly, a stag is picking his way across the pavement. He goes carefully on cloven hooves, tall and rust-red and wearing his antlers like a crown. There's a glint in his eyes that says he's out of place and afraid, and I know that look for I've worn it a thousand times.

I fly down the steps before Jack can stop me. Bystanders back away from the stag, wary of his crown, and they part before me like ripples around a rock.

We meet in empty space, he and I, set apart from the watching crowds, and there's an animal sort of confusion in the way the creature tosses his head that tugs at my heart.

"Come here," I murmur, reaching out to him. "Have you lost your way?"

Without hesitation, the stag steps forward and noses his elegant velvet muzzle into the palm of my hand. I put an arm around his ruffed neck and we sink to the pavement together, to sit side by side. I hear a sigh go up from the waiting crowd, and I know the Woodlands look is on me, that I've briefly become a fey and untouchable creature, the sort of girl who slips between worlds.

The stag lays his great head in my lap and I rest one hand between his antlers.

"We'll wait together," I tell him. "Until you find your fate, or it finds you."

We haven't long to wait, as it turns out. There's a flurry of running feet in the direction from which the stag has come, and half a dozen uniformed zookeepers appear, one with a rifle, another with a bucket of grain. The stag and I stand as one, as gracefully as we sat. He turns his head toward me and I whisper in his ear.

"Go quietly, my love. And thank you for coming."

I press a kiss to the creature's muzzle and we stand for a moment, forehead to forehead, before he swings around. The keepers hover uncertainly, but then one rattles the bucket of grain and the stag follows after her, mannerly as a house pet. It's not until they reach the square's edge that he stops and turns back to look at me.

I raise a hand and the stag stretches his neck and bellows. His full-throated roar reverberates from one end of the square to the other.

Then he turns a corner and is lost from view.

The groups of people hanging back throughout the square begin to speak again, and I feel more than see that they turn to watch me as I climb the Gallery steps and sit at Jack's side.

He looks at me, and his face is troubled. "Philippa Hapwell, who are you?"

I sigh, and rest my head on his shoulder.

"I've been asking myself that question for a very long time."

The restoration room is empty. It's late, and the other restorers have gone home, and I stand in front of the far wall, looking up at the pictures on it.

The *Lady of Shalott* sits in her little boat, one hand still on the chain that bound it to the bank. She wears white, and a hopeless expression. Around her lie the drapes and folds of her tapestry, in which she wove images of the lives she longed to live, and which was her undoing in the end. At the prow of the vessel are three candles, two burned out, one still guttering in the wind. I want to ask her who those candles are, which one of us is still alight and which two have gone dark and cold, but she refuses to meet my eyes.

Ophelia is worse. She floats on her back, and perhaps her gown was once white, but it's gone grey from the water. Fallen flowers lie around her, as if she'd picked her own funeral bouquet on the way into the river. Her open eyes stare skyward, her cold lips part, and I long to read relief in her expression. I ache to see peace, rest, calm at last, but there's nothing. Her face is a mask, and gives no quarter in death. She bears no secrets, as badly as I want to find them.

I linger in front of her, loath to move on to the painting that separates her and the *Lady*. But at last I step once to the side and confront it.

Watts's *Found Drowned* is not a beautiful picture, but it is an evocative one. The stone arch of the bridge. The bare and comfortless bit of shoreline. The clear light that illuminates the prone form on the sand, so focused it seems to radiate out from her. The gloomy city, uncaring in the distance. The serene, untroubled expression on the woman's face, and the perfection of her features. She doesn't look at all like the poor soul I saw at Scotland Yard—the scene is sterile and antiseptic, a drowning with its teeth taken out.

I can't see truth here either, because inside me there is a thing with fangs always gnawing away at my stomach, my lungs, my heart.

59

I DREAM OF A BIRCH RING THAT IS AT ONCE IN THIS world and the other. In it, Evelyn stands before me, and Cervus stands beside her. I walk toward them, but mist rises and shrouds the clearing, and when it passes, they've gone. The whole birch ring has vanished, and left me alone on a pebbled riverbank, watching the darkly rushing water as it rises up and tugs at my ankles with longing hands.

On the opposite bank stand my family, and Jack, and Presswick, and everyone I knew at St. Agatha's, but from upstream comes a little boat, carried by the current. Evelyn sits in it, clad all in white, and she reaches out a hand to me. The water pulls harder as I wade further in. It ripples around my knees, my waist, my ribs, my shoulders, then laps hungrily at my hair, my neck, my lips—

The last thing I see as the river closes over my face is Evelyn, peering down from above the surface and still reaching out to me.

60

THE TULIPS HAVE NEARLY FINISHED THEIR BLOOM IN St. James's Park and fledglings are busy in the trees the day I take my seat and Presswick pushes a sealed envelope toward me.

"It's not for copying," she says, watching me closely. "It came for you."

I slit the envelope open. There are two pages inside, one on stationery, bearing familiar handwriting, and the other an invitation printed on thick parchment paper.

Dear Philippa, the handwritten letter begins.

> *I hope you don't think your father and I haven't been to the Gallery to see you because we're angry. Truly, we want nothing more than for you to come home. But since the war we've been at a loss as to what to do with the three of you children, and since Evelyn, more than a little afraid of any misstep we might make.*
>
> *I don't want to push you, Philippa, but when you're ready, we'd like to see you. If not at home, perhaps we could meet*

elsewhere. Enclosed you'll find an invitation that came for you from St. Agatha's. We've had one as well—they're holding a candlelight service for your sister, which your father and I plan to attend. If you and Jamie came, it would mean the world to us.

Whatever you decide, we hope you're happy. We hope you're well.

Love,

Mum

The invitation lists a time and date, two weeks from now. I stare down at it, and at the letter, until Presswick glances up. "What is it?"

"A letter from my mother, and an invitation to a service for my sister."

Presswick takes off her spectacles and gives me a long, searching look. "Will you go?"

"I can't think of anything worse and it'll mean another day off, the Friday after next."

"Good girl," Presswick says approvingly. "You won't regret being there, I promise you."

"May I take a few minutes?" I ask. Presswick nods and turns back to her work.

I walk through one of the reference rooms on my way upstairs, full of waiting masterpieces. The air in the room is still, hushed with anticipation. It's the same on the Main Floor, and I wonder if a storm's about to break outside.

Rembrandt's *Woman Bathing in a Stream* is waiting for me. I stand by as an elderly couple finishes with her, then step up to the silk cord that separates us.

Now the painting's been cleaned, there's a luminous quality to the light that strikes her. It picks out gold everywhere—in her hair, in the folds of her shirt, in the ripples of the water as she steps forward. I still can't quite tell what she's thinking, but it's easy to see from the expression on her face what she doesn't feel.

She's not afraid. She's not overwrought. There is a calmness, a deliberateness to her posture. She's at peace, and she holds up the hem of her linen shirt the way a queen holds her royal robes. I may not know what the bather is about to do—may not know if she's grieving or glad—but I know she's come to this place of her own volition. The riverbank is no surprise to her. And she looks down at the water the way one might look at an old friend.

I stop at the front desk on my way back through the Gallery. Kitty waves a languid greeting and I lean against the counter. "Mind if I use the phone?"

"*Mi casa es su casa,*" Kitty quips, and passes me the telephone. I turn the dial and wait as the phone rings, and rings, and rings.

"Hello?" says Jamie's voice on the other end of the line.

"Jamie. It's Phil."

"I know."

I pause. "Do you?"

"Yes, St. Agatha's sent me an invitation. I'm assuming you've got one, too."

I shift, trying to keep out of Kitty's way as she dispenses guidebooks.

"Are we going?" Jamie asks.

"I don't want to," I admit. "But I think I need to. I'm not asking you to come."

Jamie's quiet for a moment before speaking again. "Of course I'm coming. I'll meet you at the station next week Friday. It's going to be dreadful, but strength in numbers and all that."

"Friday, then."

"Friday."

61

I DON'T TELL JACK UNTIL EARLY THE DAY OF, WHEN HE'S dressed for work and I'm dressed for the train. I've come down from the attic and we sit side by side on his couch eating muffins and eggs and having a morning cup of tea, because there isn't room for a table and chairs.

"I'm going to a service for Evelyn today," I blurt out, because there's no way to lead into it. Jack's hand, holding a teacup, stops halfway to his mouth. Then he sets the cup aside and shifts to look at me straight on.

"Do you want me to come?"

I reach up and brush one hand against his face. Yes, I do. Of course I do. But this is the last of my pentimenti, the last of my repentances, and it ought to be done alone. "You're a lamb to offer, but my brother will be there. I'll stay at the inn in town, and come back Saturday."

Jack hesitates.

"Will you?" he asks after a moment, and there's something unspoken in the question.

He's not sure I'll come back. On the inside, he's started to wonder if I'll vanish—if one day, he'll turn around and I'll be gone. And I lived through that sort of wondering for enough years that I hate to think of another person feeling it.

Leaning forward, I put my arms around him and hold tight. After a moment, he does the same.

"I'm not going anywhere," I say. I'm on the brink of tears because there's a slow tug in my bones that feels terribly like goodbye. It's a pull that began with a three a.m. phone call, and it's been building ever since, made stronger by painted forests and drowned girls and stags in Trafalgar Square. "I promise I'll come back to you."

I need the words to be true, but they taste of ashes on my tongue. How many promises have I made and broken?

"Good," Jack says, and clears his throat. "Because I've been meaning to ask you something."

I push away, wide-eyed. Jack grins.

"Philippa Hapwell, when you get back, will you . . . go to dinner with me?"

I shake my head and smile, though my eyes are damp. "What, that's it? I thought you might ask the other thing."

"Well. I don't want to frighten you away."

I haven't kissed him since the night he brought me here. I've been ever so well-behaved, but I kiss him now in earnest, with a promise on my lips—the one I've already spoken, that I'll come back, that this leaving is only for a little while.

But when we've said goodbye and I sit on the train, watching the glorious spring countryside fly past, I'm cold enough to freeze the woods for a hundred years. And because of where I'm going, because I'm on my way to confront Evelyn's ghosts, I permit myself to recall a day I hate remembering.

Evelyn and Jamie and I are on the beach, beyond the woods below Palace Beautiful. It's an overcast afternoon in midsummer, and the surface of the sea is alive with rain, a mosaic of ripples glinting grey and blue and white.

Ev walks barefoot by the water's edge, a smile on her face. The war with the Tarsin Empire is won. She has grieved for our dead and her tears are spent. A calm lies over the kingdom, and even Ev's dreams of Venndarien Tarsin's death have begun to subside.

But I can't lay hold of the peace she feels, at least not in this world. We were born elsewhere, and while Evelyn may have all but forgotten, I've never stopped remembering. Even Jamie is growing restless. There is an urgency in me now the Great Wood is safe, to get back home. To return to that night of sirens and shelling. To pick up our story where it left off.

Jamie and I have made a decision, after weeks' worth of conversations stretching past midnight. It's time to go. All that's left is to tell Evelyn, but for once, I can't find the right words. I've known, since the first week we spent here, that this place means something to her it doesn't to Jamie or me. That it will break her heart to be torn away.

What can we do, though? We can't possibly leave her behind. I barely remember the child she was in England. I can remember myself, and Jamie. I remember our parents, our house, that other war. But images of Evelyn in the Woodlands always come to the forefront when I try to think of who she was back then. It's so much easier to see her here, and that frightens me.

Ev comes up alongside me, silent on bare feet. Of the three of us, she's the only one who's learned that trick, of walking the Woodlands way. She puts her arm through mine and we watch the waves sighing onto the shore.

"He's here," Jamie says from where he waits a few yards off, hands in his pockets, rain glinting on his fair hair.

I'm meant to have warned Evelyn, and it's cruel that I haven't. I look one last time for a way to explain, but there are still no words for this within me. They all fall empty and flat, leaving me hollow. I haven't felt so bleak since I came within an inch of betraying the Great Wood.

Cervus is coming toward us on the beach, and our time here is running out. Perhaps this will be better in the end, to tear the plaster off all in one go.

Inside me something aches and aches, and I wonder if it will ever stop. I reach out and hold tight to my sister's hand because I can't fathom going home without her, but can't imagine her anywhere but here.

62 ~

GOOD TO HIS WORD, JAMIE'S WAITING AT THE STATION. The road to St. Agatha's is a verdant tunnel, trees overhanging the laneway and filtering the late afternoon sunlight into motes of soft green. I can barely tell where I am, if this is the English countryside, or if we've driven into the Great Wood itself.

"Drive a little more?" I ask when we're close to the school, because the service won't start for an hour and I'm not ready, not yet. Jamie turns off down a side road and we carry on through the countryside, over hills and past sheep fields until the shadows grow long and the sun rests in the boughs of the tallest trees. When it can't be put off any longer, we crunch down St. Agatha's gravel drive and Jamie parks near the dormitory.

People are already filtering into the refectory—girls in uniform, adults in somber clothes, St. Agatha's faculty. I wonder if our parents are here yet. I'm sorry for leaving them, though I'm not sure I could have borne it if I'd stayed—I'm sorry for so many things.

Jamie and I step through the open doors, and it all feels as mournful and final as I'd feared. Candles burn in the wall sconces and at the front of the room. Chairs are set up with white ribbons tied to them. There are photographs of Evelyn on a table at the front, and someone—Georgie, I suspect—has carefully written out half a dozen Teasdale poems in curling script on heavy paper.

When the first vaguely familiar girl approaches me, I can feel the person I was at school falling into place, stifling me. She's careful, collected. Every word and gesture calculated to hide the real Philippa from sight, and to ensure my defenses are unassailable. Trouble is, I haven't been that Philippa for months, and I'm not sure I can be her again. I smile and nod and excuse myself, ducking out of the refectory just as the Curmudgeon calls for everyone to be seated.

I walk a little way, still in view of the door but far enough from the trickle of late arrivals, and lean against the building's cool stone wall. I'm not surprised to find Jamie already outside, though it does surprise me to find him smoking.

"I didn't know you did that," I say. Jamie takes a last drag on his cigarette and stubs it out against the wall.

"I don't, at least not anymore. I gave it up after St. Joe's. This is a special occasion."

"Aren't we full of secrets?"

It's not exactly dark yet, but everything's growing dim. Though I can't see the expression on Jamie's face, there's an uncharacteristically bitter edge to his voice.

"I'm an open book compared to you and Ev. Mum and Dad are sitting up front—they said you're not living at home anymore."

"No."

"You might have told me."

I stay silent, because Jamie ought not to throw stones. He's always been the one who had the luxury of distancing himself from Ev and her troubles, of finding his own way, forging his own path.

"How bad was it with her, Phil?" he asks.

"Pretty bad," I say. I want to go home. I want to sit next to Jack on the couch in his tiny flat, drinking tea and reading mysteries that all end in a satisfying, tidy way. I never should have come here, to this place where sorrow and regret and something larger are tugging at my bones. "Sometimes I thought I'd lose her. It was all I could do to hold her together."

A match flares in the dusk as Jamie lights another cigarette. "I can't believe you never said anything."

"I'm sorry. That I didn't, and that I left. Are things ever going to be alright again, do you think?"

Jamie doesn't answer. A battered lorry pulls into the quad, and a familiar family climbs out. There are five of them, and they form a hedge of protection around a gangly boy with freckles, who's pale-faced but decidedly less unhappy-looking than when I last saw him.

"That's Tom Harper," Jamie tells me, though of course I know. "I'd better go in with him. It's my fault he got caught up in this, after all."

"It's not your fault," I chide gently. "He didn't have to stand by Ev. He had a choice we never did."

Jamie laughs, a short brittle sound. "No one's ever had a choice around you and Ev. The two of you are like gravity. It's impossible to get free once you're caught."

He walks off across the quad, and shakes hands with Tom. I

watch them go in, but I can't follow. I can't lay her to rest, can't speak final words about her I don't know to be true, and there's something bewitching in the way the wind has risen up in the nearby trees. It sighs in their leafy branches and I can't resist that call. So I take off my pumps and walk barefoot through the meadow, to the back gate with its rusted hinges, where I slip out into the darkening forest.

63

THE NIGHTTIME WOOD STRIPS ME BARE, PEELS AWAY
the Philippas I've been and leaves me only myself, a lost girl wandering in the dark. I'm not frightened or grief-stricken, just quiet and empty.

I follow a familiar track through the forest that Evelyn once haunted. There were many nights that I drifted along behind her, an invisible guardian watching as she made her way through the trees. I'm still following in her footsteps, walking where she walked, trying to get far enough down the road to see where she ended up.

When the white birch ring gleams ahead of me in the dark, I slow my pace, hesitant to enter. They told me her trail ended at the river, but she spent so much time here that surely a little of her has been left behind.

A musky, wild smell hangs on the air, redolent of forest earth and decaying wood and hidden wildflowers. There's a moon near to full sailing between gaps in the clouds, and when I finally step out into the ring, it illuminates the clearing with brilliant silver light. It shines on the pale trees, their fine leaves, the dew-wet grass.

All this loveliness holds nothing of my sister. I find as little of her here as I did in the Gallery's paintings, or in her carefully copied lines of poetry. The clearing is muggy with tension, and the trees tremble as they wait.

Reluctantly, I cross the greensward to where a narrow track weaves darkly through the undergrowth. The birches dusk and shiver, and I reach out to run one hand against smooth white bark. Above me, the tree's branches shudder. Barefoot and soundless, I start down the river path.

Phantom shapes flit through the woods. They might be shadows, or memories, or milk-white hinds grazing in the moonlight. Leaves gust along the winding trail, tugging at my skirt, blustering past my ankles like skittish cats. The charge in the air builds and builds until rain begins to fall in cold and scattered drops. I pull my sweater tight and carry on.

Briars snag my nylons, branches catch at my hair. Out-of-place sounds drift through the wood, little rills of music like bells or chimes. A leaf brushes against my face, feather-light and gentle as a kiss.

Once asleep, the wood is waking.

I walk along the river path, and I'm not sure I could stop if I tried. Fear is a cold, round pebble in my throat, making it hard to swallow, hard to breathe, but still I press forward, through the whispers, the rain, the woodland ghosts. I should be to the river by now, to the place where the Went runs deep and dangerous among the trees.

The leaves surround me like a cloud, a cloak, an honor guard, and bear me on. Pale light glints ahead of us.

A last few stumbling steps and here I am.

I know this place.

64 ⁓

TREES ARCH OVERHEAD AND RAIN BEADS ON MY HAIR like jewels. I stand for a moment in the shadow of the woods and look out at the spit of grey sand before me, the froth of grey waves, the long stretch of grey sky. Over the sea the clouds give way and the moon gleams on water that stretches to the horizon.

I step out of the shelter of the wood and onto damp sand. Stopping to look over one shoulder, I see scudding leaves swirl together, forming the shape of a girl. She raises one hand in greeting and with a gust of wind, is gone.

Waves weep against the shore as I walk along the water's edge. Ahead and above, Palace Beautiful perches on its lonely cliff, panes of glass and wet slate glittering. Smoke rises from the chimneys and the warm glow of lamplight spills from a few upper windows.

I climb the winding path up the cliffside, and in the wildflower meadow before the gate, Cervus is waiting. He seems smaller than he once did, and greyer around the muzzle, but he's still rust-red and holds his head proudly. When I look at him, a wide and hollow ache opens up inside me, a longing for truth, for peace, for home.

"Little one," Cervus says, and his voice is a wild Woodlands sound, a song in my blood and bones. "Why are you walking the worlds alone tonight?"

He wears his antlers like a crown of silver beneath the moon, and his eyes are bottomless dark wells.

"*Where is my sister?*" The question every inch of me has been asking for months on end rolls off my tongue. There's power in the words, an invocation compelling truth from the one who answers.

Light dapples Cervus's strong flanks, and that clean forest smell fills the air. I've known him through years and lives, and he's never seemed so otherworldly.

"A Woodlands heart always finds its way home," he says.

Taking a step backward, I put distance between us. "That isn't an answer. I want to know where she is now. I want to know what happened. I *need* to know."

"Are you certain?" His voice is gentle, but the question frightens me.

I wrap my arms around myself, trying to hold in the things I feel, standing here in this place I never thought I'd see again, speaking to a creature who ought not to exist.

"I'm—" I begin.

A soft voice from the dark gateway interrupts me.

"Philippa."

And the thousand pieces of my heart begin knitting together as Evelyn steps out of the shadows.

There's a stillness about her, a confidence I've only ever seen in the Woodlands. She's bareheaded and her hair hangs loose down her back, a fall of gold in a world of silver. I've never seen anyone so beautiful.

"Evelyn," I breathe. I pick my way across the meadow and stop before my sister, suddenly afraid that if I reach out and touch her, all this will vanish.

"What happened?" I ask, and Evelyn smiles, blinding as the sun.

"I crossed between the worlds, Phil. I've done it once before."

She and Cervus have always been this way—enigmatic, cut from the same mystic cloth. When I hedge, it's to hide how ordinary I am behind all my bluffs and glamour. When Evelyn and Cervus won't give an answer, it's because they know no one else sees the world quite the same way they do.

With my question still hanging between us, I gather my courage one last time. I put my arms around Evelyn and she is solid and real.

"Oh, Evie," I say when I can get the words out. "I *missed* you."

She hugs me back and presses a kiss to my cheek, and I'd nearly forgotten this version of my sister, the one who's whole and well and radiates joy.

"You said we weren't coming back," I say to Cervus. "You told us on the beach."

He lowers his head in assent. "I said I could not call you again. But your sister has a Woodlands heart, and found her way home."

I hold both of Evelyn's hands in my own, reluctant to release them. "It's been six years since we first left the Great Wood. Ev stayed in our world all that time, and suffered. We all did. Why are we here *now*?"

"I wanted to come before," Evelyn says. "But there was always something holding me back. A bit of me wanted to stay and find my feet, if only for your sake and Jamie's, and Mum's and Dad's. So I gave it one last try, without you, and—oh, Philippa. I just couldn't manage. We don't fit together anymore, your world and I."

Tears well in my eyes.

"You're not coming back, are you?" I ask Ev. She looks past me, beyond the wildflower meadow to the uncharted expanse of the Great Wood beyond.

"You know I can't. And I know you can't stay, so I won't even ask."

There's a part of me longing to deny her, to swear we can be together, and that I won't leave her here alone. But I'm no Woodlander. Unlike Evelyn, the heart that beats in my chest is not a Woodlands heart.

"What will you do, all on your own?" I ask, because I can't leave her without knowing down to my very core that she'll be alright.

"All on my own?" Evelyn laughs. "I have more friends here than I ever did in our world. I will work in the gardens at Palace Beautiful with Alfreya, plant saplings in the heart of the wood with Vaya, and stand watch through the longest night with Cervus. Perhaps I'll even convince Hector to teach me how to sail. There are a thousand things to do, and if I ever come to the end of them, I'll just sit under the trees and *be*."

I look down at the ground because I can't meet her eyes. "I'm so sorry, Evelyn. I never should have made you leave."

My sister tilts my chin up so I'm forced to look at her. "It's alright. I'm more than you think, and there's no need to worry anymore. I've made my own path and I can stand on my own."

"You're right." My sister stands before me now, rooted in the soil of another world, and she has always been more than I thought. She's always been Evelyn of the Woodlands, whose heart called its way home.

But I am plain Philippa Hapwell, and my heart belongs to no particular country. It belongs instead to all the people I've loved. A good part of it lies here and if I leave it behind, I will never be whole again. I'd be even less, though, if I stayed. More of me rests in the world to which I was born, and it's time for me, too, to find my way home.

"Are you ready, little one?" Cervus asks. "Shall I send you back again?"

I pull Evelyn close one last time and kiss her bright hair. "Promise me you'll be happy?"

"I will be the gladdest thing under the sun, but the Great Wood will be a little lonelier without you. You'll tell Jamie, won't you? That I'm home? And Philippa—" Evelyn flushes. "There was a boy. Tom Harper. If you could find something—anything—to say, to make things easier for him, and for Mum and Dad and Georgie, too?"

"Yes," I promise. "I will. I'll find the words, I swear."

A fitful gust of rain whips at us, bringing with it the smell of the forest. I cannot stay, and this is our final goodbye.

Evelyn nods, and grows solemn as Cervus steps forward. The great stag throws back his head and roars, a sound that shakes the ground beneath my feet and raises a gale that rattles all the branches in the Great Wood. The noise redoubles until it seems the very sky will split.

But Evelyn speaks, too, her words barely audible beneath Cervus's call as she says her last farewell.

"I thought of you and how you love this beauty,
And walking up the long beach all alone
I heard the waves breaking in measured thunder
As you and I once heard their monotone.

Around me were the echoing dunes, beyond me
The cold and sparkling silver of the sea—
We two will pass through death and ages lengthen
Before you hear that sound again with me."

When the echo of their joined voices dies away I stand at the edge of a birch ring, facing an empty clearing with rain soaking me to the skin. There's no magic in these trees beyond the witchery of spring, of bud and leaf and new things growing, and I love their very ordinariness.

I walk back through the forest, which is alive and vital with insects and night birds and shrilling frogs. Still in the cover of the trees, I stop for a moment at the meadow's edge and look out at St. Agatha's, at the stone building that radiates light, and the sound of young voices singing. Their words are incongruous and lovely, full of a hope I hadn't expected to find when the day began.

"All shall be well,
And all shall be well,
And all manner of thing shall be well.
From heaven and earth the refrain doth swell,
All manner of thing shall be well."

When the song dies down, I step out of the woods and into the world.

ACKNOWLEDGMENTS

THERE ARE TWO INCREDIBLE WOMEN IN THE PUBLISHING industry who were essential to the creation of this book. The first is Alice Jerman, a kindred spirit and a delight of an editor who lets me run down editorial rabbit trails and keep all the British spellings my heart desires. There's no one else I can spend over two hours on the phone with while thinking it's only been ten minutes. If anyone's been born into this world with a Woodlands heart, Alice, I think it's you.

Second is Lauren Spieller, a truly extraordinary agent who represents my work with all of the determination and energy she brings to every aspect of life. I never had a dream agent during the querying process, but I certainly do now. It is my great privilege to work with you, Lauren. I think we make a pretty unbeatable team!

Prior to *The Light Between Worlds* finding a place in publishing, Jen Fulmer and Joanna Meyer believed in it. The world's absolute best CPs, they're a sounding board for all my ideas, literary or otherwise. I don't know where I'd be without our DT group chats, which cover everything from the intricacies of battle scenes to baby sleep habits to gluten-free flour brands. Jen and Joanna, I couldn't have done it without your help along the way.

Many thanks to Barry Cunningham and Rachel Leyshon at Chicken House Books for their support and insight throughout the editorial process, and to Brent Taylor from Triada for his impassioned and enthusiastic foreign rights representation. Thanks also to Navah Wolfe, who sparked the idea for this book.

London Shah, Bethany Morrow, Kelly Tse, Steph Messa, Mike Moody, Anna Schafer, and Cindy Baldwin all read *The Light Between Worlds* at various points in the editorial process. Thanks to each one of you for your assistance, as well as to Chris Needham and Richard Wragg, archivists extraordinaire, who helped bring the National Gallery circa 1950 to life.

On the back end of things, so many people offered encouragement and moral support as I wrote, queried, and revised. My American bestie, Ashley, who's possibly the only person to ever utter the phrase "Laura, you're the coolest person I know." My wonderful sisters, Amy and Breanne, who've both put up with my nerdy ways for a lifetime and taken an interest in my weird hobbies. You both loved me when I was still just a frumpy piece of rock from Mars. My parents—Mom, I always know an idea's a keeper if you like it. Thanks for saving me from the jaws of the laundry beast, and believing I could do this. Dad, just the fact that you said you'd voluntarily read a book when this comes out is a testament to how much you support me.

Eternal thanks belong to my own quirky little family. My girls are the reason I started writing again in the first place, and a constant source of inspiration. I'd walk between worlds for the two of you. Tyler, my trophy husband/werewolf—there's no one else I have more fun with. Life's just boring when we aren't together. Let's Viking River Cruise through the rest of it side by side.

And lastly, thanks to you, dear reader, for journeying with Ev and Philippa.

I felt it shelter to speak to you.

RESOURCES IN ORDER OF APPEARANCE

POETRY IN *THE LIGHT BETWEEN WORLDS*

An End
Sara Teasdale

Let the Light Enter
Frances Ellen Watkins Harper

There Will Come Soft Rains
Sara Teasdale

I Lost a World
Emily Dickinson

Ulysses
Alfred, Lord Tennyson

Snowfall
Sara Teasdale

The Heart of a Woman
Georgia Douglas Johnson

The Two Sisters
    Pablo Picasso

Ambush in the Woods
    Jan Bruegel the Elder

The Olive Tree Wood in the Moreno Garden
    Claude Monet

Trees and Undergrowth
    Vincent van Gogh

Lakeside with Birch Trees
    Gustav Klimt

View of Dedham
    Thomas Gainsborough

The Lady of Shalott
    John William Waterhouse

Ophelia
    Sir John Everett Millais

Found Drowned
    George Frederic Watts

PROLOGUE

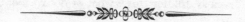

A LACE-TRIMMED WEDDING INVITATION SITS ON MY nightstand and I know, beyond the shadow of a doubt, that Mama is not coming back. It was inevitable, but so far in life, ignoring the inevitable has always been easy for me.

Until now.

There's no avoiding the truth anymore. There it is, stamped in gold ink, wafting the lingering traces of rose-scented eau de toilette toward me.

Curled up on my side in bed, I stare at the invitation as if it's a snake.

"Violet." Wyn, my father's ward, calls softly from the other side of the bedroom door. "Can I come in?"

He may not be able to see me nod, but the House can. There's a click as it turns back the lock and a gentle scrape of hinges as it swings the door wide. I glance over and see Wyn crossing the room carefully, holding a cup of water with two hands so as not to spill. He's always walked so since coming to Burleigh House—as if the ground beneath his feet is strewn with invisible bits of broken glass, and he might damage himself with a single wrong step.

Wyn sets the cup down on my nightstand, in front of Mama's invitation, so that the print looks strange and distorted when seen through the glass. We may both be only eight and surrounded by servants—Jed and Mira, Papa's steward and housekeeper, are never far off—but even as children this is what we do. We look after each other.

As Wyn takes a seat at my side, the comforting ivy Burleigh House has blanketed me with rustles and pulls away from him— they've never got on that well, Burleigh and Wyn. Flames flare deep purple on the hearth and the lamplight glows in the same shade. Poor old House—it hates to see me unhappy just as much as Wyn does. I sometimes forget in these moments when Burleigh's so kind and solicitous that it's one of the five Great Houses, whose vast magic governs the well-being of England. To me, my House has always been both more and less than that. Burleigh, like Wyn, is simply this: both family, and a friend.

Wyn shifts, putting a little more space between himself and Burleigh's retreating leaves. If he were anyone else, he'd ask if I'm alright. But Wyn's been a quiet child since the day Papa brought him back to Burleigh House from a Taunton foundling home. Papa found him in a Taunton alley and brought him home. Which is just as well, if you ask me—I've never seen much use in endlessly talking over troubles. I don't want to talk about how Papa's gone yet again, off in London on House business. I don't want to talk about how Burleigh House's worries have been seeping into me through the floors, and how sometimes they make my heart pound so fast I can hardly breathe.

I absolutely do not want to talk about Mama.

Instead, I hug my legs tighter, wishing to make myself so small I'll disappear. Wyn looks down at me, solemn and wide-eyed. I know he and the House will stay with me all night and dog my steps tomorrow. They never abandon me, at any rate. The House will wrap me in flowers and lull me to sleep with nightingale song, and Wyn—well. Wyn never sleeps in his own bed. He prefers a pile of blankets and a pillow in my airing cupboard.

I can't help but remember how Mama felt about all of this. My mother and father fought about everything, but the way I feel about Burleigh and Wyn came up often.

"She *should* put the House first, Eloise," Papa would say. "Vi will be Caretaker of this place when she's grown. Burleigh will choose her, I'll pass on the key when I'm ready, and His Majesty will certainly approve of the arrangement—you know the king's always taken an interest in Vi. This is who she's meant to be."

"She doesn't know who she is *now*, let alone who she ought to be in the future," Mama always argued back. "And how will she ever sort herself out if you keep her tethered to Burleigh House and never let her be with ordinary children?"

"Wyn keeps her company."

"He is *not* an ordinary child."

They'd go on and on like that, in endless circles, arguing behind closed doors. Perhaps they didn't know Wyn and I sat outside listening, or perhaps they were past caring.

But now all the fighting has come to an end, and Mama's off in Switzerland, planning her second wedding to some foreign baron.

"Wyn." I sit up and look at him. I need to know that all this is worth it. I need to know that no matter what I've lost, I've lost it for the greater good.

"Yes?" he says, all untidy sandy hair and serious grey eyes.

"Do you think I'll be a good Caretaker for Burleigh House?"

Wyn doesn't answer. He fixes his gaze on the blanket of ivy still covering my bed, except for the conspicuously empty space around him.

"A good Caretaker puts her House first," I say, half to myself.

"Always?" Wyn asks.

I reach out a hand and a strand of green ivy twines around my wrist, a near match for the latticework birthmark of slick pink skin that stamps me there, like a bracelet. "Always. Papa says so—a good Caretaker puts her House before king. Before country. Before family. Before her own life, even."

"But what if you change your mind?"

Now that is unthinkable. Mama may leave, I may grow up, but the one thing that will never change is my resolve to serve Burleigh House. My father, George Sterling, is a perfect Caretaker, and in the rare moments when he's at home, he sees to it that I learn my place. That one day I'll follow after him: the best Caretaker England has ever known. Under Papa's watchful tenure, Burleigh has thrived. The counties our House governs have known peace and prosperity.

"I will *never* change my mind," I tell Wyn. "I'll put Burleigh first all my life, because this place is greater than you or me or any one person."

And though I've learned this lesson by rote under the watchful eye of my stern father, my heart still swells when I repeat it. For as long as I can remember, Burleigh has been everything to me. This

House is like a mother, father, comforter, and friend. I intend to repay the favor someday, when I'm able.

"We may not understand the House, we may not be able to speak with it, but Burleigh House was here watching over the West Country before you or I were born, and it will be here long after we're gone. It is my duty as a Sterling to serve this place, and to help it care for the countryside. Mama *knew* that, Wyn. She knew it. But she was always jealous of Burleigh. She couldn't see why it's worth looking after." I stop and swallow fiercely, past the heat burning in the back of my throat and behind my eyes.

Wyn stares down at the floor, looking as small and miserable as I feel.

"And what about a good House?" he asks after a long silence. I frown as he plucks an ivy leaf and shreds it to bits. "What does a good House do? Shouldn't you get something in return?"

I run a finger across the ivy, soothing the place where Wyn marred it, and the leaves turn to my touch like flowers toward sun. "I don't expect anything. A good House puts *itself* first, because the well-being of the countryside is bound up in the health of its House. And so a good House chooses its Caretaker wisely, and doesn't spare them when trouble comes."

The fire flickers in the hearth, as if to confirm my words.

"Violet."

When I glance up at Wyn, the expression in his eyes makes my stomach clench. He always looks just so—restless, ill at ease, like an animal poised for flight—before making the suggestion I know is coming. "Let's run away. You don't have to stay here, or be a Caretaker, if you don't want to. We could go to Switzerland, to your mother. Or somewhere else—you can choose, just . . . let's leave."

Wind moans in the chimney, like a sob, and the ivy on my bed begins to recede, sliding sadly away toward the windows it crept in through. Out of habit and out of practice, all my self-pity shifts as my heart goes out to Burleigh House.

"You shouldn't say such things," I tell Wyn, my tone a reproach. "You know I'll never go, and you know even talking about leaving upsets Burleigh."

Wyn hangs his head and looks so woebegone I don't know who I feel for more—him, or my keening House.

"Oh, stop it, Burleigh," I say, and the wailing wind subsides even as I speak. "I'm not going anywhere."

But it's Wyn who I throw my arms around, and he relaxes just a little. As much as Wyn ever does, at any rate.

"I'm sorry about your mother," he whispers, and I hold him tighter.

"I'm not." The words come out so fiercely I almost believe them. "I'm not, I'm not. I've got you and Burleigh, and Papa when he's not working on House business. What more could I possibly want?"

After Wyn climbs off the bed and retreats to his makeshift cot in the cupboard, I get up. Opening the drawer in the nightstand, I pull out a letter Mama enclosed with the wedding invitation. It carries even more of her scent than the invitation itself, and I breathe in that aroma of roses, remembering the feel of her arms around me.

One sentence stands out, for the ink has run and spotted, as if tears were shed when it was written.

Come to me, my Violet—let me make a home for you here.

But I have a home. I am a Sterling—I was born on the grounds of Burleigh House, and someday, I hope to be as brilliant a Caretaker as Papa.

A good Caretaker puts her House first. Before king, before country.

Before family.

Kneeling next to the hearth, I feed Mama's letter to the sympathetic flames, which shift to blue as I scrub the sleeve of my nightgown across my eyes.

"Think about something else. Anything else. It helps," Wyn's voice says from the shadows of the cupboard.

I take a shaky breath and begin to hum. It's a song Papa always sings for me when he's at home.

Blood for a beginning
Mortar for an end
Speak out your binding,
Be you foe or friend

Take up the deed
Take it well in hand
And bind a House's power
Bind it to the land

Blood for an ending
Mortar for a start
Unmake a binding
At your House's heart

Unleash a House's power
Let it all run free
Leave naught for the king
Naught for you or me

First House for a prison
Second for ladies' rest
Third for a palace
Fourth to be blessed

Fifth House holds quicksilver
The Sixth ruins all
But for blood in its mortar
But for breath in its walls

But this time it doesn't have the usual effect, not even when I fix my mind on the words.

All I see is Mama's handwriting. All I can think of is the fact that she's never coming back.

"Once upon a time there was a Great House," I begin somewhat desperately. I haven't told Wyn a story in over a year, not since he grew used to life here at Burleigh. But it grounds me, the sound of him settling in to listen, and the feeling of the immense, brooding presence that is my beloved Burleigh turning its attention in my direction. "There were the Sterlings, too, who lived and died for it. Their blood ran with its mortar. Their bones rested in its ground."

When I turn away from the fireplace, every inch of the bedroom floor is carpeted with new-sprouted daisies. Slowly, I lock up the sadness of my mother's leaving deep inside, because I know I would give anything for this place. One day, my blood will run with its mortar. One day, my bones will rest in its ground.

1

Nine Years Later

BENEATH ME, THE FLAT BOTTOM OF MY BOAT THRUMS ever so slightly as a fenland pike bumps against it. The long, gleaming creature is focused on its fishy business, and I've been motionless for near an hour, letting gentle currents in the marsh water carry me this way and that. I'm all but invisible to the pike, and an invisible fisher is a successful one.

Sun beats down on my bare head, and heats the long rope of my braid. Sweat trickles between my shoulder blades and down my raised arm, which holds a sharp-tipped fishing spear aloft. This is the one thing that affords me relief—this moment where everything comes together and all of me fixes on a single goal. I'm no longer Violet Sterling, dispossessed daughter of a treasonous nobleman, too long separated from her family home. All the aching worry over Papa and Wyn and my House recedes, and I become whole instead of fractured—Vi of the Fens, who never ends the day empty-handed.

In this moment, I distill into my most elemental self. A level head. A keen set of eyes. A pair of hands that move like quicksilver, or summer lightning. The fish turns over on its side, exposing a glistening expanse of scales.

In an explosion of spear and net and brackish water, I haul the pike aboard. It thrashes ferociously and the boat rocks, but a quick blow from the hatchet I keep under my low seat puts an end to that. Shoving my braid back over one shoulder, I finally allow myself to grin, to wipe the sweat from my forehead, and to feel that my nose has burned terribly yet again. It'll peel and freckle, and Mira will scold, but so be it. We'll eat for half a week thanks to this fish. And in this moment of clarity I've found a way to shed the creeping anxiety that's plagued me these past years. At least for a little while.

But even as I straighten and stand above my catch, the sense returns—that I am too far from home, but still bound to it by a long, taut stretch of line. It's not just Burleigh I can't get past, either.

"What do you think of that, Wyn?" I murmur. I only indulge the habit of speaking to him when I'm alone on the fens, careful to make sure no one hears. God knows who actually talks to Wyn now—who takes his silences and his moods into account, who lets him stay close when the night is too long and too dark, full of noises and shadows that remind him of things he'll never speak of. I hope it helps, that I send my voice to him when I can.

With the trackless expanse of the East Fens surrounding me, there's only a miry waste of bogs and silt deposits and tidal estuaries to hear my secret conversations. In places, the land's been shored up and laid to pasture, so that farmhouses and sheep enclosures stand out incongruously against the marshland. It's all a jumble and a maze, but I know this place better than any other save one. The currents speak a language I've learned, the seabirds call to me, and the brassy blue sky above is a map waiting to be read. The marshes are honest, if you understand them, and they always play by their own particular set of rules.

But they are not the West Country, which encompasses the five most southwesterly of England's counties, and which Burleigh House nurtures and governs. This land is wide and flat and straightforward in its wildness. It's unlike the Blackdown Hills I grew up among, which look tame at first, checkered with enclosed pastures and apple orchards, but which hide old shrines in their valleys and bone-wrought charms in their hedgerows. And nothing could compare to Burleigh's strange, enchanted grounds. The truth is, though I take up the oars and begin sculling back to shore, it doesn't feel like heading for home. It never does.

By the time I make it back to our little cottage on a raised hump of land in the middle of absolutely nowhere, the light's growing long and golden away inland. Mira has the shutters thrown open, and Jed sits on the front stoop whittling. He wasn't a whittler before our exile, but I suppose I wasn't much of a fisherwoman, either.

"Find your luck, then?" Jed asks as I tie the boat to our bit of dock. In answer, I sling the pike up, and it takes two hands for me to lift it.

Jed lets out a low whistle. He's a thickset, bearded man with a florid white complexion and close-cropped hair that long ago went grey, and though he's stood by me through good times and bad, I love him best for how he was with my father. There never was a more devoted steward, whether Papa was present or absent. When the king sentenced my father to House arrest, it took six men to hold Jed back. He shouted and struggled as they sealed George

Sterling away behind Burleigh's walls, and he never stopped fighting, not till the front gate vanished, replaced by unbreachable stone.

"Mira's waiting inside," Jed says. "She's—we—have something you need to hear."

I can feel the smile fade from my face at his words. "What—"

But before I'm able to ask, Mira's voice calls from within the cottage, cutting me off. "Bring that fish in here at once and wash the stink of it off your hands."

As I step into the close confines of the cottage, she tuts at me. "I expected you home hours ago."

Mira does rule us with a bit of an iron fist, but Jed and I would be lost without her. We're a family—an odd one, to be sure, but time and tide have bound us together and it would break my heart to lose them.

I cross the cottage's tiny downstairs room—just the one space for cooking and eating and living, with a curtain drawn across the nook that holds Jed and Mira's bed. A ladder leads up to a loft for me, and that's all there is to it.

With a weighty thud, I let my pike fall onto the kitchen table, and Mira turns. Horror writes itself across her face.

"Violet Sterling, you're a sight, and today of all days I wanted you home early."

Leaning against the table that holds my rather splendid fish, I hunch my shoulders, as if doing so can protect me from what's surely coming. If Wyn were here, he'd appear and just stand at my side, a silent ally in all things. And if we were home, the House would already have a carpet of reassuring flowers around my feet.

Will I never feel whole without them?

"Why? What's happened?" I finally summon the courage to ask.

Jed ducks into the cottage, and the whole space feels suddenly smaller. "Mira had a visitor come looking for you today. A messenger from the king."

All the air goes out of me. I drop onto my chair, ignoring the fish now lying forgotten on the table.

"His Majesty's back from Belgium and stopping at the Knight's Arms in Thiswick tonight," Mira says. "Apparently he'd be much obliged if his only goddaughter would pay him a visit tomorrow at noon, before he journeys on. The messenger said—he said there's news from Burleigh House."

"News." My voice breaks on the word. There's been no news from Burleigh House for seven years. And every sun that sets without it is a relief to me, because it means that across the country, my father and Burleigh and Wyn have survived another day of House arrest.

Jed steps up behind me and puts his enormous hands on my shoulders. "He didn't give any particulars, but I don't think we have to tell you what to expect."

I choke back questions I know Jed and Mira have no answers to, and mechanically lay the table for supper. But when we've eaten and the dishes have been cleared, I duck out of the cottage the instant Mira's back is turned. Jed watches, saying nothing as I shove our dory into the water and scramble aboard. I ship the oars and haul back on them and the boat reluctantly begins to move.

"Violet!" Mira calls through the open cottage doorway. "Just where do you think you're going so close to nightfall?"

"Away!" I answer back, sculling for all I'm worth. The dory pulls steadily forward, building momentum until I'm skimming across the water, dragging the welter of my emotions behind me like a length of tangled net. Movement is the best thing for me, I know—to still the aching of my heart, the clenching of my stomach, the furious grinding of my teeth. I scull until my arms and back ache—till sweat drips between my shoulders again and the last of the day's sun adds freckles to my freckles.

And when I've rowed for so long that each oar seems weighted with lead, I drop anchor in the middle of a tidal floodplain. Water stretches ahead of me to the very edge of the eastern sky, which has gone dark. I turn away from it, and from the vast, uneasy North Sea, looking westward instead, toward the setting sun. Beyond that blaze of splendor lies my past. Beyond it lies my future. Beyond it lies my House.

Blood and mortar, I miss it with everything in me. Every bone and every breath. I thought the end of Papa's House arrest might taint things between Burleigh and me, but even knowing what's surely happened—that my father must be dead, finally killed by the House itself—all I feel when I think of Burleigh is an agonizing desire to be with it.

So I know in the morning I'll visit His Majesty. I'll sit in front of him while he feigns pity and tells me Papa's protracted death sentence has ended, and a new Caretaker must assume his place. I'll do what must be done, choking down my hatred and fear of the king, all for the sake of Burleigh House.